# STEPULI CHRONICLES:
# THE TRACKS WE LEAVE

MAGGIE MAXFIELD

ISBN: 979-8-9868794-1-3

# ACKNOWLEDGMENTS

To Anastasia, thanks for lending me your name kiddo. And to Ian. Thanks for saying I could make you the lackey if I wanted, love you babe. And finally, to mom, the most dedicated reader anyone could have. Seriously. Stop asking me for chapters, they'll come when they come.

# CHAPTER 1
## STASIA

T wo stone guard shacks stood like sentinels. I drove up to the base gate on the narrow lane between them with my registration, insurance, and state ID in hand. Nostalgia hit me, the whole scene reminiscent of my military days. My foot tapped restlessly against the floorboard while bittersweet memories played through my mind.

I don't know why a weight dropped in my gut. I had mostly enjoyed my time in the service. I was coming back as a contractor and wouldn't have the same restrictions as when I was enlisted. This was a great opportunity, the pay was outrageous, and so far, everything I saw of Washington I loved. I hadn't even started work, so it's not like I could blame the hospital for this feeling. Regardless, something triggered my fight or flight response.

Before I could dwell on that, traffic moved forward. I took a deep breath and rolled my window down. As I pulled up to the gate, a large black man, broad-shouldered and decked out in camouflage with an M4 slung lazily across his front, leaned down to take my information.

"Morning," he said jovially. Jesus, he looked like GI Joe and sounded like Mr. Rogers.

I smiled, his energy putting me at ease. Holding my paperwork in easy reach for him, I said, "Hi, I'm here for my first day at the hospital. Christopher Shaw is my liaison. He's supposed to be meeting me here."

The man, Jacob, I read on his nametag, said, "Ah, you were supposed to go to the Passing ID Office." He pointed toward a building I could now see just through the trees. I bit my lip but offered him a tense smile. I was going to be late. I hated being late.

"Thanks so much, I must have missed the turnoff. Do I just turn around or...?"

Jacob waved away my words. "Nah, I know Chris, I'll just radio him to come to the gate. Pull into the turnoff up there," he pointed, "I'll let you know when he comes through, and you can follow him out."

Giving him a more genuine smile, I said, "Thank you." He winked, already talking into his radio. I moved forward to where he indicated, putting my car in park to wait for Mr. Shaw.

He drove through in a black Impala sedan. He lowered his passenger window and waved at me. Nodding back, I put the car in drive and threw a thumbs up back to Jacob.

Shaw led me to a four-story building set in boring angular lines. It was designed like a typical hospital with a straightforward layout. That impression continued inside with plain white floors and walls, low hanging ceilings, and a musty odor that gave away the building's age. It didn't turn me off. It wouldn't be the first old low-budget hospital I'd worked in.

"I'll introduce you to the charge nurse," Chris said as I followed along. "They're very short today, and we heard you'd done some travel nursing in the past and would be comfortable with no clinical orientation."

I nodded because it was true, but I was still surprised. Usually, permanent jobs loved to show you the difference between staff and travel work. They insisted on orientation I wouldn't need as a new grad.

Chris made quick introductions to a woman named Ava. Her brown hair varied shades, and she was a little heavy in the waist. She smiled at me, her pretty, made-up face looking harried. I smiled back because her expression told me exactly what kind of day she was having.

"Where do you want me?" I asked.

She looked at Chris and said, "Thanks I've got it from here," dismissing him without another look. "What are you comfortable with?"

"Anything." I shrugged, watching curiously as Chris walked away grumbling.

"I have no psych nurses today, and we have more boarders than usual. Our regular staff really aren't great with them. We normally ship them so quickly. Can you go to that hall?"

Psych was where I excelled. My ability to sense people, or my good intuition, helped me de-escalate sticky situations. I could pivot between a schizophrenic and a borderline patient like a pro. "Sure thing. What room numbers? I'll head over."

She waved that away. "I'm not going to let you drown completely. Let's do a quick tour of the ER. I'll show you the stock rooms, your closest med cart, and introduce you to Shelly. You can shadow her for the last hour of her shift just to get the ropes. Then you can take over her assignment. Sound good?"

"Yeah, that's perfect."

Her stressed face relaxed the more we spoke, and her energy lightened from the frenetic quality it had been when I'd first walked up to her.

"Fantastic. I'm so sorry you're getting no more introduction than this your first day."

I shrugged, not bothered. Answering truthfully, I said, "I prefer it this way. Lead on."

As promised, she showed me around the Emergency Room and introduced me to Shelly. We made short work of catching up with her patients' orders. Eleven came by in a blink, then I was taking care of a four-room psych assignment. An easy day, really.

As I thought this, the alarm sounded for an incoming ambulance. I finished off my charting and got up from the desk to go prepare the room. On my way I read the page. *Violent patient, in restraints with military police, recent history of schizophrenia.*

I had just finished clearing the room of sharps and projectiles when the EMTs rolled the patient in. Police hovered at the door. The room filled with people: security, patient care technicians, another RN, and the physician. The EMTs gave a patient report as everyone moved the man to the ER stretcher.

They went about the typical duties involved in triaging a psychiatric patient. Vital signs, change the clothes, take the belongings. The process stopped abruptly when the patient shouted, "I don't wanna be here! This is bullshit! Stop, get the FUCK away from me you BITCH. Fuck you!"

The doctor attempted to interrupt the patient's tirade, aimed at the patient care tech, who backed away fearfully. I stayed at my computer, feeling bombarded by the patient's panicked and confused energy. There were already too many people in the room. This man didn't need anyone closer to him. Emily, the RN who had come in to help, didn't seem to realize that though.

When the doctor's attempts to explain the process didn't work, Emily stepped up next to the patient and said, "You need to stop yelling. You aren't the only one in this hospital. Security, get the restraints. Listen, if you don't stop yelling, I'm going to put you in restraints."

My mind boggled. She hadn't even given the patient time to respond. Not to mention, he wasn't currently being aggressive. Sure, he had screamed profanities, and no, it wasn't acceptable. But she was making it worse. And she was actively threatening the patient. She was aggressively handling a paranoid schizophrenic in psychosis.

The doctor shrugged, looking bored. "Emily when you get it handled come and get me. Anxiety medications if you need it." Then he walked out. He hadn't even spoken to me, the primary nurse.

"All right, let's get the locked restraints," Emily said to a heavyset older man. The type of security guard who was ten years retired from the force. She walked out with him to retrieve the restraints, confusing me even more. If she was so worried about this patient's aggression, why would she leave the room? With one of the security guards?

I looked at the door, hoping I had time. "Let's clear the room. You and you stay," I indicated to the scared patient care technician and one of the three security guards, "everyone else, mind stepping out the door?"

There were a lot of grumbles, and plenty of incredulous stares, but my confidant tone encouraged them to obey. Sensing the patient's panic and distrust, I stayed out of his space. Instead, I leaned against the back counter, keeping my body language relaxed. The raised side rails provided a barrier and time to get out of the room if he erupted.

"Hi, I'm Stasia, what's your name?"

He ignored me, not making eye contact. Typical, but it was important to know he was concentrating on me, not the voices speaking in his head. "Hey bud," I said, using my usual moniker. "Bud, look at me. Can you look at me?"

Finally, he did. I smiled warmly. I didn't stare him down, briefly keeping my gaze on his eyes then shifting to his chin. "Hey, I'm Stasia. I'm going to be one of your nurses. Do you know why you're here?"

He yelled again. "Yeah, it's bullshit. My dad called. I wasn't doin' nothin'! I was just fuckin' chillin'!"

I nodded as if this was perfectly understandable.

"I get it." I used a calm voice in low tones, purposefully designed to put him at ease. "Are you having thoughts of hurting yourself or anyone else today?"

"NO. Fuck! This isn't fair. I want to go!" His eyes were wide, panicked to even the casual observer. The feeling I got from him was terrifying. Not violence or meanness, but soul-deep fear.

I smiled slightly. "It's not. I'm sorry. That's good you aren't having those thoughts. You've been here before for stuff like this right?" I hadn't had a chance to look up his chart, but I didn't have a lot of time before Emily got back with restraints.

He nodded. He teared up, his aggression making way

to his underlying emotions. Perfect. That meant I was making progress. The fear rolling off him lessened in intensity, corroborating my assessment.

I continued. "So you know the drill bud. Just let us get all the necessary stuff done. The sooner we do, the sooner you can talk to psych and get out of here. How about we get your vitals, your lab work. Let you get changed. I'll bring a turkey sandwich and some apple juice. You can chill and watch TV or whatever you want to do in the room."

I worded it carefully so he understood he had boundaries but also options. It would make him feel more in control and help prevent him from pushing his limits.

"I'm hungry," he said instantly.

This was typical, and I used it as a bargaining chip. "I'll get you the food as soon as we get your blood pressure, blood work, and clothes."

He thought about that. From my vantage point, I saw Emily coming from up the hall and moved to intercept her at the doorway. I leaned against the door jam, standing as if I had all the time in the world for his decision. In the meantime, my position blocked Emily from getting in the room.

Just in time, he said, "Okay."

I looked over at the patient care tech as I felt Emily at my back. The tech looked at me like I was a voodoo priestess. I forced back a laugh. I smiled at her and said to the patient, "This young lady will help you get started. Just a second."

I felt comfortable leaving the tech with the security guard in the room. I turned to Emily, who barely left me any personal space. She had locked restraints in her hand and a pinched face.

"He's good now," I said. "Consenting to care."

Her pinched face became derisive. The portly guard stood at her back. She said, "Bullshit, I don't trust him. Not the way he was yelling. I'm going to tie him down for a while."

The guard at her back looked bored, like he didn't mind either way. I began to feel a little violent myself at her misuse of care.

"Excuse me?" I said, moving so she had to back further from the door.

"That guy was just yelling like a lunatic." Her own voice rose. "I'm putting him in restraints!"

I breathed in through my nose and out through my mouth. The irony of her shouting his need for restraints wasn't lost on me. I had seen this all too often in healthcare. It wasn't that she didn't know how to handle psych patients, she got off on the power. Violating someone's body, someone's autonomy, was as simple as her convenience, and not actually about safety at all.

"This is my patient. You are going to back away. You are going to stay away from the room if he begins to escalate." I didn't say anything else. I didn't trust myself to. I hated that tears burned at the back of my eyes because of the anger burning up my chest.

Emily's eyes bugged out. "I'm going to get the charge nurse. You're new here, maybe you didn't handle psych patients where you came from but—"

"Get the charge nurse." My flat tone cut her off without room for argument. She stormed off.

\*\*\*

On my way home, exhaustion weighed down my shoulders. This must have been what the stone in my stomach had been about. The charge nurse had been underselling it when she said her typical ER staff weren't good with psych patients. They were one of the most vulnerable and misunderstood populations. They were also one of the largest any ER saw, and the small military hospital treated them with borderline abuse.

Ava, after hearing our argument, had sided with me. It helped my case that for the rest of the shift he was an easy patient, sweet even. Emily was going to hate me for life. Considering this was a permanent position, that could prove to be a problem.

Pulling into the driveway of my oceanfront home, I looked to the right. I hadn't met the neighbor yet. I had gotten in late last night with an early morning today and hadn't had much time to explore.

I started up the walk, my head hung from exhaustion. My lower back and calves ached from being on my feet for twelve hours. I looked up as I hit the walkway to the front door and investigated the front windows out of habit. Stopping short, I dropped my bag and laughed. Flynn panted excitedly in the window, the blinds down around his neck like a coat.

This dog could test the patience of a saint. I adopted Flynn from a couple on Craigslist on a particularly lonely night at one of my lowest points. I blame the wine for thinking I could tame a nine-week-old wolfdog. His first two months he tore up my entire carpet, ate my couch, and ripped down my blinds. At first, I had told myself the kind thing would be to give him back to the couple I'd adopted him from, to a shelter, to anyone but my own very unprepared hands. In the end though, I couldn't. I knew from experience there was no worse feeling than being given back.

He had gotten better, but the abrupt change from Florida must have triggered his anxiety. After freeing him from the blinds, we headed to the back yard so he could burn off some of his nervous energy. He danced next to me, rushing out when I opened the back slider. I smiled and followed him.

Flynn took his time smelling around the yard, getting to know his new home. I took a deep breath. My exhaustion melted away with the crisp air. This view was the reason I'd parted with the lion's share of my savings. Scattered Douglas fir trees offered shade. Lush green grass covered the yard with a small pond set back before the land dropped off to the ocean below.

I went to sit on the deck steps, but Flynn's head shot up, pointing to the yard next door. He took off. I cursed under my breath and called, "Flynnstone!"

He didn't even look back. I groaned, rushing after him. He ran to the neighbor's deck where a man had walked out. I tried calling his name a couple more times as I walked over, but Flynn continued ignoring me.

"I'm so sorry," I called as I got closer.

The man had an easy smile on his face, a beer on the wide arm of his Adirondack chair, and his hands buried in Flynn's thick gray mane. Dark eyes, dark hair, lightly tanned skin. His smile brightened his face, and his eyes crinkled at the corners. I rubbed my hand across the back of my neck, my cheeks warming. I was nearing thirty, but a handsome man could still turn my cheeks red.

"It's not a problem, he's adorable," the man said as I climbed the steps to his deck. Stubble shaded his defined jaw. His large hands found a particular spot that made Flynn's back leg kick. I smiled at the picture of the two of them, his words putting me at ease.

"Thanks, he normally doesn't wander. I think he's just restless from the move. I'm Stasia, your new neighbor. I'm so sorry he barged over here." The smooth lines of the man's defined shoulders tightened, and the corners of his lips turned down.

"It's okay," he said slowly, giving me a searching look. "He made my evening much more exciting. I'm Jack." His polite words were incongruous to the tense energy coming off him. The sudden change confused me.

My smile strained as I wondered what I'd missed. I tried finding something to do with my hands, embarrassment and uncertainty suffusing me. My hand landed on Flynn's backside, absently scratching him. He panted happily, soaking up the attention, oblivious to the growing awkwardness between me and Jack.

"You just moved in last night, right?" Jack peered up at me. He furrowed his brow like someone trying to solve a puzzle.

"Yeah, I got in kind of late, right before dark." Jack's change in demeanor and questions made anxiety curl in my chest. I started to extract myself from the situation when I heard a young voice calling.

"Jack!"

He turned his head and sighed. The slider to his house opened, and a young girl, probably in her midteens, popped out. Her red hair, freckled skin, and brown eyes were adorable. She brightened when she saw me but was quickly distracted by Flynn.

"Who's this cutie?" she squealed.

Flynn immediately abandoned Jack and ran for her, as excited as her for the attention. Jack chuckled softly and straightened. He rubbed the back of his head. "What is it Lill?"

She looked up at me and asked, "Who's this?"

Jack gave her a meaningful look. "This is Stasia, our new neighbor." I wondered if Jack took care of his sister or if he lived with his parents.

Lilly knelt, scratching her way around Flynn's ears. She looked up at me, smiling so wide dimples creased her right cheek. "Hey Stasia, I'm Lilly. Can I dog sit for you?"

I laughed at her abruptness as Jack gazed skyward. "Anytime Lilly, but he's a handful. He busted up your poor brother's peaceful night."

Lilly baby-talked to Flynn. "You can bust up our night anytime. Yes, you can. Aren't you a pretty boy?"

Flynn's tail went wild as he rubbed his head against her hip.

Lilly looked over at Jack. "Soooooo, I was going to see if I could talk you into starting dinner."

Jack stood, beer bottle in hand. "Figured as much when I heard you hollering. Is Brandon home yet?"

Lilly nodded, still absorbed by Flynn.

"Right. Well, it was nice to meet you, Stasia. Let's go, Lilly."

Lilly, oblivious to his shepherding, continued scratching Flynn's ears. "Do you want to come to dinner, big guy?" She turned to me. "And you too Stasia."

Jack shifted his weight at her question, looking uncomfortable.

"Thank you so much, but I had a long day. Another time."

Jack's hand landed on Lilly's shoulder, steering her inside. "Have a good night," he said. I felt his need to usher her in.

I called Flynn, this time he followed, and was walking off the porch stairs as they reached the slider. I turned back to wave, but Jack never looked back.

# CHAPTER 2

## Jack

The new neighbor was beautiful, with big green eyes, blonde hair, and a short, athletic body. At first, I had been excited. Finally, another Stepuli family came to Whidbey. One that lived independently and not under the government's thumb. At least not directly under it. It helped that one look from her had set my blood on fire. Her dog, energetic and free with his love, also charmed me. I'd been eager to welcome her. And then she'd stepped onto my porch. Human.

A human living next door to my sister. My sister who was going through puberty with unpredictable powers we were trying desperately to hide. Living next door to my brother who had a chip on his shoulder the size of Mount Vesuvius, and whose mood swings similarly erupted. Brandon had already slipped up and got himself on the Stepuli Eugenics Project's radar. I was barely keeping him together, and the SEP warned if I couldn't keep him together, they would take him permanently.

I went through the motions, mindlessly making

dinner, when Lilly pulled me from my thoughts. "The new neighbor is pretty, and oh, my God, Jack, that dog!" She chattered away as usual with too much energy. I had to wake up before dawn just to caffeinate enough to keep up with her.

"It's weird, she didn't feel like a Stepuli. And I kind of expected you to be more excited," Lilly said.

Nervousness churned my gut. She should be able to tell immediately if someone was human, or one of our kind. We could tell another Stepuli by feeling an elemental affinity. Even if their element differed from our own, we all vibrated to an inherent energy. Though Lilly had only ever been around me and Brandon, she could recognize the affinity from us.

I said slowly, "Lilly, she isn't Stepuli."

Lilly scrunched her small, upturned nose. "You said this part of the island was reserved for Stepuli families. That's why we've never had neighbors."

I rubbed my forehead, relieved she had only assumed. Sometimes I forgot she was young and didn't always listen to her instincts before diving into a situation. I set the pasta to boil and turned around to face her, leaning against the counter.

"I know. And I don't know what happened. But Stasia is human Lills."

She considered this. My chest ached as her face dropped. I knew Lilly was lonely, I just didn't know how to fix it. "Oh," she said, unnaturally subdued.

I reached across to ruffle her hair. Her eyes were glassy, but she didn't cry. Not my tough girl. She coughed to clear her throat, but she wasn't fooling me.

"It would have been nice to have another girl around."

Her voice slowly got stronger. "Ugh, and I would have loved to play with that dog."

Trying to lighten the mood, I teased, "I can't believe you burst out asking her to watch her dog like that."

Lilly shrugged. "He was adorable, and the goodest boy."

I rolled my eyes and turned back to the stove to finish dinner.

As I was plating the food, Brandon came into the kitchen looking like hell, his face drawn and a little pale. He practically threw himself onto the barstool next to Lilly. She wordlessly pushed him her lemonade. I did the same with his plate of dinner. He dug in, determinedly not looking at either of us.

I didn't know what to do with him. He had always seemed lost. The water in him was like an ocean constantly beating him with waves of his loss and fear. No matter how strict I'd been, how hard I'd come down on him, I still hadn't been able to keep him safe. I had backed off last fall when it had stopped mattering. One idiotic moment at a Stepuli event and he'd given himself away to the SEP.

The silence stretched uncomfortably. In typical Lilly fashion, she brought Brandon around without effort. "Bet you couldn't channel a stream with that hangover."

Brandon's head snapped up, and he winced. I glanced at the sliding doors, but I had already drawn the blinds. I'd have to talk with Brandon later about the neighbor, but for now, I could let him do the one thing that made him happy. Commune with water.

Smirking at him, I said, "I'll double that," and moved to the sink, turning it on to a slow stream. His dull eyes came to life. His slack face, though still pale, lit with anticipation. Taking one drop from the sink, he inhaled slowly.

He used his hands to focus himself, a bad habit left over from his early days at the Stepul School. I was trying to reteach him to not depend on hand and arm motions, but now wasn't the time. With his first three fingers pinched, he beckoned the drop closer, and then to his right, as if to lay a soft kiss to Lilly's cheek, making her giggle.

Then, with a smirk, he moved the drop toward me. As I watched the small drop warily, a bucket worth of water dumped over my head. Lilly dissolved into laughter, and even Brandon joined in.

I tried to look stern, but I smiled too. I was soaked and cold, but his playfulness made me happy. "You're cleaning that up asshole," I called over my shoulder, heading upstairs to dry off and change. I walked away to the musical sound of Brandon and Lilly laughing.

As I walked out of my room after drying off, I ran into Brandon in the hall. I looked over his shoulder, but Lilly hadn't made it upstairs yet. I heard the distant sound of the TV in the living room.

I reached out and grabbed his arm as he tried to move past me, head down. "B, we need to talk."

His shoulders hitched, and when he turned toward me, his jaw tightened. His wariness ate at me. Since our parents died, I had taken on the parental role. But becoming a father at nineteen hadn't given me the perspective I needed to raise well-adjusted kids. Instead, I'd driven a wedge between us that never healed.

"Yeah?"

"You've got to stop," I said without preamble.

He didn't pretend to not know what I was talking about. He took a deep breath and his shoulders dropped, all the defensiveness leaking out of him.

"I know. I just don't know what else to do."

"I get it B. But you aren't even living anymore. You're even starting to scare Lill."

Brandon dragged a hand down his face, looking ashamed. Lilly was the one thing that always united us. "Maybe I should take a break from the bar."

Relief washed through me. If I had suggested it, he'd resist. He'd managed the family bar after he turned twenty-one. When Brandon was discovered, he at least managed to hide the strength of his powers, and the SEP kept his involvement minimal so far. I had hoped putting him in charge of the business would give him a feeling of normalcy. But instead, he'd buried all his anger and disappointment in the free booze, withdrawing until I hardly recognized him.

"Let's switch jobs. I'll take over the bar, you keep Lilly on a schedule."

"Okay."

Brandon started to move past me to his room. I called out, stopping him. "Oh, and B, we're going to need to stop her training for a while." He looked at me quizzically. Keeping Lilly on a strict schedule was important. My neck ached from the tension as I told him about the new human neighbor.

***

I rubbed my forehead, a headache starting at my temples. I stared at the books. Walker's Place, the bar I had bought with reparations from my mother's death, was a mess. It had been a couple days since Brandon and I changed places, and I had started going through everything. Supply orders were behind, and we were edging into the red.

I sat back and sighed. Looking up at the corkboard over my desk, I took a break to stare at the family pictures. Mostly pictures of Lilly growing up, carefree and laughing. Sprinkled in were images of Brandon brooding. To the right, almost hidden under other photos, was one of mom and dad.

I ran a hand down my face and rolled the chair back from the desk, standing up to stretch my legs. I intended to go do inventory, something active to alleviate the cramp in my thighs from sitting so long. I wasn't made to be in a closeted office.

I walked out of the office, positioned at the furthest end of a dimly lit hall, and stepped past the bathrooms to my left, the walk-in cooler and liquor closet to my right. Rays of light beckoned me toward the main room of the bar, and already I felt a little less claustrophobic. An open concept room, booths lined the far wall with high tops scattered in between. A green felt pool table stood directly in front of me, a box stage to the back right for open mic nights or bands. To my left was the live oak bar.

I had spent so much on the live oak I couldn't afford to renovate behind the bar. The original mirrored backsplash sat behind rows of liquor bottles. We only had a few beer taps, the classics, and a rotating supply of local microbreweries. As much as I intrinsically hated this place, bought with blood money, it was hard to fail at a bar in a military town. When my parents had died, I'd needed to secure income. It provided Lilly with a better future, and Brandon an inheritance. Until he started drinking it.

Ian, my main bartender, gave me a nod but kept at his

task. We were opening soon. On a Saturday, it would be filled with a mixture of sailors from base wanting to get trashed early and hikers looking for an afternoon beer. Wordlessly, I walked along the bar, polishing the oak. Then I helped put away the dishes Ian had cleaned and dusted off the liquor bottles.

We opened at two in the afternoon, and as usual, customers came in as soon as the doors were unlocked. Ian had it in hand, so I grabbed myself a Wicked Teuton IPA and sat in the booth closest to the stage. Putting both hands around the pint, I let the coolness seep into my palms and listened to the chatter.

"Hey, fuck face," Ian called to one of the younger junior sailors. I hid a grin in a sip.

"Yo, what's up Ian? Can I get two Jack and Cokes?"

"Jack and Coke. Bit early for the hard juice, don't you think, Liam?"

Liam laughed. "Never too early for me, Ian."

Ian smiled contemptuously, but Liam didn't pick it up. He poured the drinks and offered them over the bar, taking the young sailor's cash.

"The rest is a tip, right?" he called in the same sardonic voice.

Liam's brows lowered, but he said, his voice a little less sure, "Yeah...you got it Ian." They did a hand slap thing I always found idiotic, and Liam went to sit with his friends.

After the customers vacated the bar, my eyes met Ian's. He winked, and I shook my head with a rueful smile. Ian was an abrasive bartender. In fact, he was downright insulting. But he had a big personality, and he pulled it off. The customers all thought they were in on some kind of joke when he spewed profanities at them or called them names. They liked the inclusiveness and tipped him more. He meant every word.

The afternoon progressed as it normally did. It was too early for the usual bar bunnies to be sloshed, but it was getting to that hour, so I prepared to make my escape. I was still seated at the rear booth, now with the ledgers in front of me and a coffee in my hand. Even with the noise and distractions, it was better than being trapped in the office.

Just as I was getting ready to stand up, my new neighbor walked through the door in a group of people. I recognized Angela, the real estate agent who took care of our mortgage, but didn't recognize the other male with them. Tall and painfully thin, he had a wide smile on his long face. I stayed put for a moment, curious to observe.

I'd managed to avoid Stasia for the last couple days. After a long conversation with Brandon and more stern warnings for the ever-curious Lilly, I made sure the rest of my family stayed away too. I missed my early mornings on the deck, but Stasia seemed to be an early riser as well. She often puttered around the yard with that adorable dog of hers.

The threesome walked to the bar and ordered their drinks. They all ordered a pint and headed to a high top. The sun coming in through the glass window flashed off Stasia's hair, and it struck me again how pretty she was. Her full lips accented her large eyes. Angela said something that made her smile, and the burn in my chest told me that might be her most attractive feature. I still wasn't sure what she did, but she worked long hours. I guessed she was a DOD employee of some kind. Shaking my head at my stalker tendencies, I pushed myself up to put away the ledger.

\*\*\*

I had been in the office longer than I meant to be. Lately I'd been dodging calls from Dr. Galton's direct line. This time, he'd left a message informing me he was considering bringing Lilly in to test for latent abilities. He had informed me my medical appointment was moved up and we could talk about it then. The bottom dropped out from under me at the news. I sat in my office questioning his reasons and lost track of time.

When I made it back out to the bar, I looked for Ian. He gazed intently over at Stasia's table. I reflexively turned that way. Ian might be abrasive, but part of what made him a great bartender was his ability to read people. We rarely had fights or police presence despite being generous with the booze, primarily because Ian was so good at de-escalating situations before they got out of hand. The way he was staring told me something needed de-escalating.

A mousy girl with brown hair and a mean face stood next to Stasia's table holding a mixed drink. Stasia's shoulders were drawn up and tense. Around the table, Angela was about to go off. The tall skinny man had his hand on the table. He leaned toward the mousy girl, his eyes narrowed. I moved closer to listen.

"—who you think you are. You're going to get us all hurt one day."

Stasia had her hands around a pint glass, no condensation on it. I wondered if she was still nursing the first beer she'd ordered when she came in. Stasia didn't respond for a moment, so I took a seat at the bar and looked toward Ian. He got the message and came to stand near me. I faced him like we were talking but watched the table in the mirror. Stasia's voice picked up.

"I'm not going to argue with you, Emily. Not in a public place like this. Besides, it's already been resolved. Why don't you go enjoy your day?"

I waited to find out what they were talking about. Stasia's body language screamed discomfort, but her tones were soothing, almost melodic. I felt myself relaxing even from a distance. The mousy-haired girl simmered down as well, but not enough for her to take Stasia's suggestion.

"Listen. You're a new nurse in this area. I'm not going to be a bitch. But just know not to do that again. I've been at that hospital for four years, and I know how Dr. Ferris likes things done. I know how to handle those psycho patients."

I jerked my head around at the girl's words. Doctor? Nurse? Cold washed over me. I stared openly at Stasia, my shock destroying my discretion. A red flush rose from her neck to her cheeks. I realized it wasn't embarrassment I had seen earlier, but barely contained rage. I almost stood to intervene, before her next words stopped me.

She looked at the girl dead on, whereas before she'd been slightly averting her eyes. With a steel undertone, she said, "You obviously don't know what you're doing because what you said to that man was tantamount to assault. The charge didn't agree with me because I'm new. She agreed with me because I saved the hospital from getting in trouble. Now get away from me."

Next to Stasia, Angela smiled like the cat who ate the canary. The skinny man was still leaning forward, but now he was laughing softly. When the mousy brown-haired girl opened her mouth to say something, murder on her face, the man interrupted her.

"Run along Emily. Or it'll be me who talks with Ava.

And I've been at the hospital longer than *four* years."

The brown-haired girl, Emily, I corrected myself, went red. She walked away without another word, a petulant stomp to her foot. Stasia looked at the skinny man and said, "Thanks Pat." Her voice had gone back to its soft tenor.

He smiled at her. "Emily's always been a bitch. Ignore her. I can tell you Ava's been doing nothing but singing your praises. I heard she even put you in to be one of the charges."

Stasia's eyes widened, and she said, "I thought she liked me," which caused abrupt laughter all around the table.

I turned back toward Ian and realized he had already moved on down the bar, serving customers, satisfied there wasn't going to be a cat fight. I looked back over and caught Stasia's eye. She stared at me intently, but when our eyes met, they softened, and she gave me a small smile with a slight wave. I nodded politely in her direction. Quickly standing, I loudly called goodbye to Ian.

He waved back, and I smiled tightly at Stasia as I headed to the door. First a human neighbor. Then Galton tries to tell me he's bringing Lilly in for testing despite her never exhibiting any abilities. At least not in public. Now I find out the human next door is a nurse. Was she a spy? Did Galton plant an attractive member of the SEP next door? A temptress for a guy who spent almost all his time burdened down as a dad to his sister and brother? My face set in grim lines, and I climbed onto my bike parked out front of the bar. Taking the helmet off the handlebars, I strapped it on and let the motor drown out my thoughts as I headed home.

# CHAPTER 3
## Stasia

My face went to the table, and the flush of anger turned to embarrassment. Jack had barely acknowledged me before he walked out. It was the first time we'd run into each other since that awkward first meeting, and then he overheard that horrible conversation. It wasn't often I sought out confrontation. My first instinct was always to make peace out of a situation. But my job was one place I didn't compromise unless I thought it was necessary. Regardless, my earlier resolve began crumbling, and doubt set in.

"Girl!" Angela said gleefully. I looked up to see a huge smile on her face. Satisfaction radiated from her. "That was amazing. Emily is awful. It's nice to see her put in her place."

My face tensed into a frown. I didn't like the idea of taking praise for embarrassing somebody. I started to apologize for the scene, but Pat interrupted me.

"Don't."

My eyes widened at his command, but he had a kind

look on his face. "I've been working with that girl for the *four* years she's been at the naval hospital." Again, he emphasized the four. My lips quirked.

"She's awful to everyone. A total bully. The new grads follow her around because they're scared of her. You called it right, or Ava wouldn't have said you did. She's a good assistant nurse manager. And Emily has no right to walk up to you in a bar like that."

Was he a mind reader? It was like he'd plucked the insecurities right out of my head. I felt awkward but reassured. "Thanks, Pat."

He nodded sagely, and then his serious face broke into a grin. "You're not the first. I've seen her go through new hires like cheap bubble gum. You are the first I've seen stand up to her like that."

I shrugged. "It's such a problem. I see it all the time. Staff who either aren't properly trained and don't know how to de-escalate or this bullying culture cause we're the emergency department, so we don't have to follow the rules like everyone else."

Angela nodded along with what I said, her smile slowly dissolving into a frown. "I've heard clients complain about it. They had family members or whatever with bad experiences. But being besties with Pat, and knowing what you guys go through, I just always assumed they were exaggerating, or they were the ones in the wrong."

Pat said, "I get the culture thing. I don't go out of my way to restrain, but I'm not going to lie, I didn't think about it much either until this happened."

I smiled at him. "Their disease is the same as a congestive heart failure patient that comes in, you know? It's just in their mind instead of their heart."

Angela broke in. "Why aren't you a psych nurse?"

I thought about that. "There isn't really a reason for or against it. I'm just still trying to find my niche. I like the flexibility of emergency nursing for now." The truth was, I wasn't sure what I wanted or where I belonged. After years of growing up as a foster kid in Florida, then as a girl in a male dominated military, I felt terminally out of place. "I guess part of coming to Washington was trying to figure out where I belong."

I could tell she was touched I had shared the real reason. She gave me a soft smile before taking a sip of her beer. Angela was my real estate agent, but when I got to town knowing no one, she'd gone above and beyond to make me feel welcome. When we first met, she had tried asking me personal questions, and I'd dodged them almost aggressively. But over the last couple of weeks hanging out with her, I slowly grew used to Angela's exuberant energy and felt more comfortable with her. She had introduced me to Pat, and it turned out we worked in the same department. I wondered at the fact that, in two short weeks, I had more of a support system in Whidbey than I'd had in years in Florida.

My beer had stopped sweating long ago. Angela and Pat had both drank two to my one. The bar had too much energy coming at me to let my guard down. As nice as the day was, I said goodbye to my two friends, cashed out, and headed home.

***

I walked in the front door, thankful everything was in its place. Replacing another set of blinds was not something I wanted to do today. Flynn growled up happily at me, grabbing my arm in his mouth. He walked me into the living room to show how much he missed me. I laughed, finally calling "soft" to get him to let go. He continued dancing around me happily before deciding he'd lavished enough attention on me and abandoned me for his water bowl.

I walked past the large gray couch and blue area rug, straight back to the kitchen. After grabbing a diet Coke from the fridge, I opened the sliding glass door, and let Flynn out. I'd begun to set the yard up, but this was my first time out of a box apartment, and I hadn't been very imaginative. One red wooden Adirondack chair sat at the base of the stairs, a tea table next to it, looking out on the yard. It seemed like the quintessential Washington furniture.

I sat down in the chair, opened my Coke, and thought about how Jack seemed to be avoiding me. It felt self-centered to think so, but neither him nor Lilly had reappeared since I'd moved in, and he'd left the bar like a scalded cat after seeing me. I remembered the doubt and suspicion in his gaze for the couple seconds our eyes met.

The sound of someone walking through the grass to my right interrupted my thoughts. I wondered if I was about to be proved wrong. Lilly, not her big brother. The little redhead dragged her feet, a forlorn look on her face. It was so unlike my first introduction to Lilly that concern pricked me.

As she approached, I turned to face her. Lilly met my gaze and waved her hand awkwardly. "Hi," she said, her voice small.

I gave her a big smile and pushed as much positive energy as I could her way. "Hey," I replied.

Lilly came closer, shoulders drooped. "Do you think I could play with Flynn a little?"

My smile widened as Flynn came loping from the pond where he had been making a mess. He aimed like a missile for Lilly. I laughed. "I don't think you have a choice kiddo."

Lips lifting, Lilly leaned down with her arms wide. She met his wet, dirty embrace with gusto, burying her face in his muddy mane. A sad undertone still surrounded her, but at least she was brightening a little.

I stayed seated, wanting Lilly to feel in control of the situation. Her and Flynn alternated between playing chase and belly rubs until he was done with the attention and went back out to sniff and explore the yard.

Lilly faced me but kept looking back at her house. Finally, she said, "Thanks." She turned to walk back across the yard.

"Hey."

She stopped and turned back to me. This time I hesitated. It wasn't like me to pry, but something about the set of her shoulders ate at me.

"What's going on Lilly? You seem sad," I said, deciding to be straightforward.

Lilly's entire body turned again, almost without thought, toward her home. But she paused, turned around, and came to sit down by my chair. I opened my mouth to object; the grass was wet. "It's ok, I can't get any more wet than Flynn already got me."

Lilly absently picked grass, refusing to look me in the eye. I didn't mind, just waited her out.

Finally, Lilly said, her eyes dry but with tears in her voice, "Why don't they like me?"

My heart broke. Lilly sat hunched, looking defeated. Devastation rolled off her. I vaguely remembered being that age. When someone was mean to you or you were an outcast, it felt like your entire world was falling apart. I was struck speechless at first, her words hanging in the air, but I quickly collected myself and responded.

"Who doesn't like you, Lilly?"

"The kids at school." She shrugged as she said it, like she was trying to say she was indifferent. She so obviously wasn't.

"Is anyone hurting you, Lilly?" I asked.

She looked up at me then, moisture in the corner of her eyes. Suppressed tears. The air around me warmed as she responded. "No. I mean, they don't like, try to beat me up or whatever. But they don't talk to me. They avoid me."

Lilly's voice cracked on her last word, and my sadness for her deepened. Scooting down to the wet grass with her, I began picking grass myself. I sighed, trying to decide what to say.

"Kids can be shortsighted. I'm not sure why they ignore you. But I do know how much it sucks. I felt the same way when I was your age. I had a really hard time making friends. I can tell you this much. In the short time I've known you, it's not because anything is wrong with you. I could tell in the first five seconds I met you, your older brother adores you. I hear that's really hard to accomplish," I teased.

I met my goal when I heard a small giggle. Taking a deep breath, I continued. "Sometimes there is no reason, Lilly. Sometimes it just takes time. But you're going to be okay. I promise."

A cool breeze blew away the strange moment of warmth as a couple tears escaped her eyes. She looked up and brazenly brushed them away, a smile breaking free. "Thanks, Stasia."

Someone shouted from next door. "Lilly!" called a male voice. A man stepped out onto the back porch of her house. It wasn't Jack, but someone who looked similar, a little smaller, same dark brown hair.

Lilly looked around wide eyed, and I caught a wince. I had a feeling from her reaction she wasn't supposed to be over here. She quickly stood, waving at the man on the porch. I could see his frown from here. Looking back at me, she opened her mouth, I guessed to say bye, when suddenly she jumped forward and hugged me.

I wasn't typically a touchy-feely person, but I warmly returned her hug. She bounced back and said, "Thanks Stasia," with energy back in her voice. She pivoted and ran for the man. The spunk I'd witnessed when I first met her seemed to be back. He looked at her and back at me. I waved halfheartedly, just making out the confusion on his face. With his hand on Lilly's back, he guided her inside and firmly closed the door behind them.

I rose from the grass, my butt wet. Whistling for Flynn, I thought ruefully how little the wet jeans mattered. Grabbing his collar before he could protest, I dragged him to the side of the house for a forced bath. "This is what happens when you play in muddy ponds buddy." He responded with his husky growl.

# CHAPTER 4

## Stasia

Jacob stepped out of the guard shack rubbing his hands against the spring chill. I rolled to a stop and offered him my newly minted contractor badge along with a bag of muffins and a coffee.

"You. Are. The. Best," he said, emphasizing each word.

"Gotta keep our boys alert on post."

He scoffed at me but took the treats appreciatively, waving me on without really looking at my badge. This was our morning routine now. He stood this post more often than not, and I came in so early the morning traffic jam was at least an hour away.

I drove on to the hospital, my own coffee keeping my hand warm. I kept the window cracked, enjoying the fresh air, just a little shy of being too cold for comfort.

After parking and walking into the building, I went through the rest of my morning routine. Locker room, take out my nursing supplies: stethoscope, trauma shears, extra alcohol pads. The rest was in convenient carts positioned strategically in the department. I returned hellos to a couple other coworkers on the seven a.m. to seven p.m. shift and headed to the staff lounge where we huddled before starting.

A skinny body crashed into the seat next to me, groaning, head down on the table and hands splayed dramatically in front. Patrick McCormick, or Pat, was not a morning person. The start of every day we worked together went like this. He usually took at least an hour to work himself up to a full sentence.

In keeping with my usual luck, Emily worked on my new permanent shift.

Since the incident at the bar, Emily avoided me like the plague, which I preferred. She sat at the table furthest from me and Pat, but whenever I looked around the room, if our eyes caught, she always shot me a mean-girl glare. The juvenileness of it almost made me smile, but better not to stoke *that* fire.

Ava, it turned out, wasn't just the charge nurse, but the assistant nurse manager. She only stepped in on chaotic days like I had experienced when I first started here. Susan, an older woman with white-streaked yellow hair was charge today. She led us through daily announcements and updates before giving us our assignments and releasing us to the floor. Pat dragged behind me dramatically, groaning and shuffling his feet for affect. We found our computers, signed in, and got a report from the outgoing shift.

The day progressed as usual. I found myself getting a little bored at the hospital, its pace much slower than I was used to. I still wasn't sure what I wanted long term for a career. I had found emergency care exciting when I'd first started it, but now found it monotonous. While I excelled at psych nursing, it wasn't an environment I wanted to be in all the time. Despite my indecisiveness, the Washington State area, and friends I had made so far, made me happy I'd moved.

There was a new doctor on today, Dr. Galton, and he was good. I liked his direct style. So many doctors ordered every test imaginable, ending in a million dollar workup for the sniffles. Dr. Galton performed thorough assessments, ordering only what was necessary from his exam. He also put all his orders in together, which I appreciated.

I was moving through my routine when the alarm went off on our phones for a trauma coming in. A bicycle accident, middle-aged man with cardiac history and complaint of chest pain, unstable vital signs. He was coming to one of my rooms, so I pivoted from my more menial tasks to prepare.

Pat and the nurse technician I had worked with before, Sarah, came in after me and we set up together. Cardiac leads ready, the blood infuser out just in case, warmed fluids, and EKG at the ready. After everything that happened, Emily stayed away from my rooms even if there was something exciting.

Dr. Galton arrived shortly before EMS rolled in. "Hey team," he said in an upbeat voice. He turned on the ultrasound screen and verified jelly was on his cart.

"Hi," we all called. The naval hospital didn't have the worst relationship between physicians and nurses, but it wasn't the best either. The military hierarchy kept everyone from fraternizing too heavily. Dr. Galton seemed more like a civilian doctor in his mannerisms, casual and talkative with all the staff.

"You're new here, right?" he asked, looking at me.

"Yup, been here just under a month. I came from Florida."

I didn't try getting a read on him, I rarely dug too deep with my intuition on workdays. The feelings around me would overwhelm me if I did.

Dr. Galton asked, "What part of Florida?"

"A small town about an hour outside of Tampa."

"I love Tampa! Great baseball games."

I nodded, smiling politely. I didn't know anything about baseball except how I liked my hotdog. Luckily, EMS rolling in interrupted the painful small talk. We efficiently moved the patient from cot to stretcher, and Dr. Galton began his trauma assessment. As the primary nurse, I recorded. Sarah and Pat moved around the physician seamlessly. The patient needed to be moved to a trauma hospital. By the time we stabilized him, the flight crew had arrived.

I sat at the desk wearily after the flight team left. Trauma patients were rewarding to care for but could be physically exhausting. As I finished my charting, Dr. Galton approached me.

I assumed he had notes for me to include on the trauma or orders for another patient. But he surprised me by leaning casually against the high desk separating the nursing station from the patient rooms.

"How do you like working here?" he asked.

I always found this such an odd question for a new hire. What was I going to say? That some of the staff were hostile? That they really needed to update their de-escalation training considering the size of their substance abuse and psychiatric population?

"It's great," I said with forced cheeriness.

He laughed as if understanding my hyperbole.

"I won't beat around the bush. I've been hearing really good things about you."

I flushed with pride. I wasn't above compliments, and while it might not be what I wanted forever, I took a lot of pride in my job. Hearing that other people recognized my effort made me feel good.

"Thank you," I said sincerely.

He nodded but wasn't done. "Actually, I'm glad I caught you. I've been working on a project, a sort of clinical trial, that I think you would be perfect for. The subjects," he frowned, "patients," he corrected himself, "are sensitive. I've heard some gossip about your first day. I think someone with your ability to recognize body language and diffuse situations would be ideal."

My interest piqued, even as my cheeks heated because people were still talking about that. Clinical trials seemed like they could be interesting, but I had never been part of one before. "Is it based here in the Emergency Room?"

"No, no. I've spoken with Ava. For this, I would need to temporarily steal you from here. I know you just started, so you may not want to, but it won't jeopardize your position here. We'd have to get you a higher security clearance, so it may be a couple weeks before you could start."

The mention of a higher security clearance had me even more curious. To start at the base, I had secret clearance already. What could they possibly be doing that I needed something higher than that? I said as much to Dr. Galton.

"This is cutting-edge stuff. All staff from the physicians to the janitors have top secret clearance."

It sounded like an exaggeration. Depending on the content of the trial, I'd have access to patient charts. Maybe that accounted for the additional security. I'd been bored since starting here. Ava had started making noise about moving me into a charge nurse role, but I wasn't sure I was after management either. I had never done anything like a clinical trial.

"I'm interested," I said impulsively. Maybe getting out of my comfort zone for a while would be exactly what I needed to get some direction.

He smiled wide, and for the first time, I felt emotions coming from him. He was excited. Very excited. I smiled back. I liked a physician who enjoyed his work.

"Great. I know you're still finishing up that last patient. He was a handful. I'll email you the details for the offices you'll need to visit to begin your clearance application. I already spoke to Ava. We decided if you agreed you'd be taken off the schedule here so we can get you started as soon as possible."

I nodded, surprised she'd agreed to that. As short-staffed as they were here, I'd expect the assistant nurse manager to put up more of a fight to keep me as long as possible. Still, I was happy to have the monotony broken up.

"Sounds good, thanks for the opportunity," I said to him, professionalism taking over.

Before walking away, he said, "Welcome to SEP Stasia."

***

Pulling into my driveway, I put the car in park. Jack leaned into the back of a green Tahoe in his driveway. I seized the opportunity to find out if he was really avoiding me once and for all.

I stepped out of the vehicle and walked across the yard separating us. "Hey, need some help?" I called.

He looked my way. His forehead furrowed, and he kept his body pointed away from me. There wasn't animosity, but wariness settled into his stance as I approached. "Hey. Stasia, right?"

"Right." I smiled in what I hoped was a casual, friendly way. Jack was handsome and he me made me nervous, but we were neighbors. Moreover, neighbors on a secluded street a little way from town. It would be nice to be on speaking terms. His scruff from the other day had filled in, giving him a pleasing, rugged look. I swear beards were a man's best accessory.

"No, I'm good," he said.

I looked inside his hatchback. A baguette and lettuce peeked out of a couple paper bags next to potting soil and some empty clay pots.

"Gardening supplies?" I asked, trying to keep conversation flowing.

"Yeah."

I was surprised, it wasn't a common hobby for a guy who looked to be in his thirties. Surprise morphed into appreciation of his beautifully curated yard. "Did you landscape everything?"

Jack twiddled the edge of one of the paper bags, and I felt his reticence but ignored it.

"Yeah."

His monosyllabic responses made me feel silly for forcing this conversation. I didn't typically insert myself like this. I sighed in defeat, asking one more question before I left. "How's Lilly doing by the way?"

That got me a reaction. Jack turned from the paper

bag, giving me his full attention. "Lilly?"

I wasn't sure what the dynamic was. I guessed this was Jack's house, and maybe he helped his parents by taking his little sister often. "Yeah, she seemed kind of down when she visited the other day. Not her usual upbeat self. She probably talked to your mom about it."

Jack frowned, and he said absently, "Our Mom and Dad are dead. I take care of her." Realizing what he said, Jack shook himself. "Hey, thanks for asking after her, but I'm sure she's good. I better get these groceries inside and get dinner started."

He grabbed each bag then hit the button for the hatchback. I moved back to give him room, shock and sadness for his family moving through me. "Yeah, of course. Have a good night, Jack." I felt his discomfort. I don't think he meant to tell me about his parents.

"You too," he called without looking back.

I imagined him running for the door instead of the steady pace he moved at. Putting my arms around myself, I moved back over to my yard and headed inside to Flynn. The old insecurities seeped in. What about me made Jack so uncomfortable, so intent to stay away?

# CHAPTER 5

## Jack

I wrestled with the door, my hands full of groceries, flushed with anger, or embarrassment, I wasn't sure. Stasia had surprised me in the driveway. I had sensed she wanted to talk. I didn't want to be outright rude but had tried to keep my responses short enough to not encourage conversation. Then somehow, she had pulled the death of my parents out of me.

It was a small thing, really. They'd been dead for over a decade. But I didn't typically give people details about my personal life. I knew we were never going back to the planet our great-grandparents were from. I was born on Earth, and at this point, being Stepuli wasn't much different from being any other kind of green-carder. Except other green-carders weren't subject to compulsory clinical testing if they didn't manage to hide hereditary traits the government wanted. And they weren't obligated to keep the biggest part of themselves from their partner, if they were lucky enough to find one.

I'd had relationships over my thirty-five years, but

after taking full custody of Brandon and Lilly, never anything that lasted long. And I never invited women back to my house. After Brandon was old enough, I'd given him the same rules. I didn't want Lilly growing up in a frat house, and I wasn't sure how to reconcile having a long-term relationship with the obstacles of raising Lilly and having to hide who we were.

I hollered up the stairs as I moved through the foyer to the kitchen. Stasia had mentioned Lilly being upset, which should be impossible considering she had been given strict instructions to stay away from the neighbor.

The stairs rumbled as Lilly raced down at her usual top speed. She ran into the kitchen, flushed, hair crazy. I shook my head, almost distracted from the fact I was annoyed at her.

"What's up?" Lilly asked.

"Had an interesting conversation with the neighbor just now…" I started, letting my voice trail off.

"Stasia?" Lilly brightened.

I stopped reaching into the grocery bags in front of me and gave her an exasperated look. She wasn't even trying to hide it. "Lilly. What did I say?"

Lilly slammed her brows down as Brandon came in from the hall and sat on a barstool. Lilly put her hands on her hips, her expression mulish as she said, "I don't know, what did you say?"

Brandon's lips quirked, but he kept his head down. He knew I'd wring his neck if he encouraged her. Lilly was entering the phase of adolescence where she challenged everything. It'd be a miracle if I didn't pull all my hair out before forty.

Taking a deep breath, I kept my voice level and said,

"I said to stay away from the neighbor, Lilly. The very *human* neighbor."

Lilly's bravado faltered, and her face screwed up. I couldn't tell if she was acting or really upset. "I was just talking to her, Jack."

"Which you were expressly told not to do Lill."

Tears slipped free, tracking down her cheeks. She said in a soggy voice, "I just wanted to talk to a girl for a minute! It isn't fair. I'm not allowed to go to the Stepuli events, but you don't want me bringing home human friends either! Not that I have any because even without knowing anything about me, they all think I'm a *freak*."

She was yelling by the end of her speech. I was shocked. I had no idea she'd been feeling this way. I thought she was just having issues with her classes, normal teenage stuff. I opened my mouth to say something, though I had no idea what, but she didn't wait for me. She stormed off down the hall, stomping her feet dramatically on the stairs and slamming her door.

I shook my head at the ridiculousness of teenage girls, but Brandon's face was serious.

He said, "She talked to her the other day. She went outside, and the dog was out. I saw her playing with him and thought there was no harm with giving her a moment. Right when she was about to head back, she turned back around and talked to that neighbor girl."

I didn't know how I felt about that. When Brandon had stepped back from the bar, we switched roles. He was here more often with Lilly now, making sure she got home from school and kept to a routine. I'd gone back to managing the bar. The fact he let her break the rules and didn't mention it to me made me doubt his ability to look out for our little sister.

Brandon continued, stopping my thoughts in their tracks, "She'd been upset about something all day. Not like herself at all Jack. Then when she came back from the neighbor's, she was a live wire again. Her annoying, way-too-energetic self. I didn't tell you because I didn't want you to freak out. But it seemed good for her."

Walking around the island, the groceries abandoned, I sat down heavily. That old fear, that I was fucking up trying to raise Lilly, seeped in. I was at a loss. How did I protect her without suffocating her?

We sat in silence for a while before Brandon got twitchy. Looking over at him, I said, "What should I do B?"

He met my eyes and shrugged. "How the hell do I know Jack? I'm an alcoholic."

His self-deprecation ate at me. In some ways, Brandon had it the hardest out of all of us. After he'd revealed his elemental power, Dr. Galton had jumped on it. My mother had sacrificed herself so her kids were left alone unless one of us expressed abilities. Then we were fair game for the clinical trials. Mom was in one of the first groups of inseminations in the Eugenics Project. Something that had cost her life. But the treaty had superseded her sacrifice, and Brandon had lost the life he'd thought he was going to have.

Finally, I said, "You're already turning it around. Quit talking to yourself like that, B." I sighed heavily. Mulling it over, I said hesitantly, "Maybe we should, I don't know, invite the neighbor to dinner or something."

Brandon's eyebrows raised in surprise. Hell, I was surprised. But at least if I allowed Lilly some access to the neighbor, she'd stop trying to see her when neither of us were here. She couldn't go to the Stepuli events, thinly veiled get-togethers designed to find active powers in fourth generation Stepuli.

"I mean, Lilly would be stoked. Are you sure you want to?" he asked.

I wasn't sure. But Lilly's outburst worried me. It worried me even more that she had hinted at having a hard time with the kids at school. I didn't want to totally mess up as a parent. If she needed some girl time, I wanted her to have it. Just under my roof. Where I could control it.

***

Deciding to grill so I could maybe catch Stasia outside, I took the steaks out. There were already extra, me and Brandon ate enough for a family of four. Hedging my bets, I threw the steaks on the grill. The sides were already done and keeping warm on the stove.

A I turned the rib eye's, a mixed a howl and growl announced Flynn's presence. Stasia followed close behind him. Our yards weren't far apart, close enough that, when I called her name, she easily heard me.

Stasia seemed surprised but wasted no time heading my way. Flynn loped alongside her. As she neared the stairs to my deck, she placed a hand on the rail, but didn't step up to where I was. Flynn had no such hesitation.

I couldn't help the laugh that escaped as I ran my hands down his thick fur, appreciating his growls, his way of saying hello.

"How's it going Jack?" Stasia greeted.

I forced some of the tension out of my body. I knew my prejudice against her wasn't fair. So far, she had proved to be a normal neighbor. If anything, she seemed to go out of her way to give us privacy.

"It's good. Sorry I was short earlier, you just caught

me by surprise. I didn't know Lilly was struggling. I'm beating myself up for it."

Her face softened. I suddenly felt calm in her presence.

"No problem, I understand."

"So…" I continued, feeling awkward since I'd been trying to get away during every interaction before now. "Uhm, we were wondering. Lilly really enjoyed being over at your house the other day. I was thinking…"

I sounded like a fucking idiot. I fell over my words, wondering how I was supposed to abruptly ask her to dinner after being an ass since she moved in. She tilted her head, a small smile on her face, but waited for me. I sighed, laughing at myself.

I asked bluntly, "Want to join us for dinner tonight?"

That wide smile I'd seen the other night at the bar broke across her face. She had an amazing smile. "I'd love to," she said brightly. "Let me just bring Flynn home and get him settled."

"He can join, if you want." He had already laid down at my feet, panting at the grill.

Her brows puckered. "Are you sure? It's kind of impossible to take him places without leaving his fur behind."

I laughed but said, "Lilly will go nuts, and I have a vacuum."

She nodded, finally stepping up to the deck. Guilt pricked me that I had been such a shitty neighbor. We lived in a secluded area, and she was a single woman living alone in a new town. Just as I was about to speak again, the sliding glass door opened, and Lilly walked out.

"Stasia?"

"Hey Lilly." Stasia waved.

45

Before Lilly could talk again, I said, "Stasia is going to join us for dinner, okay Lills? Why don't you go set the table? Steaks are almost done."

I looked over my shoulder. Whether this was a good idea or not didn't matter anymore. The smile Lilly gave me made me feel, at least for a moment, like I wasn't messing up this parenting thing.

# CHAPTER 6
## Stasia

Jack's usual distrust wasn't coming off him, but I could tell he felt awkward by the way he stumbled over his words.

"Can I help with anything?" I asked.

He turned to me, a forced smile on his face, his brow slightly puckered. "No thanks." He pointed with tongs to his slider. "Why don't you head in. I'll be in with the steaks in a second."

I headed toward the door, whistling for Flynn. I didn't hear him get up, so I looked back. He concentrated the full force of his begging on Jack and the sizzling meat in front of him. I cocked a hand on my hip, ready to reprimand him when Jack looked over, then down.

He chuckled, and this time the expression seemed casual. "No worries, I'll bring him in with me. Oh, how do you like your steak?"

I'd be annoyed with Flynn later for not listening. And for begging. But for now, I silently promised him an under-the-table morsel for helping thaw the ice. "Medium rare works great, thanks."

With a nod from Jack, I headed in. To chaos.

"LILLY!" I heard the man I'd seen on the porch the other day holler. An island sat in the middle of an L-shaped kitchen with pots and bowls scattered around it. Tin foil lay haphazardly here and there. The man looked young, maybe early twenties? He hollered for Lilly who popped back in, bouncing on the balls of her feet. Instead of heading for who I assumed was another brother, she came straight to me, grabbing my hand.

"Oh, Stasia! I'm so glad you agreed to come to dinner!"

I laughed and headed over to the island. "Thanks for inviting me, Lilly."

The man looked up as I approached, serving spoon in hand. "Hi, I'm Brandon," he greeted with butter on his cheek. *How?*

I waved. "Stasia. Can I help?" I repeated my offer, but this time meant it more earnestly. This kid needed help. He wasn't really a kid, but he obviously wasn't a cook either.

"Uh…sure. Lilly, can you set the table?" He asked as he moved down the island. "I'm just trying to get this stuff served up into bowls. Jack said we should make it more presentable than the usual grab and go off the oven."

It was sweet, but Brandon was making a mess. He had dished some green beans into a large mixing bowl. Some fell over the sides. Mashed potatoes still sat in a pot with an empty mixing bowl near them.

"Show me the garbage, take the green beans to the table, and leave the rest to me." Brandon looked relieved at my direction and left me to it.

As promised, it wasn't long before Jack came in with

the steaks. We had gotten the sides to the table and the island cleaned up right before he came in with Flynn circling his ankles. He set the steaks on each of our plates at the large circular table set in a dinette off the kitchen. I sat down, Jack across from me, his shoulders stiff.

Lilly spoke, mouth half full. "So Stasia, how is living on Whidbey?"

I swallowed my bite, the food delicious. "It's been great. I come from Florida, and I'm not much for round-the-clock sun and one-hundred-degree weather." Looking across the table, I said, "Food is great Jack."

He hummed his thanks while Lilly bulldozed on. "Oooh, Florida! How cool! Do you surf? I don't really swim in the ocean here, it's too cold."

I admitted sheepishly, "No, I'm actually a horrible swimmer. Crippling fear of sharks."

Lilly had scooped a large bite of mashed potatoes and didn't respond right away. Brandon said, "Thanks for the help earlier, by the way. I was making a mess." His voice was deeper than I would have expected, like Jack's even though he seemed much younger.

Jack looked up at his admission, his eyebrows drawn down in confusion. I shrugged. "Happy to help. This dinner is amazing. Thanks for inviting me."

Jack opened his mouth to say something, but Lilly got there first. "Anytime! So, you were right. I mean, it isn't perfect, but school is getting a little better. I made a friend. A new girl who came in last week in the middle of the semester."

I turned to her, truly delighted to hear that. Growing up with only brothers had to be hard, especially at her age. Getting used to your period, starting to crush on boys.

Talking to an older brother about that would be worse than awkward.

"Lilly, that's great! What's she like?"

Lilly launched into an in-depth explanation about her new friend, dominating the dinner conversation for most of the night. At some point Flynn had laid down under the table, his chin on my foot. Jack interjected here and there. As the night wore on, his shoulders relaxed, and the tense lines of his face smoothed out.

Brandon gave me more background about this end of the island. Apparently, the land was tied up in leases with the reservation. They were surprised I'd been able to get into the house I had rented. It made me even more thankful it had been available.

When dinner was done, I stood with Brandon to clean up, but Jack stopped me. Apparently, this was a nightly ritual. Lilly stood, and Brandon and she washed up together. Jack took out a deck of cards and started shuffling. The coffee machine started to gurgle.

Jack dealt the deck. "So, we're taking advantage of you a little bit tonight, Stasia."

He had been relaxing more and more throughout dinner. His voice took on a playful edge, and my interest piqued. "Oh really?" I asked, a grin playing at my lips.

He nodded sagely, looking up only briefly. "We usually play war or something after dinner. But since you're here, we're going to play a game of spades. Ever played?"

I had, from my time in the military. Young kids at the smoke deck with nothing better to do loved trash talking over spades. Instead, I said, "Hmmm, not sure I have."

I was always a terrible liar. His cocked brow told me I

probably still was. "We'll see. Let me give you a run down." Jack explained the rules, and Brandon and Lilly returned to the table, their nightly routine done. Because of the way we were sitting, Jack and I were partners, which Lilly pouted about for a short while. Despite her complaints, he refused to budge, looking at me conspiratorially. Oh yea, Jack knew I had been lying.

\*\*\*

"NO!" Brandon roared.

"What?" Lilly asked, placing an ace of spades against the four of spades I had put down to cut hearts. "I thought aces were good?"

I bit my lower lip to hold in the chuckle and looked up at Jack. He winked as Brandon threw himself back against the chair grumbling.

"What?" Lilly asked again, looking at everyone in turn, her brows puckered in puzzlement. Jack and I laughed. Before anyone could explain why her strategy was off, Flynn stood, a low growl coming out as he dipped into a long stretch. He headed to the sliding glass door and looked at me expectantly. Surprised, I looked over at the clock on the oven. I'd been here for hours. It was close to nine p.m.

I put my cards down on the table. "Sounds like my cue. Thanks again everyone for a great dinner."

As I stood to go, coffee in hand to place in the sink, Jack stood with me. Lilly said, "Do you want to come to dinner tomorrow, Stasia?" She sounded so hopeful. I wanted to say yes. The truth was, I had a plate of pasta back home to clean up. The offer to not eat alone had been too enticing to pass up. This had been a nice night, full of laughter, and after the initial awkwardness, surprising ease.

My hesitation must have been clear because Jack spoke up. "You should." His voice was low, and for once I didn't feel any tension coming off him. He walked over, his fingers brushing mine as he took my coffee cup. I heated from the touch and couldn't help a small intake of breath. Brandon's next grumbled words covered it.

"But we aren't playing spades again. Or if we are, you're on my team."

We all laughed, and Jack moved into the kitchen toward the sink. I headed to Flynn, who was now scratching at the door, looking over at me impatiently. "Uhm, sounds good then. I'll see you tomorrow."

Jack called from in the kitchen, "Around seven? I'll send Lilly over to get you."

I smiled back. "Okay. Night guys."

"Night!" A chorus of voices returned. As I set home with Flynn, for once, the loneliness that had been my constant companion didn't feel so close.

# CHAPTER 7

## Jack

I rested my elbow on the window, head resting on my fist. Lilly sat behind me talking about her new friend at school, Letty something. "Lilly and Letty," she said. The school bus didn't reach our little beach house, so Brandon or I dropped her off every day at school. Brandon had taken over the job, but today was my day for clinical testing. I'd told him I'd drop her off on my way into the clinic, and he had taken over for me at the bar.

It was his first day back since our talk, and while I was a little worried, I felt like I needed to trust him. I had spent a lot of time dictating what he would do when he was younger, and the heavy-handedness had driven us apart. I wanted to mend that gap. Moving forward in the parent drop-off line, I forced myself to stop worrying my bottom lip and tried to tune into what Lilly was saying.

"—but I was thinking, everything went so great with Stasia last night, maybe Letty could come over too."

Fuck, what had I missed? She was right, things with Stasia had gone surprisingly well last night. Lilly had only changed the temperature slightly with her excitement. It had been subtle enough Stasia hadn't even remarked on it, and eventually, I had let my guard down completely. My thoughts strayed to touching her hand, that startled sound I'd heard her make. I warmed at the memory. Shaking myself out of it, I turned to Lilly while we were stopped. I needed to shut this down.

"Lilly, that was an exception. The *only* exception. You're required to go to human schools because of the treaty. All attempts should be made to integrate unless you're expressing powers. That's the only reason I have you go here. You're still letting your fire out in little ways. At random times."

She folded her arms and looked out her window, chin set in stubborn lines. "I'm always with you or Brandon. I just want some girl time Jack."

"I thought Stasia was girl time Lill," I said, exasperated.

Her head whipped around, her stubborn expression gone. Her eyes were augers. "It is. I mean. I had a lot of fun with Stasia at dinner last night. I was surprised you invited her again."

I took advantage of her obvious worry I'd change my mind. "Then why are you pushing it?"

"I..." she began hesitantly. We pulled up to the drop-off, she didn't have much time. Clearly deciding to err on the side of caution, she said, "You know what, never mind. Love you."

As she opened her door, I felt a vague sense of victory. "Love you!" I called to her retreating back, doubting she heard it over the slamming door. Continuing out of the parking lot, I turned for the clinic. All of a sudden, I felt queasy, and a cold, clammy sweat broke out. Any sense of victory I'd had with Lilly leaked out of me the closer I got to the clinic.

\*\*\*

Sickness settled in my gut as I looked at the nondescript building with peeling pink stucco that made my life hell. Made my family and my people's lives hell.

After generations of Stepuli-human pairings reliably producing children with elemental abilities, the government began wondering if they could harness the elemental power. Transfer it to humans somehow. When the medical teams intensified their studies, adding in practical testing of abilities, they explained the Stepuli power could do everything from reversing global warming to helping curb future wars. My parents were asked, "Isn't that why your grandparents came to our planet?"

We didn't have much of a choice. Even after decades on the planet, we were still organized into insular communities. The government ceded us land, told us we could consider it our own territory with our own rules, but the human population wasn't ready to know about life outside Earth. The Stepuli's agreed so they could live out their lives peacefully. I don't think they realized generations of children would come later, suppressed and confined.

I forced myself out of the Tahoe, knowing stalling wouldn't do any good. I walked through the glass door into a typical clinic office. A cover in case the casual passerby happened in. Rows of metal chairs on either side faced a plexiglass screen that separated the secretary in front of me from the rest of the room. I felt like I was in urgent care.

The woman looked up, her floral blouse drooping off her shoulders. The skin at the base of her neck loose, accented by a glass necklace. Her reading glasses were falling down the bridge of her small nose.

"Hey, Jack," she said and continued typing on her computer. Tilting her curly brown hair toward the door to my right, she said, "Galton's been expecting you. Go ahead."

I nodded, not returning her greeting. It always kind of sickened me how normal the human's running this office found this compulsory medical testing. The soft click sounded behind me as I moved through the door. Generic pictures hung haphazardly down the plain hallway. I walked to the end exam room on the right.

Standing in the doorway, I tapped twice on the door in front of me. Dr. Galton sat at the sink with a computer in front of him. Balding with white hair sparsely surrounding the crown of his head, white shirt accented by an ugly-patterned tie, and brown slacks, Dr. Henry Galton sat for all the world like he was at his boring office job. I felt traces of earth around me and let the element rush through my core and warm in my palms. Soothing me, centering me.

Galton looked up at my rap on the door. He smiled at me like we were old friends. "Hey, Jack. You're a hard man to get a hold of."

I grunted because we both knew I avoided him like the plague. Walking in, I took a seat in the exam chair facing the small bed that drew out to an exam table. I put down the folded side table and drew up the sleeve of my Henley, wanting this over with.

"You don't usually do the routine blood draws." It was an obvious statement, but I wanted to get this conversation over with. I hated Galton's small talk, like we were friends.

He hummed and nodded, moving away from his

computer with some supplies. "Well, we need to talk." His voice had a musical quality to it. A caricature of the kind grandfather.

"Lilly isn't coming in for testing unless she expresses abilities. Besides the deal you made with our mother, you and I had a deal."

He hummed again as he placed the tourniquet, readying me for my monthly labs. The government never figured out a way to unlock elemental powers in humans. When they'd failed, they'd started a thinly veiled breeding program, calling it the Eugenics Project. If they couldn't create elementals, they could birth them. Since they were limited by reproduction, they wanted to ensure they encouraged the strongest progeny each generation. Somehow, they were mapping this with DNA.

As the needle pierced my arm, Galton said, "An unusual number of fourth generation Stepuli are expressing late abilities. No stone unturned and all that."

Anger burned me. My mother had died buying our freedom. She had been part of the first group of inseminations after our dad died. At the time, volunteers received allowances. With a probation-type program, their families would be allowed to live outside the communities with humans, under the condition that our true nature was kept secret. She'd died giving birth to Lilly before she could realize that dream with us.

"I agreed to help you with your fifth generation." I spat it, the idea of contributing to this atrocity filling me with loathing. Of doing the same thing I had, at times, raged against my mother for doing. But since Lilly was born, I'd grown to understand you would do anything for your child. My love for my mother grew, my regret over our last year together deepened, and I knew I'd sacrifice anything to save Lilly these indignities. I wished I had saved Brandon too.

Dr. Galton nodded agreeably, taking the needle out and pressing gauze to the dot of blood trying to escape. "We've yet to begin your contributions in that area, however. So far, all we have is our promises, Jack."

Ice traced down my spine. This is why he was here collecting routine blood. He'd finally found someone he wanted to pair me with. My heart pounded, my mouth watered, nausea pooling in my gut.

The idea of doing anything to save Lilly from being a lab rat, from becoming part of the insemination program herself, had always been abstract. I had expected it in my twenties, but as I inched closer to thirty-five, Galton had never called on me to actively participate in the program. He'd never even summoned me for fertility testing. My deprivation testing had proved I was one of the strongest earth elementals since the ambassadors. I'd always wondered what was taking him so long. Apparently, I didn't need to wonder anymore.

Dr. Galton smiled, looking like a grandfather bestowing an heirloom. He held out a sterile cup. "We need a semen sample."

"Now?" I asked, my voice croaking.

"No time like the present. We're both here, and I think we've found a subject to match you with."

Sweat trickled down my neck. As years went by and he didn't call me to deliver on my promise, despite knowing he'd want my genes, I had stupidly imagined maybe my blood didn't match up to what he wanted. Maybe this day wouldn't come.

"Will I—" I coughed to clear my voice. "Will I meet the woman you're inseminating?"

Dr. Galton continued holding the cup out, the picture of patience. I just looked at it. "No. We have decided to raise this generation of children. The mother will carry the fetus to term, and we will take over care of the child. This is the agreement for you to have freedom. For Lilly to have freedom."

I had succeeded in keeping Lilly's fire under wraps. Nobody realized the things she could do. If they did, he wouldn't offer me this.

"I want it in writing. I want it in writing, and I want no more home visits." Still trying to leverage. Oh, my God, this meant I'd have a child out there. My own child. Being raised in a lab. Panic made my heart race and sweat continued trickling down my back. I couldn't think about that. *I have a child now*, I thought, *and she still has a chance.*

Dr. Galton, finally tiring of my reticence, shoved the cup into my hand. "Second door on the right. Semen sample first, and we'll expand our agreement. After we verify it's successful, I'll amend your probation."

The indignity of this ate at me. *Anything for your child*, I reminded myself as I walked down the hall. The second door. My hand reached for the handle. Turning it, I felt disgust for everything I was, everything I had to do to survive. Magazines lay next to a chair on a small side table in the dimly lit room. I closed the door behind me. The catch of the door resounded around me. It was the sound of my prison locking.

# CHAPTER 8

## Stasia

A knock on my back door had Flynn growling and rushing for the slider. I beckoned Lilly in. I was on my laptop doing some pre-employment work for the trial Dr. Galton had invited me to. He hadn't exaggerated about the increased security clearance.

"Hey Stasia." Lilly dutifully stopped to give Flynn scratches, not that she had much choice. He adopted his approach to catching me when I first walked in the door, mouth clamped gently around her wrist, growling his displeasure at her absence while she giggled and lavished love on him.

I laughed with her but called, "Soft." Flynn hadn't been around kids before Lilly. She might not be little, but I didn't want her to get hurt accidentally if he was too rough.

She sat down next to me on the newly unpackaged kitchen stools by my island. "Watcha workin' on?" She asked in a sing-song voice.

The hair at her temples was sweaty and cowlicked, and

she had that salty smell of a kid playing at recess. I chuckled inwardly. Lilly was sixteen, she had told me at dinner the other night. She was young at heart, and I loved it. I wondered if it was because she'd grown up with older brothers who probably perpetually saw her as a baby or if her spirit was just so carefree it refused to rush toward adulthood like so many did at her age.

"Some boring work stuff," I replied to her original question and closed the laptop. Partly because it turned out the trial really was top secret, and partly because I wanted to concentrate on her.

She didn't seem to mind, her grin bringing out the dimple in her right cheek as she twisted back and forth on the stool. "Jack's in a mood, and Brandon is always in a mood, so I came over early. I thought girls were supposed to be moody!"

She had me laughing in the middle of her speech, and by the time she finished, I was bent over. God, I wish the boys had heard that. I loved this girl. Standing up, I tapped her on the shoulder, tears leaking out of the corner of my left eye.

"Let's make them some brownies for their woes," I said. I walked over to the pantry to the right of my galley kitchen. By now I had stocked up.

"You know how to bake?" Lilly asked brightly, staying seated while she watched me collect everything.

My cheeks warmed a little, and I brushed a stray lock of hair behind my ear. "Well..." I paused as I bent over, grabbing mixing bowls from the cabinet under the island. "Know how is a strong word."

She looked puzzled. I gave her a sheepish smile as I straightened. "I actually didn't really know how to cook before this. Like cook anything. Except maybe ramen."

"So, what did you eat?" she asked quizzically, and I marveled at the fact that Jack must cook for her every night. I wondered what age he was when he took over her care.

"I was well-versed in takeout. I worked a lot, so it was easier." I shrugged. "Moving here, I knew I'd have a slower pace, and I decided it was time to learn. I love sweets, so I started playing around with baking first."

I finished collecting all the ingredients and we set to work making brownies from a box. Flynn pouted in the living room after sternly being ordered to the border of the kitchen. I figured we could do without brownies à la mode Flynn hair.

Lilly chatted about her day at school. They were reading *Their Eyes Were Watching God* in English class, and she was delighted by the colloquial language Hurston used in her novel. We fell into an enthusiastic discussion about the character's life, with me promising the ending would shock her. Hurston had been one of my favorites in school.

It was six thirty when the brownies were done and cooled. It may have been from a box, but I was excited the brownies were edible. Me and Lilly shared one just to be sure, giggling that Jack would never let her have dessert before dinner. We loaded the brownies onto a plate with a towel over them and headed to her house, Flynn following at Lilly's insistence.

*\*\*\**

Stepping into Lilly's house, I was struck by the unnatural quiet. The last time I'd come in for dinner there had been chaos, yelling. For a family of three, it had felt more like a scene out of *Cheaper by the Dozen*. This time, Jack sat at their dinette table, head in his hands, coffee in front of him. Delicious smells wafted from the kitchen. Chicken?

He looked up when the door opened, his eyes a little unfocused. Lilly frowned at him and said, "Jesus Jack, are you sleeping on the job?"

That shook him out of whatever daze he'd been in. Seeing me, he said lifelessly, "Hey Stasia."

I lifted the brownies in a salute and headed to the kitchen, taking a few breaths. Jack felt…empty. Like a black hole. I had seen him distrustful, suspicious, annoyed, even happy and playful at this point. His current emotions didn't touch on anything I'd seen from him before. He was scarily vacant.

The front door opened, and I looked up, forcing my smile to work.

"Hey! Sorry, I couldn't find the damn gravy anywhere in the supermarket, Jack," Brandon called as he came down the hall.

Where Jack was a rugged handsome, Brandon was more of a pretty handsome. His body had long lines of ropey muscle and his hair stuck up in various directions. His almost-golden eyes tense with worry. Something was wrong, and Brandon wasn't sure what to do.

We all plated our food from the stove at my insistence, and to Lilly's delight. "Less dishes," she explained. She hadn't caught onto Jack's mood yet, distracted by me and Flynn, and the reveal that she had helped make dessert.

Everyone sat down at the table, the conversation a low hum. Jack didn't join in and barely took his eyes off his food. As time went on, an uneasy quiet that hadn't been present last night fell over the table. Brandon and I kept exchanging worried looks without comment. Sweat trickled down my neck. I distantly wondered what the thermostat was set at but didn't say anything.

Over the course of dinner, we managed some questions, focusing on Lilly's day at school and Brandon's at the bar. Like last night, after we finished our plates, the younger siblings got up to clean the table. Jack and I hadn't really spoken outside of last night. Before that, he had outright been avoiding me. I had an idea but wasn't sure how welcome it would be.

Someone dropped a fork at the sink. Jack jumped, and that decided it for me. "Hey Jack, want to take a walk?"

He focused on my face when I spoke. His eyebrows raised slightly, his hair, a little too long in front, fell over his forehead. "I—" he began, but Brandon interrupted from the kitchen.

"You should go." Jack and I looked over at the statement. Brandon hadn't even bothered turning toward us. Lilly silently dried dishes next to him, casting worried glances at Jack over her shoulder.

Jack seemed to notice for the first time. Sweat dripped from his temple to his ear. He wiped at the moisture, surprised. Looking from his hand to me he said, "Yeah, that sounds good. Hey B, why don't you turn down the heat. I think I set it too high. It's hot as hell in here."

Brandon called over his shoulder, "You bet." Lilly stiffened next to him. I hurt for her, picking up on her brother's feelings. Flynn got up to follow us as I followed Jack's lead out the back door.

\*\*\*

I had expected we'd walk along the road, but Jack led me to the tree line at the edge of our properties. We walked to the far right of his property. I saw that they'd cut steps into the cliff face, adding wood blocks for footing, leading to the beach below. I envied his access and wondered how I hadn't noticed it before now. It was so skillfully cut into the earth it looked like a naturally grown path.

We made it to the beach quickly. Jack put his hands in his jean pockets, the neck of his dark gray Henley falling open in the wind to reveal chest hair and a collar bone I found far too attractive.

Inwardly cursing myself, I thought, *an attractive collar bone? You idiot.*

We continued in silence for a while. The beaches here were so different from Florida. Instead of white sandy beaches, it was packed sand with rocks covering the beach and large sheets of driftwood lying around. Considering I wasn't a swimmer, I found the moody setting more pleasing.

"Sorry about tonight." Jack spoke gruffly, his voice deeper than usual. He looked at me briefly, then brought one hand out of his pocket and swept his overgrown bangs back. He took a shuddering breath. "Today just kind of…sucked."

I nodded, not sure what to say. I could feel he didn't want to talk about it. But while he spoke, that black hole began feeling less empty. The emotions weren't happy ones. Grief and fear. But they were feelings. They weren't the terrifying emptiness I had felt from him all night.

"What happened?" I asked, hoping he would let more of it go.

"Just some family stuff." He looked out at the ocean for a while before continuing. "Some stuff I have to do because my parents died. Some responsibilities I have to take care of, so Lilly has what she needs."

He struggled to get out his words, like he was talking

around something rather than talking about it.

"How did your parents die?" I hoped the question wasn't too intrusive. He surprised me by answering easily.

"My mom died in childbirth with Lilly. My dad was..." He hesitated then said, "My dad was killed. Attacked."

My eyes widened as horror filled me. I stopped and turned to him. "Oh, my God, Jack. I'm so sorry."

He muttered thanks then kept walking. I fell into step with him. We continued a little longer before he spoke again. "So, what really brought you to Washington? We talked about it a little last night."

A splash caught our attention. Flynn dove into the waves after something. He walked back out of the surf, lazily following our path. Jack looked back at me and smiled. The first smile I'd seen on him tonight. Love for Flynn blossomed, and something loosened in my chest at the sight. For the first time in a long time, I opened up.

"It was just so empty for me there." I kicked a rock, absorbing the fact I was really telling him the truth. I didn't just rarely speak about this. I never spoke about it. But then, I wondered how often he talked about his parents. He stayed quiet, his hands back in his pockets, letting me speak at my own pace.

"I grew up in foster care in Florida. I was abandoned as a baby. My mom did something called safe haven. She dropped me off at a fire station." I swallowed. The old feelings of not being good enough surged even though months of therapy had made me accept it wasn't my fault.

"I...I don't know why, but I just never really bonded with any of my foster families. Usually babies, you know, they just get adopted. Well, I almost got adopted once. Or

I was, I guess. But that didn't work out, and after, I could feel that none of the families really wanted me."

Jack looked over at me, his body had been slowly relaxing as I spoke. He asked, "What happened with the adoption?"

Bile rose in my throat. That was another story I had never told. Not after the first time. I opened my mouth to tell him "nothing," but Jack's arms hung loosely at his side, his face peaceful. Seeing my story distract him from that horrible place he had been in earlier, the truth popped out.

"I had an adopted brother with that first family. We were never close. We didn't even really know each other. He was a lot older. But he had this friend who needed extra money, and so my adopted parents offered to let him babysit. I was too young for school, and the woman, my adopted mom, needed a break sometimes. It started when I was five. He started doing... things." I took a deep breath, shame and anger filling me.

"When I finally told my adopted parents, my brother said I was lying. The boy who had been babysitting me was his best friend. He raged at his parents until they told the agency the adoption wasn't working out, and I was put back in the foster system. When people asked why they said it was because I made up stories. After that, I bounced around a lot." I ended there, unable to go further. It was my biggest secret. The fear of being hated for what the boy had done to me. For what, what would have been my brother claimed I lied about. Even now, it was too strong.

I looked over at Jack, afraid to see his expression, his revulsion or discomfort at my oversharing. Maybe I had been projecting and he hadn't needed me to keep talking at all. He had stopped walking and turned to me slightly.

His shoulders were tight, his arm flexed. I looked down and realized his hands were fisted.

Taking in my reaction, he opened his hands and intentionally relaxed. Tears burned my eyes, and I looked away from him, not understanding his reaction and feeling humiliated at my own story. His feet moved, but I kept my eyes fastened on the angry gray ocean, seeming to reflect my own emotions. I felt his hand on my arm. His rough fingers, callused from some kind of work, wrapped around my bicep and compelled me to look up at him.

"I'm sorry that happened." His voice was deep, and I looked up into his chocolate eyes. "Those people were idiots and cowards. None of that was your fault." My throat was too choked to speak without completely humiliating myself, so I just nodded. His face blurred slightly, but I took large breaths through my nose, and as subtly as possible let them out my mouth to hold back the tears. He reached up with his thumb and caught an escaped tear. His eyes searched my face a second longer before he surprised me and pulled me into a hug.

His strong arms wrapped around my small frame. It took me a second, but my arms reached up, my palms flat on his back. I heard his sharp intake of breath and his arms tightened slightly. Giving in, I buried my face in his shirt, breathing in his crisp, clean scent, like a forest on a spring day.

Just as I was beginning to wish the hug would never end, Flynn barked. His large paws landed on our arms, crashing us apart. I caught myself from falling. Flynn crouched down, his butt in the air, tail wagging, thinking this was some fun new game. I looked over at Jack and we burst out laughing.

# CHAPTER 9

## Stasia

It was black. It was all black. My breath quickened. I heard that. I could hear my breathing. I tried to touch something, but I was floating. I was floating in an endless expanse of space, weightless.

I listened for a drip. For the murmur of voices. For any sounds of life. But there was nothing.

I hyperventilated as fear crept in. Panic danced at the edges of my consciousness. My heart pounded in my ears. I wanted out. I reached up, but there was no lid. I dropped my leg to stand, but instead, my face dipped below the water. There was nothing solid to bounce my foot off, to buoy me back to the surface.

I wondered if I'd drown. If I would drown in this weightless, lonely, silent place.

My thoughts unconsciously relaxed my body, and it naturally floated back to the surface, the salt in the water wanting my solid form to float. I took a breath, the sound of *my gasp the only sound in the room. In the world.*

*In the blackness, in the water, the most real feeling, the only feeling, was the trickle of my tears sliding from my eyes to my temples and into my hair.*

I woke up crying. It had been a long time since I'd done that. Flynn whined beside my bed, confused. If anything, the sound of him, the gray tones of the room bringing my dresser and nightstand into focus, made me cry harder. Big racking sobs, my hand to my chest, sweet relief coursing through me.

Eventually, the sobs eased. Flynn had jumped onto the bed, his head resting on my leg. I sat up to scratch him, reassure him everything was okay. After washing my tear-stained face in the bathroom, I walked him downstairs into the predawn light. I was starting early today for my clearance interviews and an in-depth employee health screening.

Stepping onto the wet grass, feet barefoot, I let my toes sink in. The dream had been so visceral I was still celebrating every sensation I could absorb. A noise came from the house next door. Jack stepped out, coffee mug in hand, and walked to the chair I had seen him in when I'd first moved in. He took a seat and noticed me. He raised his mug to me. I smiled and raised mine back.

We moved at the same time, him standing and stepping off his porch, me meeting him halfway. We stood in the grass near our property line, and without needing to agree, turned to watch Flynn sniff his way to the tree line.

"Sleep well?" His baritone moved through me. My favorite sensation so far this morning.

"Like a baby," I lied, "you?"

He chuckled. "Better than I would have thought." He turned his head to look at me, his eyes soft, and butterflies took flight in my stomach.

"Jack!" Lilly called shrilly from their deck.

Dropping his shoulders and looking at the sky, he said, "Jesus, can't she sleep until her alarm like a normal freakin' teenager."

I laughed. Fat chance. Everything I had learned about Lilly said she had boundless energy.

"Jack, I need my gym shirt. I get marked down if I don't dress out."

"I'm coming!" He called, cutting her off. Rolling his eyes, the corner of his mouth picked up, and he said, "See you later?"

I smiled back. "I'm sure we'll see each other around."

*** 

"Hi," I greeted, "I'm Anastasia Smith. I'm here for employee health."

I looked through the plexiglass window at the woman. She was older, with wiry curly hair. She nodded pleasantly. "You're all checked in dear, take a seat."

I nodded back, wondering at the fact I didn't have to give more information. It was a small town. The military community made it even smaller, I decided. I turned to the chairs, looking for a seat. Surprise pricked me. In the back row, chin practically touching his chest, for all the world looking asleep, sat Pat's long lanky body. I headed to the seat next to him.

I sat down loudly, making Pat jump. He wiped his mouth as if he'd been drooling. Looking around wide eyed, he finally seemed to realize who sat next to him. His brow furrowed in confusion. "Stasia?"

I smiled brightly at him. He hated when I flaunted my morning happiness. "What's a guy like you doing in a place like this?" I asked, purposefully adding pep to my voice.

His eyes came together in annoyance, and I laughed, relaxing my posture. He turned the side of his mouth suspiciously, waiting for the cheeriness to return but settled back into his seat. Finally, he said, "I could ask you the same question."

I had forgotten to tell him, I realized. He'd been sent home early due to low census the day Dr. Galton had asked me to join the trial, and we hadn't gotten together since that last day at work. "They're moving me to a different department for a little while. For some reason it requires doing all the employee health testing over."

"Me too…"

Suspicion accompanied by cautious excitement bubbled in my chest. "What department?" I asked, dragging my words out.

"I can't really say."

We finished together, "Dr. Galton."

Neither of us pushed it past that admission, which only strengthened my belief he'd been tapped for the same trial. Pat may be a horrible morning person and a goofy dork, but he was a consummate professional. If he wasn't giving me more, I'd lay a bet it was for the same reason I wasn't.

We settled into our chairs, but we didn't have long to wait before both our names were called. The health screening process was straightforward. Someone took my blood, and I gave a urine sample. They did a vision test, and a basic physical. They took a hair sample, which was new, but I shrugged it off.

I waited inside the exam room on the bench that stretched into a bed, kicking my heels against the metal base. I was scrolling absently through my phone when Dr. Galton himself stepped into the room.

I straightened, shocked to see him here. "Hey doctor."

"Henry, please," he returned, confirming my belief he must be a contractor. He didn't have the normal rigidity of an officer.

"Henry. What are you doing here?"

I was glad I was dressed. I had been required to get into a gown for the physical. I hopped down from the exam table, not liking the dynamic. Something about it gave me an uneasy feeling. He didn't comment, just moved to one of the two chairs in the room. The rolling provider chair. I took the other and rested on the plastic arm.

"I came to help you get off to the next phase of your training today."

My head cocked. "Training? I thought today was the interview for the security clearance." What kind of training was required that I didn't already have? All the additional testing for the job began to unsettle me. I was used to silly requirements from when I contracted, but this seemed above and beyond anything I'd been asked to do before.

"No, no. I managed to fast-track that a little. We contacted your old employers for your character reviews and had everything buttoned up yesterday."

"So... training?"

He clapped his hands together. "Yes! So, you'll find we do a lot of unorthodox testing in this clinical trial. In fact, the subject matter of the trial itself is unorthodox. We put you through a shorter version of the testing required of the subjects for you to understand their mindsets, the results, and what we're trying to achieve."

I noticed he said subjects again, but figured it was his way of compartmentalizing, something many clinicians did. "Okay." So far everything was vague, and I had a pit in my stomach, similar to the one I'd had on my first day at the naval hospital. "When will it be explained exactly what this trial is for? Excuse me Dr.— Henry, but so far there's already been a lot of unorthodox testing. Repeat blood work, hair samples?"

Dr. Galton didn't seem taken aback by my directness. He ran his hand through his sparse balding hair, looking almost abashed. "Ah, yes. I'm sorry, it's been a while since we brought on new recruits, and sometimes I forget how strange it all is in the beginning. There will be a full orientation in a few days where everything is explained. It's important we do this at the training facility with a demonstration, to really help everyone understand. Doing all of this first allows you to get started directly after that."

They didn't want to tell everyone everything twice. I felt better that he at least acknowledged the strangeness of everything. "You said a couple days?"

Dr. Galton put his hand on my arm reassuringly. "You're going to report to headquarters now. Dr. Kimi Alver will meet you for the training we want to conduct today. She'll give you instructions for orientation at the end of your day."

I thanked him, and we said our goodbyes. When I walked out to the lobby of the clinic, Pat was nowhere to be seen. Disappointed, I headed to the address I'd been given to do this mysterious testing. The day had just started, but for some reason, I already felt emotionally and physically exhausted.

\*\*\*

Pat's familiar face waited at a reception desk. Relief suffused me to see him waving at me, and relief was clear on his face as well. No one sat behind the desk. As I reached him, he whispered, "This trial is getting freaking weird."

His words confirmed, if his presence hadn't already, that he was here for the same thing I was. I agreed with him, but any more conversation was cut off as the receptionist, or maybe security guard, returned to the desk; a tall man, well built, with typical military crew cut and clean-shaven features.

"Anastasia Smith and Patrick McCormick?" he asked, his voice gruff, but not deep. Pat brushed my shoulder. I appreciated the solidarity.

"Follow me," the guard said.

Pat and I looked at each other but followed him obediently through the large open room. The only lights came from overhead fluorescents, no windows in view. The building went up two or three stories, but all we could see was the tall ceilings and walls as we walked over to the elevator bank. He hit the button to call the elevator car, and we waited in awkward silence. The man looked bored.

"So—" I finally started to say, the quiet resounding uncomfortably in my ears, but the man cut me off. He hadn't offered a name, and he had no nametag. Just a collared shirt and utility pants with a belt.

"You'll take this down to the basement. They'll get you started. Good luck." The doors opened, and he turned—a right left, definitely military—and walked away without another word.

Pat and I looked at each other again. His mouth was turned to the side. The doors started closing, and impulsively, I caught them. The ding of the doors opening back up got us moving. We stepped onto the elevator car, and Pat leaned forward, tapping the button for the basement.

The doors opened to bustling activity. People sat at stations with computers and helmet shaped headsets with attached wires surrounding the body. A large pool took up the center of the room, and in it floated four pods. The black pool lining made it impossible to see the bottom. Pat comfortingly put his hand on my low back, and we started forward.

A dark-haired woman with bold, proud features walked toward us in a white lab coat. "Hi, you must be Stasia and Pat," she said, using both our nicknames. "I'm Dr. Kimi Alver."

We nodded our assent and she continued. "Dr. Galton let me know you were coming today. We had some openings with the deprivation chambers, so it worked out perfectly."

She talked quickly and efficiently. She was poised and a little intimidating. Next to me, Pat shifted. Dr. Alver walked us through what the deprivation chambers were: complete sensory deprivation that would help put us into a meditative state. She would then take a reading of our brainwaves and explained that the headsets with the wires attached were portable EEGs.

"What's the purpose of these tests? What are you trying to discover with them?" I asked, curious as to what they were trying to glean from our brainwaves in that state.

"A lot of that will be explained in your orientation. Today, we aren't really trying to read anything. We want you to understand the experience your patients will have."

Pat interjected next to me, "Will any of this hurt? Is it dangerous?"

Dr. Alver chuckled. "No, it's all safe."

I swallowed, her openness easing my nerves at the strangeness of it all. "How long will we be in the deprivation chamber?"

"About ten minutes. Just a short exhibition of what patients experience on their deprivation day."

I looked at Pat, and he gazed back into my eyes. His tight mouth showed his uncertainty. I gave him a strained smile, and we nodded to each other. I turned back to Dr. Alver. "Ok, let's get started."

After changing into standard-issue bathing suits, Pat and I were led back to the pool. There was some kind of machine hidden beneath the black water that brought the small pods to the edge of the pool on a track. The whir of the metal echoed in the chamber-like room.

The person at the control panel on the edge of the pool moved efficiently, clearly having done this before, and often. He hit a button that opened the lid of the pod and instructed me how to get in. I was able to walk around a small lip until I could sit in the pod. There was a floor to the pod, the pool inside shallow.

Dr. Kimi explained to us that we would be floating in a consistency of water greater than the Dead Sea, and it would allow us to float without fear of drowning. I felt comfortable stepping into the shallow pool, knowing I could stand at any time. We weren't given much more instruction than that, other than we would be brought back in after ten minutes. This was just a taste of what our patients in the trial experienced.

The door slowly lowered, and the whirring machine

sending the pod back out to the pool echoed loudly around me. I laid back, and sure enough, the salt in the water let me float effortlessly on top. The pod came to a jerky stop, and the sound bouncing off the pod's walls slowly dissipated.

As I listened to the air sawing in and out of my chest, I realized I couldn't hear anything else. They had warned us this was a deprivation chamber, but for some reason the meaning didn't sink in until now. I listened for anything, a drip of condensation, a murmur of voices. My breathing picked up, and panic clawed at my chest. I went to stand up, unable to take the clawing emotion, when my head submerged under the water, the floor making this a shallow pool suddenly gone. My dream from last night was my last thought before I blacked out.

# CHAPTER 10
## Stasia

I sat on the hard barstool at a high top, Pat on one side of me and Angela on the other. Her beautiful mocha face, kinky curls, and curvy body were turned to me. Every part of her radiated concern as Pat told her the story about the deprivation chamber. Well, the sanitized version we could tell outside of the top secret security clearance. Basically, he told her I'd fallen at work and passed out.

I shuddered while he talked, thinking about how my experience mirrored my dream. It wasn't the first time I'd had a sense of déjà vu after one of my vivid dreams, but never that strong. Never that exact.

Pat slapped his hand on the table, catching my attention. "Damn girl, but you scared the hell out of me."

I looked at him, still feeling exhausted, but too afraid to go home. "I scared myself."

Angela put her hand on my arm, her fingers beautifully manicured. I should really ask her some style questions. Angela had being a girl down.

"Hun, you look like crap. You sure you don't want to

go home? I can give you a ride and bring you back to your car in the morning."

I shook my head. The idea of being in the house, the echo off the walls. I didn't know what I wanted, but I didn't want that right now.

Seeing my expression, Pat said, "Nah, Angela, I think what Stasia wants is a shot." He went up to the bar before I could stop him.

Angela read something in my face and said, "You can just tell him no. We can stay out a while longer, we don't need to drink."

I felt stupid. I didn't like letting go. I had made a few mistakes in the military after nights of too much alcohol, and it made me reticent to touch it. But after a day like today, if there was ever an occasion to drink, it was now. "He's not wrong."

Angela's look of concern turned into a mischievous smile. "In that case..." she said right as three shots of tequila landed in the middle of the table. A glass of hot sauce landed next to them. We each took up a glass, hot sauce dabbed on our thumbs like salt, and called, "Cheers!"

*** 

At some point, my willingness to take a shot had turned into my inability to see one person at a time. Two Pats said to me, "Stasia, I love you so much."

I nodded sagely back to him. "I love you too."

Angela's arms wrapped around me, and I accepted the embrace in a way I never did when I was sober. She laughed and said, "You two are a riot. But I think it's time to get you home."

Two Pats looked offended. "Hey, they didn't cut me off."

Angela rolled all four of her eyes. "Ian is working tonight, Pat. He's never going to cut you off. You'll be dead in a ditch, and he'll still be making you an appletini."

Two Pats scoffed. "I only drank an appletini that one time. And you never let me forget it."

Angela turned her head, but her four puffed out cheeks told me she was holding in a laugh.

Suddenly I felt a presence behind me, solid and warm. Something about it brought calm and focus. Once again, only one Pat sat next to me, and Angela only had two cheeks and two eyes. A warm hand laid against my lower back, and a clean woodsy scent made me stop from recoiling. I knew that smell. I remembered it from the beach.

"Hey guys," Jack said behind me, amusement in his voice.

Angela looked over at him, her eyes brightening, giving him an appreciative once-over. I felt a prick of something ugly at that, but my drunk mind didn't have time to focus on it before Pat said, "Jack!" His tone inferred they were long-lost pals.

Jack looked at Angela and said, "Having fun?"

It must have been clear she was the only sober one, because even though I wasn't seeing doubles anymore, my thoughts still flitted from one thing to another, and I leaned heavily with my left arm on the table. Looking up at Pat, I corrected myself, I was lying on the table.

Angela laughed. "These two had a rough day at work. Stasia fell and blacked out, scaring the hell out of Pat. I've been letting them blow off steam. I'm going to get them home."

Jack had removed his hand while he was talking, but it returned to my shoulder. He looked down at me, concern etched in the lines of his chiseled face. "Should you be drinking? Are you okay?"

Angela spoke for me while I smiled dreamily up at him, replaying his hug in my mind.

"Pat said she was fine. They seemed pretty spooked by whatever happened to her though. I couldn't get Stasia to talk until she was two tequila shots in."

Jack moved closer. His gaze seemed focused on the bar, but I could feel the heat of him along my back. When he found whatever he was looking for, he pointed at me and hooked his thumb at the door. Turning his focus back to the table, he said to Angela, "Why don't you take Pat, and I'll stake Stasia. I was getting ready to head home anyway. This gets me out of work faster."

I couldn't see Angela's face, turned as I was to Jack and Pat, but she must have agreed because Jack's hand moved to my lower back again. Taking my hand, he encouraged, "Let's get you home to Flynn, Stasia."

I stood with him, swaying a little once I was upright. He wrapped his arm around my back, settling his hand on my hip. I lay my head in the dip of his shoulder, too short to come up high enough to lay it on top.

"You're hot," I said. Someone snorted behind me.

Jack smiled widely and said, "I'll remind you, you said that later. Come on, Miss Tequila."

I must have fallen asleep on the drive because, the next thing I knew, Jack was at the passenger door of his Tahoe helping me out. It was dark, and I wondered how long I had been at the bar after work. Worrying about Flynn and feeling guilty, I said, "Oh shit, what time—"

Jack cut me off, arm around me again. "I had Lilly come next door and grab him. The back door was unlocked. He's at our house, hope that's okay."

I nodded, gratefulness overcoming me. I had sobered up a little bit. Enough to remember why I had been so upset, but not enough to process it in any kind of healthy way. Jack got me into the house, and after I directed him to my room, he walked me up the stairs.

He sat me on the edge of my bed. Just as he asked me if I would be okay, and I began to tell him yes and thank him for offering to take Flynn for the night, bile rose at the back of my throat. Slapping a hand over my mouth, I raced for the bathroom.

Or tried to race. I stumbled against the door frame and used the sink for support, barely making it to the toilet before the tequila made a reappearance. My hair scraped away from my face, and that warm hand returned to my back. I let my arm fall across the toilet seat, grateful I had cleaned the bathroom recently, and groaned.

"I'm okay," I said finally. I was getting tired. The act of getting home, vomiting, and the emotionally wrought day took its final toll.

"What happened today, Stasia?" the concerned voice said behind me, the baritone soothing me, making me feel safe. I drifted into a semi-dreaming wakeful state. Drifting in the comfort of that voice.

"The dream came true. They barely ever come true. The pod was so dark. It was so quiet. The silence Jack. I never want to return to that silence."

The hand that had been rubbing my back stopped suddenly. I didn't hear whatever he said though, because sleep won its battle and took over.

# CHAPTER 11

## Jack

"Stasia," I said again. I held her hair in a ponytail away from her face. Her head rested on her arm, slung across the toilet seat. A bit of bile stuck to the corner of her mouth, and the thought of letting her stay here, as clean as it looked, was disgusting.

Standing from my crouch, I scooped her tiny frame into my arms. She weighed nothing. Though she was short, something about her presence always filled a room. Like this, asleep with sickness on her face, her fear in the last thing she said, she looked delicate. Breakable.

I laid her on the bed and ran cool water on a washcloth I'd found rummaging through cabinets. I washed her face and hands, took her shoes off, and raised the covers over her shoulders. Dropping down next to her, knees steadying me against her bed, I folded my hands together and rested my chin on them, staring at her intently.

She had said pod. Fuck if I'm wrong, but she had described the deprivation chambers. Those evil pods they put us in for hours. They forced us into a state of psychosis when we were young to force the most violent of our powers to release. Since Stepuli had been suppressing their powers, it had become a standard first step in our training.

I sat back on my butt, the implications of what I was thinking putting me into a cold sweat. I ran a hand down my face. I couldn't take my eyes off her. The delicate slope of her straight nose. Her full, perfectly-shaped lips. When she was awake, those lips stretched into one of the widest smiles I'd ever seen. Her shoulders were thin, her hands tucked under her head. Her light blonde hair like a halo. I thought about the pods and the silence she'd described. Could she be Stepuli?

I cursed at myself as soon as I thought it, knowing part of it was just hope. I liked Stasia. And I had already made peace with the fact I couldn't see myself being with a human. I couldn't see myself hiding the biggest part of who I was from someone I loved. I couldn't see falling in love with someone who didn't really know me. And the brainwashed nature of most of the Stepuli I met in this area—submitting to the government's subjugation without question like they were doing us a favor—no, I couldn't see myself with someone like that either.

I ran my hand along the beard I had grown, thinking. Thinking back to all the little things about Stasia I may have missed. I tried to feel an affinity like I had on that first day but still felt nothing. Well, that wasn't quite true. It never had been. I didn't feel an elemental affinity, but she also didn't feel like a normal human. I had dismissed the sensation when I determined she wasn't alien, figuring it had to do with the ass I tried getting a look at every time I thought nobody was watching.

I thought back to the bar. The fight that wasn't a fight

with Emily. How she'd used her voice to calm Emily, but the effect had been so strong, I imagined even my own heart rate slowing. I remembered when I had called her over the first time I had invited her to dinner. How I'd been so nervous I could barely get my words out. How with one smile my frayed nerves had knit together.

There was something none of us knew about, not the Stepuli, not the humans, not even the government hacks who'd been stealing our blood and whatever other samples they could get a hold of to map our DNA. A spirit Stepuli. My parents hadn't even known much about them. The original ambassadors refused to speak of them. Even back then, before they knew the depth of the depravity the humans would stoop to against our people, they hadn't been willing to give up any information on the spiritual advisers of our planet.

All I knew was all anybody knew. The spirit Stepuli never left Stepul. They didn't go on goodwill missions to help fledgling planets. They were kept on our planet, keeping the balance of all Stepuli elementals. Cherished. Revered. The ambassadors had never disclosed exactly what they did. They had never thought we'd need to know, and they didn't want the humans to know.

I looked closer at Stasia's face. She made a small, discontented sound and then jerked. Her voice mewling then getting clearer. "No," she pleaded. I moved forward, unable to help myself, and took one of the hands she had reached out, as if to ward someone off. I squeezed it tight and sat with my back against the nightstand, keeping watch over her.

***

I woke to an abrupt brightness, a crick in my neck, and my

ass numb. What woke me was a softly worded question.

"Jack?" she asked again.

I was still holding Stasia's hand. She rubbed her forehead with the other one and looked at me questioningly. As beautiful as I thought she was, she looked like shit. Her lips were pale, her eyes sunken, and her hair lay limply across her cheek, greasy at the top.

"Hey," I said, wincing as I sat up and feeling began returning to my back area.

"What happened?" She sat up in bed as I did, the blanket falling around her waist. She looked down and realized she was still wearing the same clothes she had on yesterday, a tank top over navy blue scrub pants. I noticed there were no pictures on the walls, just two nightstands, her bed, and a dresser. Like she had ordered an adult bedroom off a catalog.

Behind me sat one single photo on the nightstand of Flynn and her hiking. I remembered what she'd told me that night on the beach. I had never felt so violent toward a little boy before. It comforted me a little that he was now an adult, and the intensity with which I'd wanted to wring his neck was less immoral than if I were to do it to his adolescent self.

"You remember anything about last night?" I asked as I kicked out my legs, stood, and moved to her doorway to give her room.

She shook her head then winced.

"Stasia, don't you have curtains?" I asked gently, again looking around her room.

She squinted against the sunlight flooding her room and shook her head more gently this time. "I don't know how to put them up. I wake up early anyway. I figured I'd eventually YouTube it like I did with the blinds."

I cursed myself again for being a horrible neighbor. "Do you remember being at the bar last night with Pat and Angela?"

She started nodding, then stopped and covered her face with both hands. "Oh, no."

Her pale face suffused with red. She would never be able to hide her embarrassment, the evidence traveled all the way to her chest. I bit my lip. "Angela got Pat, and I offered to take you home."

"Thank you," she started slowly, and then suddenly she panicked. "Where's Flynn? Oh, my God, I've never left him like that. Flynn!" she called with tears in her voice. She rushed toward me, toward the door.

I caught her shoulders and looked down at her. "Stasia, stop. Stop. Flynn is at my house. We talked about this last night. Lilly picked him up. He's fine. She got his bowls and dog food. She was excited for the sleepover."

Stasia tilted her head up to me, her breathing slowing. Her pain left behind in her panic over forgetting to walk or feed her dog. My stomach turned, and I wanted to pull her into a hug. I wanted to do more than that. Instead, I stepped back.

She put her arm against the door jam, absorbing my words. She leaned her head against her arm and didn't look at me as she said, "I'm so sorry Jack. This is so embarrassing. It was just a hard day at work yesterday. Pat suggested shots, and I don't really drink. I don't know what I was thinking. I'm so sorry you had to clean up after me like that." Misery laced her words.

"Stasia, no big deal. I didn't mind."

"God, you stayed on the floor all night."

I closed the distance between us again. I couldn't help myself. I put my hand under her chin and guided her gaze to mine. "I was happy to. Now, I'm going to need you to go into that bathroom," I pointed, "and clean up. I'm going to get breakfast, a hangover breakfast, ready for you downstairs and put on a pot of coffee. I'll be gone before you get down there. Flynn will already be walked and home. You don't have to work today?"

Her mouth turned down like she wanted to cry, but she obediently shook her head no, no work. She was so adorable. I wanted to touch her, which meant it was time to go.

"On board with my plan?" I asked before leaving.

Her mouth was still turned down, but more like she was hiding a smile now, amusement twinkling in her eyes. She nodded, staying mute. I chucked her under the chin before I made myself let go completely, and then walked downstairs to deliver on my promises. She couldn't remember last night. She wouldn't remember telling me about the pod. The whole time, a question circled my brain: *Could she be Stepuli?*

# CHAPTER 12

## Jack

"Have a good night?" Brandon stood at the kitchen counter with a smirk on his face.

I looked at the clock behind him and realized what he must think. He already got Lilly off to school judging by the quiet and the hour.

"Brandon—"

"Bro, I mean. She's hot. High five, for real. I didn't think you had it in you. You're always so uptight about your hookups. Hope this doesn't—"

"I think she's Stepuli."

I walked over to the island. His assumptions, and the way he talked about Stasia, didn't sit well with me. Either way, there were more important things we needed to discuss.

Brandon's grin dropped and his face screwed up in doubt. "Jack, just because you had a good night with a girl in bed doesn't mean she's part of the very scarce alien race on Earth."

I rolled my eyes at his flippant attitude and explained

what she had said last night, pointing out moments I thought could have been displays of power.

"I never mentioned it because I thought maybe it was just attraction making me stupid. But think about it. When you've been around her, I know she doesn't feel Stepuli, but does she feel human to you?"

As I had gone on, Brandon's doubt had slowly morphed into contemplation. He slouched over the kitchen island now, braced on his forearms, looking at his hands. "I haven't put much thought into it, Jack. She wasn't Stepuli, and I stopped there. She looks at you with hearts in her eyes, and I catch you staring at her ass every time she's not looking. I wasn't interested in diving deeper."

For a brief moment, I appreciated his observation skills. I wasn't sure how I'd feel if he had mentioned an attraction toward her. But I shoved it aside quickly. *More important things to discuss*, I reminded myself.

"Do you think it's possible a Stepuli female got away from one of the communities? Managed to hide a baby?" I asked.

"I think the better question is, how the hell did the government succeed in possibly creating a spirit? And if they did, or even were trying to, how could they have lost track of the subject?"

It jarred me that he used that term. Subject. That's what Galton's sterile doctors always called us when testing our abilities. While Brandon had spent his early adolescence in the Stepul School, designed to groom Stepuli to be good boys and girls and follow the government's initiative, Dove had gotten him out. Dove, our mom, had allowed herself to be inseminated with the hope her children would have some freedom from the SEP's systematic grooming.

Shaking it off, I said, "How could we find out? On the down low. Not that I'm sure it matters if he already has her in pods."

Brandon's mouth twisted. "Do you really think she could be a Stepuli Jack? We don't know anything about spirits, but if their only powers were calming tense situations, I don't see why the ambassadors wouldn't have talked about them."

I swallowed. I thought of how distraught she'd been. "I don't know for sure. But she described a dark pod with scary silence."

Brandon nodded. "There's a community meeting in an hour. I was thinking about going cause there's this air I wanted to meet up with. I can try to poke around."

In contrast to my reticence to date other Stepuli in our community who were drinking the Kool-Aid, Brandon was all too happy to dive in headfirst. It was what had gotten him into trouble in the first place. He loved showing off, he loved using his powers and sharing them with others. Different Stepuli events, like community meetings, were his one chance to do so without being locked down.

I hesitated. I hadn't been to a Stepuli event since I'd stepped down as a council member when Lilly turned six and was ready to start first grade. I had grown jaded with everyone's acceptance, and she had begun wondering where I went during the day. But maybe if I went, I could get a sense of how the communities were doing. Overhear some talk about trying to find a missing Stepuli.

"How about I come with?"

Brandon looked at me skeptically. "It's been a long time since you were around that scene. You didn't exactly leave in the best way."

I hadn't just resigned as a council member. I also let the other members know what direction I thought they were headed before taking the last bit of coveted freedom offered to a Stepuli family in Washington State.

"I have to do something. I'll go crazy here at home alone."

Brandon shrugged. I grabbed the keys, and we headed out.

\*\*\*

It was obvious when we drove past the border. Nestled in the heart of the island, near South Whidbey State Park, was the Washington State Stepuli Community. There were no gates or guard shacks. Our shackles were less obvious and far more restrictive.

We didn't appear as thrown away as Native Americans in this country. Our communities were well-tended, with newer buildings, movie theaters, and activity centers. Stepuli children weren't separated into grades. They attended one large school that looked like a university campus, and they moved through a ten-year education together.

But we were required to wear a band. It looked like a watch. Hell, it was a watch for the most part. But it didn't have a clasp. It was waterproof, and it always stayed on. It was connected to a perimeter that dug around the circumference of the land we'd been given to live on. It alerted a central command anytime we left the Stepuli community or tried to take it off. Keeping that band off Brandon's and my wrists, and ensuring it never went around Lilly's, occupied my mind most days.

As we turned into the parking lot of a building that said "City Hall," I shook my head at the irony. It wasn't a city. It was a prison. Remembering the playacting I'd participated in, being a "community leader" turned my gut. I stepped out of the car.

"Do we have a plan?" I asked as we circled the hood and met up.

Brandon sighed. "Yeah, don't talk a lot. There's still a lot of resentment that Galton hasn't forced our return. Nobody really understands how you do it, and the fact you act like you're better than everyone doesn't help."

I grunted. I couldn't really argue his point. "Maybe I shouldn't have come?"

"Too late now. Besides, things seem to be changing, Jack. Everyone's always been all gung-ho about the government's 'missions.' You know, integrating in with hotshots to combat wildfires in California. Getting month-long details to Antarctica to help slow melting ice caps. But now, it's all they talk about. The ability testing has gotten more intensive. More...militaristic."

Nervousness turned in my gut. It had always been headed this way. That's why they only educated us for ten years. We didn't have the option for college or different careers. After our education, we were integrated into various teams that matched our skills and level of ability. We were taught to like it, taught it was our purpose.

When mom got us out, I'd deprogrammed myself. I learned all the things they decided we didn't need to know and realized our education left us dependent on them. They taught us the minimum to integrate for short periods of time in the human world, and the rest was propaganda to make us think our only purpose was our elements.

"They aren't more militaristic B. SEP is integrating them into the actual military." I reaffirmed in my head Lilly would never be a part of this.

We walked toward the doors. "Yeah, it's just, I don't know. It's the way they talk. The devotion." He ran his hand through his hair. He needed a damn haircut. It was sticking up in all directions. "It's like they don't have minds of their own."

I sighed as I opened the door for Brandon to step through. "B, when did they?"

\*\*\*

We sat through the entire meeting for no reason. They prattled on about daily matters of the community. The usual: Trash pickup needed to be adjusted over the holiday season. The community garden was going by the wayside and earth children needed to be corralled and monitored more on their duties. That one irked me.

Brandon moved through the crowd doing his usual schmoozing. He could coax a smile as easily from an air as a water. A giggle from an earth. Fires were never allowed outside the Stepul School. It's not that we purposefully segregated ourselves. Our affinities were naturally stronger toward those of our same element.

Families tended to be the same one or two elements.

Brandon took after our mother with water, and me after our dad with earth. Lilly didn't know how she was fire. I had never let her step foot inside this community, so she didn't even realize it was unusual that all three of us had affinities to different elements. And as far as the community was concerned, she had never expressed ability toward any element, completely human in traits.

I stood stiffly against the wall, waiting for B to finish up. He walked over to me flanked by a man and woman around his age. The man's long black hair was pulled back in a ponytail, the woman's features so similar I realized they were twins. I vaguely remembered a pair of twins around Brandon's age before we left. This must be the air he had wanted to meet up with.

As they reached me, the man spoke up. "If it isn't the infamous Jack, deigning to visit with the hopeless sheep."

My jaw tightened, my eyes cutting to Brandon. Looking back, I said, "You are?"

"You don't recognize me?" He put a hand against his chest and mock hurt painted his face. "Lucy, your favorite little hellion."

I grunted. I remembered now. The air twins. The boy had always been a troublemaker growing up. Lola, his sister, had always been sweet.

Brandon cut in. "We were just about to head out, Lucy. It was nice seeing you guys. Maybe we can catch up sometime soon." He looked between the two, and I tried figuring out which one he had been here pursuing.

Brandon and the twins said their goodbyes. We were just turning to walk out when a man stopped us, deep lines in his face a map of his age. He wasn't physically imposing, but he was solid, and the air of disapproval around him filled up the room.

My shoulders tensed, and my jaw hardened. "Robert."

"What are you doing here Jack? When you left, telling us all we were blind sheep for following Galton's rules, we didn't expect to see you back."

His tone and posture screamed disapproval. I was stupid for coming here. Brandon had been accepted back because he integrated with the community. Though he enjoyed the freedom our mother and I had bought with our agreement, he wasn't derisive toward the community itself. I think part of them hoped he'd take a partner and bring them out of the community too.

"Just spending some time with my brother. He wanted to come."

"Yes, Brandon does his part. He isn't selfish. Doesn't think only of his needs."

His blatant reprimand ate at me, but I didn't want to get into a fight. Robert was mad because I wouldn't take a Stepuli wife, and because when everyone else was called back, the clauses in the treaty revoking their probation, me and my family had stayed free. As an elder and one of the most powerful earth Stepuli, I had been expected to return. When I didn't, they had hoped I would bring someone else out of the community with me. The fact I eschewed my own people wasn't forgivable in his eyes.

Brandon coughed next to me. All eyes drew to him, and he shifted. "We have to get back, don't we Jack? Lilly needs to be picked up from school."

I held my hand out for Robert. "He's right, we've got to go." Robert looked down at the peace offering. He gave me a cold look and walked past me, saying nothing.

"Well, that was awkward." I shot Lucy an annoyed look at the obvious comment. I looked at Brandon and cocked my head toward the door. He nodded, and we headed out.

Neither of us talked as we drove home. Brandon hadn't been able to find any gossip about long-ago Stepuli runaways. We turned onto our street, not a community, but still land bought by the government to keep us away from general human neighborhoods.

As usual, they claimed it was for us, to help prevent anyone from ever seeing us express our abilities. I remembered how shocked I had been that they'd let someone move in next door. It only affirmed my gut feeling: Galton knew all along Stasia was Stepuli.

I parked in the driveway, pushing the gear shift into park. I sat back and let the silence stretch between me and Brandon. He was looking at his hands, palms up, in his lap.

"Do you really think she could be a spirit, Jack?"

I paused for a second. "Yeah. Yeah, I do."

Brandon looked up through the windshield and shook his head. "A fucking spirit. God, we don't even know what they can do."

I had been waiting to let the thought creep in. As it did, an overprotective anger unlike anything I had ever felt before burned up my chest. It was like what I felt for Lill. But that weightlessness in my gut like I was on a rollercoaster didn't usually accompany it.

"There's one problem, B." I laughed. "Or at least another problem."

He looked over at me. "What's that?"

I met his gaze and said, "I don't think she knows what she is. And Galton's already experimenting on her."

# CHAPTER 13
## Stasia

I turned down various streets, the buildings becoming newer and more modern. My GPS brought me to a collection of red brick buildings that resembled a university campus, though this wasn't any university I had ever heard of. The community college was at the other end of the island, near Deception Pass. The large state university was in Seattle. I read the sign, Stepul School.

I pulled into the sparsely used parking lot and easily spotted Pat's car. Again, I thanked fate for having him put in this trial with me. I had wanted something new and exciting in my life, but I was beginning to feel like I had bitten off more than I could chew.

Walking up next to his driver-side window, I barked out a laugh. His head hung back against the headrest and his mouth hung wide open. This time, there was no questioning the line of drool dripping from the left corner of his mouth. I rapped on his window. He jumped, his long body hitting the roof of his car. His forehead drew down into an annoyed expression while his hand rubbed the top of his head. He turned to me. His face immediately cleared when he saw the to-go cup of coffee I held out.

He wiped his mouth as he exited the car, fingers wiggling in a gimme gesture. "You are a saint," he said, taking a long pull.

I laughed. "Jacob says the same thing."

"Who?"

"Never mind." We fell into step with each other walking toward the pretty campus. Pacific madrone trees accented the lush green grass. Wild lilacs added pops of blues and purples to the hedges. Somewhere, there must have been a groundcover of jasmine. The scent reached out to me on the breeze.

"This is a step up from the hospital grounds," I remarked as Pat held the door to the main building open for me. He hummed, ignoring me as usual as he caffeinated sufficiently to be a person.

The greeter at the main building's central desk directed us upstairs to the right, and we walked along a row of offices and classrooms until we reached the room orientation would be held in. A sign on the door said, "SEP Orientation." Pat and I walked in and took seats in the back, side by side.

The room slowly filled with others, but I didn't recognize anyone else. Some people wore lab coats, others wore street clothes. I looked around curiously, tapping my thumbs on the table while I waited to understand what the pool had been all about.

When Pat was at the bottom of his cup of coffee, just beginning to perk up, in walked Dr. Henry Galton himself. I was surprised how much hands-on involvement he had in the project. Even more surprising, Christopher

Shaw walked in with him and took a seat in one of the chairs against the back wall to the left of me.

"Hello, everyone," greeted Dr. Galton. The room quieted down, and everyone focused on the front of the room. Dr. Galton launched into an explanation of the clinical trial, double-blind studies, and the fact that we were part of a small group of specially selected individuals tapped to participate. I wondered if anyone else noticed he never really explained what the trial was about.

"Now, before I introduce you to the subjects, I need to warn you. What I am about to reveal, and what you are about to see, is going to suspend your belief. That is why we are going to explain with the proof before your eyes. We've found over the years there's really no other way to help you understand."

The mysterious words unsettled me more. What kind of scientific trial was this? Nevertheless, we all filed out obediently when Dr. Galton instructed. Christopher Shaw brought up the rear. Having Pat at my back helped assuage some of the nervousness that churned in my gut.

We walked along a viewing platform, the glass window opening to a series of pools. No pods lay in these, but there were individuals of varying ages standing next to them. They looked like kids. One middle-aged instructor in the front gesticulated with his hands and spoke to the group.

Dr. Galton took up a stance at the front of our group, his back to the glass. Shaw stood at the door, leaning against the jam. We all alternated focus between the crowd below and Galton.

"There are things the government have always kept hidden. For various reasons, from the interest of national security to the prevention of widespread panic in the general population. Altered statistics, a slower rollout of technology than we possessed. But there is one secret that we have been hiding from the American people that you are all about to be made privy to."

I shifted. His speech grew wilder, and this situation felt more wrong. Beside me, Pat stood on the balls of his feet, unconsciously leaning forward, captivated by the doctor's words.

"You are about to see a demonstration. After that, I will explain what I mean." At this, Dr. Galton turned around to watch the people below with us.

The instructor brought his hands together, and the group below snapped to attention. As one, they brought their right hands forward. It was difficult to see, but they seemed to be doing something with the fingers of their right hand. I gasped.

Water from the pools came up in a slow funnel, straight into the air in a waterspout formation. There were varying degrees of circumference and height. The youngest-looking one's spout collapsed in a splash. A girl who looked a little older reached her spout higher. Suddenly, it too collapsed, and she fell back on her butt. Her shoulders moved as if she was breathing heavily. I looked over at Pat wide eyed. He returned my shock.

Dr. Galton spoke at the front. "We are not alone. As it turns out, we never have been. Since 1947, we've been in direct contact with an alien race from a planet called Stepul. It turns out, the conspiracy theorists are right." He chuckled, and someone laughed behind me as well. Shaw stood with his arms crossed, a smile on his face.

I looked forward again. "It was indeed the Stepuli, not

a hot air balloon that crashed in the desert. The Stepuli are a peaceful race with elemental powers. When they realized they'd be unable to fix their ship, and would be finishing their lives on Earth, the government tried to make them as at home as possible. The Stepuli offered an exchange of technology for shelter, and we set up communities, integrating them with the human population as much as possible.

The political climate taught us to tread slowly. So, at first, only government employees integrated into the communities. Over time, they forged relationships with the Stepuli, and to all our surprise, children resulted. We created the SEP, or Stepuli Eugenics Project, to help the children of the original ambassadors understand their history and accomplish the mission their ancestors were sent here to complete."

You could hear a pin drop after his life-altering words. Nobody spoke for a while, and our attention quickly diverted to more maneuvers from the pool. The individuals below brought water droplets up from the pool. They ran through various exercises directed by the instructor, then the class was called to a close. Single file, the children headed to a medical station, then headed out of the gym.

When the first person spoke, breaking the silence, it was like a dam broke. Everyone spoke at once. Dr. Galton chuckled and held his arm out toward the door. "Let's go back to the classroom, and we'll get started."

***

I drove home that night in a daze. Dr. Galton had given us more history on the Stepuli, explaining they had been coming to Earth and other planets in various galaxies throughout the centuries. Their mission was to help struggling planets in their infancy.

He explained their elemental gifts, a hereditary trait on their planet, helped them further civilizations in amazing ways. He gave us examples ranging from sustainable crop farming to irrigation techniques and finding clean water. He explained how Stepuli had helped the Harrapan's with metallurgy, helped the Tamana survive the floods, and taught the Aztecs floating farming.

He had told us how, after the Stepuli were stranded on Earth, they struggled with their purpose. As the volatility of the fifties progressed, the government had felt it would be unsafe to integrate the Stepuli into the general public. The original ambassador's children had grown restless in their enclosed communities. The clinical trial was a way to understand their DNA, protect their legacy, and give them a continued purpose.

I turned into my drive, still unable to really wrap my head around the enormity of my day and what I had learned. Stepping out of the car, I heard Lilly call my name. Twigs stuck out of her wild hair. Flynn followed close behind, covered in mud. Since the other night, I had let Lilly know I left the back door open, and she was welcome to grab Flynn anytime she wanted to play with him.

The stress of everything dissolved and I barked out a laugh, holding up my hands to ward off the dirty pair. I soon discovered my efforts were pointless. Lilly came running, wrapping her arms around me in a bear hug, while Flynn rubbed his muddy fur all along the side of my scrubs. I laughed helplessly, groaning against the onslaught.

"Hope you don't mind," Jack said, following them

from the backyard. He was still clean, I noted with chagrin. He had an easy smile on his face, and my heart hammered at seeing him for the first time since the morning I'd woken up hungover. I'd been so embarrassed I was avoiding him.

"Mind?" I asked as he got closer.

"Lilly wanted to play with Flynn. We were taking a walk on the beach, so I told her to go ahead and get him."

Lilly had let me go, her attention grabbed by the pup in question. Flynn nipped at her heels, chasing her around to the back again. Her peals of laughter put me at ease; she wasn't in any real distress. By now, I was confident she could handle his antics, even when he played aggressively.

I brushed some of the dirt off my scrub pants, forcing myself to look up into Jack's face. "Not at all, I appreciate it."

Jack had a playful smile on his face that reminded me of the night we played spades. He stepped close, making my chest feel weightless. Butterflies swarmed in my belly. He lifted his hand and tucked a strand of hair that had come loose from my ponytail behind my ear. My breath caught.

"You've been avoiding me." His deep voice lowered; my eyes caught in a trance in his chocolate brown gaze.

"I was so stupid the other night."

He tutted and stepped even closer. I wasn't sure I was even still breathing. His gaze became so focused, flicking down to my lips and back to my eyes. My lips parted. I wasn't sure whether to ask a question or kiss him.

Suddenly, Lilly and Flynn burst back around the house. Lilly bent over gasping and calling, "Hey Jack, when's dinner? I'm starving!"

Her voice broke us apart, my gaze startled, his

annoyed. "In a little while," he called.

Looking back at me, he smiled ruefully. He didn't try to move close again, but asked in that same low voice, "Dinner tonight?"

My heart raced. Looking up into his handsome face, covered in a light coating of beard, I answered without even thinking. "Yes."

# CHAPTER 14
## Jack

I couldn't stop thinking about Stasia. She had been avoiding me, which frustrated me to no end. I had tried catching her in the mornings. Tried sending Lilly over as a spy. Lilly was a horrible spy. She loved Stasia and ended up spending time with her without bringing back any information or the woman herself.

I finished preparing dinner, an easy basil pesto chicken pasta, too distracted to try something complicated. I made Lilly go wash Flynn so Stasia would have more time to get ready and come over. I was anxious to have her over here, to have her in my space.

I thought about our moment on the lawn. Of how close she'd been. Of how close I'd been. The way I had tried feeling for an affinity. The way her lips had distracted me. My breathing picked up, and I had to shift toward the stove, hiding the evidence of the direction my thoughts had taken. Lilly was right outside on the deck drying Flynn with a towel. I needed to get a hold of myself.

The more I came to believe Stasia was Stepuli, the

more my walls cracked. At this point, I was pretty sure a slight breeze would crumble them to dust. I couldn't help the excitement. The hope.

I heard a commotion outside, and the object of my thoughts walked into view, laughing with Lilly and patting the large gray dog who had also become a fixture in our lives in such a short time. The food was ready, so I turned off the heat. Excitement burned in my chest as I called Brandon's name and pulled out plates and utensils for dinner.

***

Brandon and Lilly finished the cleanup, and I had just dealt the cards when my cell lit up. I frowned at it. Ian was calling, which was rare. Stasia was distracted, discussing something with Lilly about school. Brandon noticed the name flashing and looked at me questioningly.

I shrugged at him and picked up the call.

"Hey, Jack." Ian's voice sounded tense. Unusual for him, he was perpetually at ease.

"What's up, Ian?" I asked.

"We got a problem down here. I think you're going to need to come down."

Unease turned in my gut. Ian would update me, usually by text, if there was an incident at the bar. But he almost never needed my help. The few times he had, it had been bad.

"Give me a run down."

"Liam's probably done in the military. He was drunk. Fucking stupid. Got into a fight with an officer. The place is swarming with Whidbey police *and* military police."

I cursed, getting the attention of everyone at the table. Brandon started to stand, but I shook my head. He was casual friends with Liam. Since our original conversation, he hadn't touched a drop of alcohol, and I didn't want him there, compelled to be a shoulder for the guy.

"I'm on my way," I said.

"What's up?" Brandon finally asked when I hung up the phone.

"Ian has an issue down at the bar. I'll handle it."

Brandon's mouth turned to the side. He knew I was keeping him away for a reason, but warmth spread knowing he wasn't going to fight me. We had slowly started mending the distrust between us.

"Don't forget I got called in, in the morning. You've got Lilly's drop-off." I cursed. It was going to be a late night straightening this out.

"I can drop her off for you if you want." Stasia's voice brought my head around. She looked uncertain. The warmth that had started spread further.

"Thanks, that would be great. Before I head out, can I walk you home?" I wasn't done being in her presence and regretted that our night was cut short. I had been looking forward to cards, to being on her team. I was looking forward to being near her.

Her uncertain look morphed into a smile, her green eyes sparkling, the beginning of crow's feet at the corners. My heart beat faster.

"Sure, let's go." She pointed at my phone. "That sounded urgent."

I nodded, no longer caring. Ian could hold down the bar for a while until I got there.

We walked across the wet grass, our shoulders brushing as we talked about Lilly. About Flynn. About nothing and everything. The simple parts of our days.

Something I'd never done with a woman before.

She opened her slider, and I followed her in. I wasn't ready to let her go. The outside light dimly lit the kitchen. We stood so close to each other I could smell the sweet vanilla from her soap.

The light reflected off her face, brightening her green eyes. My gut clenched, heat moving through me. My fingers tingled. Her smile slowly faded. I felt more than heard her breathing pick up. Small puffs against my chest. She swallowed, and my eyes tracked the movement. Her pulse jumped, and I couldn't help myself. I put my hand against her throat. Her intake of breath reminded me of that first dinner. I felt my arousal grow, and this time it was me who swallowed. I took another step closer.

"Jack," she said, her voice plaintive.

Her fingers curled into my shirt, forcing me to close the last of the gap between us. We didn't talk, I just stared at her for a moment as my fingers trailed from her throat to the back of her head. I don't know when it happened, but suddenly our bodies were flush.

Her color was high. I heard her mutter, "Fuck this." And I agreed. Our lips were on each other's in an instant. I didn't ever want to come up for air.

\*\*\*

I pulled up in front of Walker's Place, cursing. As much as I hadn't wanted to leave Stasia, I knew if Ian had called, he needed me. Judging by the fact a cop was walking him out the door in handcuffs, he probably could have used me a little earlier.

I hopped off the bike, pulling my helmet off and moved toward the officer. "What's going on?"

The officer looked over at me. Ian's face was fixed in

a scowl, his right eye red and swollen, and he had a cut on his bottom lip. The officer said, "Who are you?"

"I'm the owner." I held my palms up in a gesture of peace.

The officer nodded but didn't look any less hostile. Indicating Ian with his head, he still held one hand on the bracelets and one on Ian's shoulder. "This asshole shoved a police officer."

"It was an accident," Ian said sharply.

"Tell it to the judge," the officer snapped back as he pushed Ian toward the police cars with their lights flashing.

Another officer stepped out of the bar with a notepad in his hand. I'd have to deal with the Ian situation later. "Hi," I greeted. The officer's head came up. Broad-shouldered and well-muscled, his face set in a stern mask. His name tag read Jacob Scales. His camo suggested military police.

"I'm the owner of the bar. Can you tell me what happened?"

He pulled me aside from the busy doorway. I looked inside anxiously. Now that my bartender was out of commission, I would need to deal with that crowd soon.

"One of our junior sailor's was drunk. Punched a captain in the face. Things apparently got a little wild. Nothing in there was too broken but some overturned tables and chairs. The bartender allegedly shoved one officer who was trying to break it up."

"Did anyone see him shove them?"

"No. It was a madhouse. The bartender had waded into the fray trying to get everyone to break it up."

I ran my hand down my face. Jesus. I'd have to bail Ian out soon, but at least it sounded easy enough to sort out. "Where is Liam and the officer? Is everyone okay? I don't see any ambulances."

The officer placed a hand on my shoulder. "Everyone was fine. We don't have a jail, so Liam was arrested by civilian police. The officer is giving his statement to MPs. It's busted up now. We're all about to head out."

I gave a word of thanks and headed into the bar. Inside, customers were righting tables and setting broken chairs against the back wall near the stage. Nadine, one of the weekend bartenders, stood behind the bar. She laughed at something someone just said then walked up and down the bar, taking orders, slinging drinks. Her movements were graceful, her body willowy. She looked unruffled despite the drama that had just unfolded.

I walked behind the bar, and her eyes lit up when she noticed me. "This isn't your normal workday," I said, dry humor lacing my words.

She laughed. "Thank God, Jack. Ian got arrested. This place was a madhouse. I was here drinking, and when they took him away in cuffs, I jumped in." She shrugged her shoulders as a few people from the crowd called out hellos. I waved back absentmindedly.

I ran my hand through my hair. "Thanks, Nadine. You're a lifesaver. Ian's going to be stuck in booking a while anyway. I'll help you catch everything up, but could I talk you into staying? Closing up tonight?"

She walked closer to me, titling her face up so she could see. Her eyes were exotic, her features delicate. She put her hand on my arm, softly smiling up at me. "Of course. I'm happy to help."

I thought of Stasia in this position not too long ago, and heat moved through me, wishing I was still in her kitchen. "You, ok?" Nadine asked, her smile turning wicked.

I shook myself out of it and nodded, moving around her. I called a thank you over my shoulder and got to work. Nadine and I had had a short fling, and she still harbored a crush. I took orders, and we worked side by side. We caught up on people's drinks and listened to them recount the epic fight.

It turned out the captain, who never came back into the bar to settle his tab, was kind of an asshole. He had made a move on Liam's girl of the night right in front of him. Liam had told him to back off, and the captain had said, with a cocky smile on his face, that he could do whatever he wanted. Liam had been drunk enough to make him prove it.

Once everyone was settled in their seats, and Nadine wasn't running to keep up with orders, I slipped to the back office. I wanted to review the security footage to see if anything was on there that could help Ian. Sure enough, he waded into the crowd, his face red from yelling. Knowing Ian, he took it personally his customers weren't behaving when he told them to. He said all the time he felt more like he ran a kindergarten than a bar. Someone shoved him, and he landed on a police officer's back, who fell to the ground. The officer stood up, snapping his baton from his belt, screaming back at Ian. Ian tried to hold his hands up, but the officer threw him to the ground, roughly slapping cuffs on him.

I must have showed up right after because the officer walked Ian directly to the door of the bar from there. I shook my head, downloaded the clip onto the cloud, and made sure I could access it from my phone. I called out a goodbye to Nadine as I headed for the door. She gave me two thumbs up and a hopeful smile. I just waved and headed out.

# CHAPTER 15
## Stasia

I rubbed my thumb against my bottom lip. Music played in the background. Lilly was talking her usual mile a minute next to me. I was a morning person, but this kid had too much energy even for me. I would definitely need more than half a cup of coffee to keep up with her this early.

I looked at the tree line to the left as I thought about last night. About the way Jack had held me in his arms, how he'd felt flush against me. How I couldn't take a second longer without his lips on mine, and I'd reached for him in my haste. How he'd met me halfway, mouth hungry, tongue hot, making my body come alive.

"Did you hear me?" Lilly asked, confusion on her face in the passenger seat.

My cheeks flooded with heat, and I dropped my arm, placing both hands on the wheel and saying, "Mmmhmm. Well, I think I missed that last part."

Lilly huffed, but repeated, "I said Letty's been acting weird these last couple days. She didn't even sit with me yesterday. I had a lot of homework to catch up on, so I didn't really pay attention to it."

My gut felt sick. Teenage girls could be cruel, but Lilly's stories at dinner had sounded like she'd made a friend. The girl was new to town, and Lilly had been showing her the ropes. She'd even tried to get me on board with talking Jack into having her over. I had wondered why he would be against the idea in the first place and had promised to conspire with Lilly to get him to agree. Until he had distracted me so completely with his hands and lips and tongue that is.

"I'm not sure kiddo. Was she just having a bad day?"

Lilly bit her lip. "Maybe." But she didn't sound certain. She looked out the window as I drove along her school building, getting closer to the drop-off.

"Oh! She's there!" Lilly said. "Do you mind if I just get out here?"

We were four or five cars down from the actual drop-off with a car boxing me in, but we were along a sidewalk, so it was safe enough for her to get out.

"Go ahead, I'll see you later. Have a good day at school!" I called the last out to her as she dashed out of the car, swinging the door behind her. She ran over to the girl she had indicated.

A young girl with dark brown hair stood with her back to me. I watched as Lilly approached her, talking animatedly with a big smile on her face. The girl turned her head to Lilly and frowned. The loose circle the kids stood in didn't open to let Lilly in. The sick feeling sank like a stone in my gut as I watched, chanting, "Please don't be mean, please don't be mean."

The car alongside me keeping me in the parent pickup

line moved. I didn't turn my car to exit but watched the scene apprehensively. Lilly's shoulders began to drop. She was turning away when a bottle-blonde girl with a mean look on her face said something.

Lilly turned back to her, the sad droop to her shoulders stiffening. I couldn't see Lilly's expression anymore with her back turned toward me. But something about Lilly had changed. There was a haze around her body, like asphalt on a hot day in Florida. Sparks traced along one of Lilly's hands, both fisted tightly at her side. The events of SEP orientation still fresh in my mind, I gasped and ran out of the car, leaving it blocking the line.

I ignored the horn honking and ran for Lilly, calling her name. The commotion made her turn. Her face was dark, her lips pressed together tightly, and eyebrows drawn in concentration. I reached her, shaking her shoulders, ignoring the children laughing behind her. Shaking her again, I said, "Lilly!"

Finally, she focused on me. She paled, her freckles a stark contrast against her now colorless face.

*Oh, my God, oh, my God, oh, my God*, I thought. "Let's go."

I hurried her along back to the car, looking around to see if anyone was watching. They were, but not for the reasons I feared from what I could tell. Looks of confusion, not alarm, followed us. Lilly let me guide her, walking mechanically. I put her into the back seat, buckled her in, and ran around to the front. I waved at the person behind me and pulled out.

We were silent on the drive back to the house. Lilly had been almost hyperventilating, but her breaths were slowing. She was looking at her folded hands. I took my eyes off her in the rearview mirror as I pulled into Jack's driveway. I put the car in park and turned it off, and we just sat there for a minute. Lilly didn't take her eyes off her hands. I opened my mouth to say something, but she opened the car door and ran for the house.

I watched her go, mouth still open. My hands cramped. They were still tightly clamped on the wheel. I took a bracing breath and forced my white knuckles to relax. When I looked back up, Jack stood on the front step, pajama pants slung loosely on his hips, no shirt on. One hand was on his hip, the other brushing through his hair. It was a nervous tick I'd noticed. His expression was worried, but not angry. I opened the car door and walked toward him. He took his arm from his hip and reached for me. I took the offered hand and let him lead me into the house.

He didn't say anything at first. He led me to the kitchen, to one of the barstools. I took the seat and he walked to the coffee pot. It was nine a.m., and I imagined this was a late start for him. Since that first dinner, I saw him most mornings on his porch when I came out at the break of dawn with Flynn.

The burble of the machine echoed through the silent kitchen. Finally, he walked around the kitchen island and took the seat next to me.

"Lilly told me what happened." He let the words hang there. I wondered how much she could have told him so fast. I was staring at my hands, so I couldn't see his expression, but he leaned one arm on the tabletop, and his body leaned toward me. I wanted to pretend I didn't know what he was talking about, but it was so obvious I did. I felt sick. I had just been brought on to a clinical trial to study a race of people. A race of aliens. A race of aliens it turned out I'd been falling for.

Because I had. I had fallen for Lilly's exuberant energy, carefree smile, and the generous way she shared all her thoughts and dreams. I had fallen for Brandon and his moody countenance that was surprisingly funny and perceptive. And I had fallen for Jack. For a brave man who had been a caretaker to his siblings. The only father Lilly had ever known. And how I had never seen an ounce of bitterness for what he may have missed due to that.

"Jack I—" I started at the same time he began to speak.

We both stopped, and I finally looked up into his face. We looked at each other, his expression pensive. Mine, I imagined, was much the same, and the ridiculousness of it seemed to pop the bubble of pressure that had built between us. We both laughed, his shoulders sagging with the release. I realized he still didn't have a shirt on, and despite everything, that managed to distract me for a moment. His well-defined muscles sloped into a narrow waist. I looked away, needing to focus.

He walked over to the beeping coffee pot. He poured us both mugs and came back, setting it in front of me. "Lilly told me what happened, Stasia." He repeated what he'd said before, so I just looked at him, brow wrinkled, wondering how I was going to tell him I was part of a clinical project that studied him. That studied his people.

"Do you understand what happened?" he asked.

"Not…not really," I began truthfully. I had only seen the demonstration of those people using water so far. Dr. Galton had explained that the aliens who had landed were an elemental people with four distinct powers.

Remembering the sparks and haze around Lilly, I could guess which hers was. But I didn't really understand why she was going to a human school. I didn't understand how Jack's family was living next door to me when all the Stepuli people lived in their community near the national park.

"What do you think you saw?" Jack asked, taking a sip. I could tell he was worried. I really wished he'd put a shirt on.

"Lilly's hands sparked. She was too far away. I couldn't hear what the kids were saying. She's been having trouble with that new friend she made. The new girl, I think she fell in with the crowd who had been excluding Lilly. Or, from the look of it, maybe flat out harassing her. Whatever they said, Lilly was angry. The air around her changed. I ran for her when her hand started sparking."

Jack looked more worried as I went on. He rubbed his hand down his face, and then through his hair. The vein in his neck popped out. "Fuck," he muttered. "Did anyone else see?"

I shook my head, but my brow furrowed. He was taking this all very well. We were talking about this like it was natural. This was not natural. He must have read something on my face because his hand went to my knee, and he concentrated on me. "Stasia, do you remember the night I brought you home from the bar?"

My head jerked back, confused that his mind had gone there. What did that have to do with the fact I was pretty sure his little sister could create fire? Which didn't make sense by itself. Dr. Galton had explained that elementals manipulated the elements around them. They didn't create it. There had been no fire around Lilly to cause those sparks.

"Yes," I said, frustration and confusion in my voice. But Jack plowed on.

"That night, before you fell asleep, you said something about pods. You described, well, you described a deprivation chamber. Do you remember that at all?"

I shook my head. That was the day I had blacked out in the pool and almost drowned. Thank God the consistency of the water was so dense. Once I'd lost consciousness, my body had relaxed enough for me to float to the surface. I had only inhaled a small amount of water. It had quickly come back up, and with prophylactic antibiotics, I'd been fine.

"Well, that night you mentioned pods. Pods like what we're put in to help get us to a meditative state to express abilities for the first time. Abilities that— Fuck, I'm messing this up. Stasia, me and Brandon and Lilly…we're—"

"Jack. Jack stop." I held a hand up. He was struggling to tell me something that I already knew. But explaining to him how I knew might change the way he saw me.

Jack looked like he wanted to say more but he obeyed, waiting for me.

"I know what you're talking about. At least the abilities part of it." His face seemed to clear, which only made my stomach sink lower. "A few weeks ago, a doctor at my work tapped me to join this clinical project. I've never mentioned it because it was top secret, I wasn't allowed to." I swallowed as his pensive face relaxed. His expression became blank.

"That day, we were put in the pods because they told us they wanted us to experience what our patients would. So we could understand the purpose of them. I had a…a bad reaction. I passed out in the pool."

Jack's solid form was motionless. I forced myself to continue. "I had orientation yesterday. The man who runs it, Dr. Galton—"

Jack flinched when I said that name, making me falter. I swallowed. "He explained to us the purpose of the trial. He said we're trying to help a people called the Stepuli continue their race and fulfill their purpose. He told us it was an alien race of elemental people. Are you...is that you?" I asked finally.

At some point during my speech, and I couldn't really pinpoint where, Jack had drawn away from me. He didn't answer, which worried me. A small voice came from the hall.

"You know Dr. Galton?" I looked over my shoulder. Lilly's tear-stained face looked suspicious, which I hadn't expected. Her eyes were red, but she'd dried her cheeks. She narrowed her eyes.

"Yeah, hon. He's my boss."

Jack was stiff. His eyes moved back and forth, searching my expression for something.

"I thought...I thought maybe you had abilities." I jerked back, the comment so unexpected. "You don't feel like another Stepuli with an affinity, but you don't feel human either. I feel calm in your presence. You're an orphan..."

His voice trailed off. I looked at him helplessly. The anger that had been tightening Lilly's face was gone, and she looked hopeful as well. I turned back to Jack, touched I made him feel calm, but knowing that it couldn't be for the reasons he hoped.

"Jack, I tracked my mom down in my early twenties. I hired a private investigator. I wanted to know who I was from and why she had left me. She was a young girl, about to go to college. Her father was strict, and she didn't want her parents to know she had gotten pregnant. The man she had me with never even knew. I tried to track him down too, but he had died in a car accident. I didn't know my parents, but they were human."

His face looked shocked. Then sick.

Behind me, Lilly spoke again. "You work for Dr. Galton?" This time, I didn't imagine it, I heard the anger plain in her voice.

I turned back around, fear creeping in, making it hard to breathe. "Yeah, Lilly."

I turned back to Jack to ask why that was bad, but his face shut down. He stood and walked over to Lilly. Instead of standing next to her, he stood in front of her. Almost shielding her. "I think you should go."

I searched his expression. Confusion and helplessness filled me, "Jack, why—"

He interrupted me as I began to ask what I had done wrong. Why were they looking at me with anger and distrust? I knew finding out I was studying their people might be weird, but I hadn't expected them to react like I was going to hurt them. I had started to get up to walk toward him, but he held a hand up, warding me off. Lilly didn't try to step around his back.

"Dr. Galton isn't a friend to our people. The eugenics program isn't a nice program to help our people find their purpose." He twisted the last word. "It's a breeding program to help the government get individuals with elemental powers they can use for their own needs. I've been hiding the fact Lilly has powers. It's the only thing that's kept her out of a lab. I thought you were a goddamn

Stepuli. That's the only reason I let you so close."

He stopped, running his hand through his hair again. "I'm an idiot." He looked down at the floor. "I should have known you were a spy. You got what you came for. Just leave."

My eyes wide, I opened my mouth to deny it. I wasn't a spy. That was crazy. It was just a sick coincidence I'd started at SEP. And what did he mean a breeding program? Or about Lilly being in a lab? I stood up off the stool, the scrape of it against the tile echoing as I reached for Jack. He shook his head, keeping his hand up between us.

"Just fucking go, Stasia," he said, the anger leaking out of him, leaving him defeated. Tears gathered in my eyes, and my chest grew heavy with sadness. I wanted to say more, but I knew now wasn't the time. So, I went.

# CHAPTER 16
## Stasia

I watched the sun rise by inches of light gained on my ceiling. My thoughts circled around the conversation with Jack yesterday. He said he'd thought I might be Stepuli. I went over and over our interactions, wondering why he'd think that. I thought of how he'd said I made him feel calm, and instead of the warmth that had spread through my chest yesterday, a weightless feeling settled.

The kind you get when you're falling, and you don't know when you'll land. Because the last thing I remembered, the thing that stood out stark in my mind, was the betrayal on Jack's face. The disgust.

Flynn's growls jolted me from my thoughts. His way of saying it was time to go outside. I threw the covers off to get up and walk him. I hoped Jack would be outside this morning. He had needed time to cool down, but I wanted to talk. So, I could explain the misunderstanding. I had just joined this project. I wasn't a spy. I could understand what he meant when he said the SEP wasn't a program trying to help the Stepuli.

In a week, I had learned not only that aliens lived on Earth, but that they'd been here for generations. More than that, I lived next door to a family of them. And I thought I might be falling in love with one of them.

We walked out into the early morning light, but Jack's back door was firmly closed, his curtains drawn. That weightless feeling yawned in my chest. Part of me wanted so badly to go knock on his door. Insist he hear me out. But, remembering the look on his face, the way Lilly had stood behind him, stopped me.

Flynn trotted up to me after doing his business and whined. His nose pointed in the air, enjoying the breeze. He looked over at the neighbor's house, getting more vocal the way huskies do. I tore my eyes away. "Not today boy. Come on."

\*\*\*

I pulled into what I now knew was the Pacific Northwest Stepuli Community. Today was my first actual day of work. I grabbed my bag and dragged myself out of the car. Confusion and dread shrouded me, dogging my every step. I heard Jack's accusing voice calling me a spy. I thought about his accusation that the Eugenics Project was a breeding program.

I juxtaposed that against the energy and excitement in yesterday's orientation. A room full of people who had taken oaths, whose entire careers were built on their desire to help others. Then again, I knew eugenics hadn't exactly been used ethically in the past, and by similar people who had taken similar oaths.

So lost in my thoughts, I almost didn't hear Pat behind me, running up calling my name. It finally permeated the fog, and I looked back. Two cups of coffee spilled over his fingers in his haste to reach me, his long lanky form disheveled.

When he finally caught up, he was breathing hard, his wrinkled brow giving away his annoyance. "You don't deserve this coffee," he said, shoving it at me. I could smell the hazelnut.

I murmured my thanks, and we fell into step. As we walked, Pat eyed me sideways.

"What's eating you this morning?" he finally asked as we reached the steps of the school.

I started to answer, but snapped my mouth shut before any words made it out. What could I say? Jack thought I was a spy. I was starting to doubt this project, already shrouded in so much mystery, after his words. I still didn't even know how his family was free to live among humans. In orientation, we were told Stepuli lived within a few scattered communities around the United States.

I bit my lip as we finally reached the doors. He held it open for me, his gaze questioning. I knew his naturally nosy personality would soon demand answers.

"I just slept wrong. Forgot my coffee." I saluted him with the to-go cup he'd brought me. "You're a lifesaver."

He beamed at me, accepting my excuse and enjoying the praise. We walked into the building, him with more energy than usual for the morning. He carried the conversation, encouraged enough by a nod here or there.

Dr. Kimi met us the lobby and explained she split her time between the school and the research center we had done our initial deprivation training in. She told us she'd be assigning us to different elemental classes. They ranged by age and type of ability.

"Kids start young working out their element," she said

as she took the group I'd been assigned to toward the gym area where we had seen the water demonstration. "The oldest classes you'll be dealing with are the new graduates of Stepul School. They get sent on training missions but still haven't joined any of the environmental teams."

"For the most part, your job is to make sure they aren't overexerting themselves. When the Stepuli use their elemental powers, it's like working out for a human. It physically tires them. Each elemental has a different strength with their element, the same as a human does in a sport. We help them develop that strength, and depending on their level of ability, they are assigned to different missions around the world."

"How have humans not realized they're here by now?" I asked.

The group—made up of two other nurses, me, and Dr. Kimi—stopped. She looked back at me and frowned a little. I shifted, feeling like I'd done something wrong by asking, but it seemed like an obvious question.

"We've gone to great lengths to ensure that they don't. If the humans found out, the Stepuli wouldn't be able to live in peace. They'd be hunted, or worse. They're a peaceful people. We keep them safe."

She turned abruptly on her heel and continued to the gym. The other two nurses I walked with murmured between each other. I fell back a little. It sounded like a company line. They had told an entire group of civilian-contracted nurses the Stepuli secret without any of the negative outcomes she mentioned.

Once we reached the gym, Dr. Kimi set us each up at a station. The other two nurses, I hadn't caught their names, were set up at the water station. Dr. Kimi walked me over to the air station. I was working with the youngest age group today. Dr. Kimi had explained there were three different rotations of age groups: eight to twelve, thirteen to seventeen, and eighteen to twenty-two. It helped keep everyone with similar capabilities in the same workout.

The bay windows at the top of the cavernous room stood open. Industrial fans sat against the wall, and smaller standing fans stood out in front of us. They were plugged in and spaced a few feet apart.

A young girl stood in front of me. Her dark, almost-black hair framed her almond-shaped eyes. Next to her, a blond boy who smacked his gum and drummed on his thighs, looking bored. Thinking of Jack's words, I watched them closely, but none of these kids looked in distress.

"So," Dr. Kimi brought my attention back around to her. "Don't interfere with the trainers unless absolutely necessary. After the kids complete their exercises, you'll get vital signs on all of them and record them in the chart."

As she spoke, she pointed to the vital sign machine next to a chair in front of a portable computer. We were on an internal charting system that they had given us a tutorial of yesterday as part of our orientation. I nodded along with her, my eyes straying to the children who seemed like any other elementary school class, fidgeting and bored while they waited for classes to begin.

Dr. Kimi snapped her fingers in front of my face. The rude gesture brought my eyes back to her.

"This is serious. This is these kids' lives. They aren't specimens for you to examine."

My eyes widened as I realized why she thought my attention had been diverted. I bristled at her suggestion that I saw them that way. Opening my mouth to refute her judgment, the words died before they left my mouth.

Dr. Kimi had seemed like a cold clinical scientist giving us an obligatory rundown. I had been so distracted and caught up in my internal thoughts I hadn't tuned into her. She felt distressed. Conflicted and worried. From her comments, I realized she was worried about the kids in front of me. Maybe she believed what she had said when I asked why they hadn't told the general population about the Stepuli.

Instead of responding defensively, I gave her honesty. "I was just thinking how they look like any other elementary class, bored waiting for their teacher. They're in good hands, Dr. Kimi. I'll make sure they aren't overworked."

Her frown only deepened, her brow furrowing. She gave one sharp nod and said, "Lunch is after workouts are complete. Then they go to their normal classes. When you rotate to the older classes, you'll find they start after lunch. They're usually too keyed up after their exercises to return to academics."

I nodded my understanding, and she walked forward, saying a warm hello to the children. Her arms on their shoulders, she crouched down to their level. The kids seemed excited to see her. The little dark-haired girl circled her arms around Dr. Kimi's neck. The boy excitedly slapped her back, trying to show her a rock he had taken from his pocket. Kimi oohed and ahhed over it and warmly hugged the girl back. She said hello to a few other kids in the lineup. Nodding to me, she left back the direction she came.

I stared after her for a moment, but my attention was quickly diverted by a young voice asking, "Who are you?"

The little blond boy tossed his rock into the air and

caught it. The dark-haired girl scuffed her shoe, looking at the ground. Two other kids to the little girl's right huddled together, talking and casting glances my way.

Following Dr. Kimi's lead, I crouched down to their eye level and said, "I'm Stasia. What's your name?"

The little boy tossed his rock up and down, smacking his bubble gum, scrutinizing me. His face broke into a wet smile, drool from the gum bubbling around his teeth. "I'm Caleb."

I couldn't help a laugh. "Hi, Caleb, how old are you?"

He stood, chest puffed out, pride in his voice. "I'm eight."

I nodded as if impressed and looked to the shy girl who peeked at me through the curtain of her hair. "And how about you?"

She darted her eyes back to her feet, but Caleb nudged her with his shoulder. She looked over at him and then shyly back at me. "I'm Elle. I'm nine."

I gave her a soft smile and said hi. Before we could talk further, a woman came into the room. She wore a utility uniform of dark blue pants and a gray shirt. Black shiny combat boots noisily announced her presence. I stood up straight, looking around. So did everyone else.

"Hey kids," she said in a stern, gravelly voice. She sounded like she smoked a lot. "Let's get started."

Her name was Sue, and she led the children gifted in air through a series of exercises. Their job was mostly to contain objects. They started with large innocuous objects like plastic bags. Sue would put the plastic bag in front of the fan, on low, and let it go. Each child would practice containing the bag before it reached a yellow line. They would then practice this on different fan speeds, and sometimes Sue would throw in an extra plastic or paper bag.

Caleb's bags never hit his yellow line. As he worked, he held his rock behind his back. It seemed like a comfort item. Sue praised him highly, spurring the other children to reach his level of success. The other two children I hadn't had a chance to speak to stood to Elle's left now, and they were able to catch their bags about half the time. Elle struggled to catch hers at all. One time, the bag smacked her in the face. She dripped with sweat, her hair matted on the right side of her head.

I felt anxious as I watched her breathing. Her respirations were high, as if she'd been running on a track, but her color was good, and her shoulders weren't drooping. I wanted to stop the session but worried I was overreacting. I tried to get a sense of how the other kids were feeling. Caleb seemed to be having fun. Elle seemed tired. The other two kids varying degrees of both. Finally, my nerves stretched taut, Sue called the training session.

The kids turned to me, almost in a military maneuver, and filed in a line to my station. Impressed with their discipline after a long morning, I waited for each one to step up. There hadn't been a chair near, so I stood from mine and sat it next to the vital machine. One of the two kids I hadn't gotten the name of approached first and stayed mostly silent as I took their vitals.

I asked a few questions: how they were feeling, if they had any pain. They answered in short sentences, bouncing up and down in their haste to have this part over with.

Next was Elle. She had me a little worried. Her vital signs were elevated, and her cheeks had flushed a dark red. She looked almost like she had heat stroke. I grabbed an ice pack from the first aid cart at my station and put it against her forehead. I started telling her to stay seated until she recovered when Sue came up beside us.

Looking over my shoulder at my chart where I had written the vital signs, she said, "She's fine. Elle doesn't have any stamina. We're working on it. This is about where she is after every workout. She's good to go to lunch."

My lips turned down. I looked at Elle and asked, "How do you feel?"

She looked up at Sue and back at me. I tensed when I felt her hesitancy, but when she spoke, her voice was firm. "I'm ok. I'm hungry."

I nodded slowly and told her okay, letting her go. She stumbled a little, and I almost called her back, but she straightened and continued after the first two kids, brushing her wet hair back from her temples.

Last was Caleb. Sue had wandered away since Caleb looked the least winded of everyone. I put on the blood pressure cuff and pulse oximeter, giving him a strained smile, still a little uncertain about my interaction with Elle. There hadn't been anything dangerous about her vitals, but I would have rather given her a rest before sending her to lunch.

Caleb sat in the chair, his rock held in a loose fist. "You feeling okay kiddo?" I asked. It struck me that he hadn't looked at me directly, and he seemed stiff. I hoped he wasn't hiding a muscle strain.

"Any pain?" I continued when he didn't answer.

Finally, he looked at me, but his eyes were colder than an eight-year-old's should be.

"Elle didn't feel good."

I frowned at the comment, my concern for the girl

sinking into my skin, making me mad at myself. I had felt pressured to let her go. I didn't understand my job yet, and I hadn't seen anything dangerous enough to contradict the trainer. Her assurance she wanted to go to lunch had tilted me in the direction of letting her go.

"I'm sorry, Caleb. I know she was tired, but she said she wanted to go to lunch."

He looked at me, his gaze no less cold. "That's because she's scared of Sue. I thought you were like Dr. Kimi."

His words opened that weightless feeling in my chest from this morning. It seemed like lately I constantly felt like I was falling.

"I'm sorry, Caleb, I didn't realize. I'll be more careful next time." I unstrapped the monitor from him as I spoke. He didn't say anything else to me, just shrugged off the chair and headed toward the cafeteria.

I stared so intently at Caleb, I noticed his little fist had opened. The rock he had been holding hovered in his loosely curled palm. Nothing touched it as it rotated in the middle of Caleb's hand.

# CHAPTER 17

## Jack

I stood in Lilly's doorway watching her sleep. The blanket was pulled up over her head, her fingers just visible. The bundle moved up and down as she breathed, deep and even. I rubbed my hand over the ache in my chest. It had been two days. She was still low on energy and depressed. Brandon came down the hall, distracting me. I closed her door and jerked my head, wordlessly telling him to follow me downstairs.

In the kitchen, I grabbed a cup of coffee and sat down with him at the table.

"She doing any better?" he asked.

"Not really. She's just sleeping a lot. I pulled her out of school for the week with the flu."

"It doesn't seem like she used enough power for this much of a dump."

I dragged my hand through my hair. I had been thinking the same thing. "I think it has to do with Stasia too. Lilly was really attached to her."

Brandon nodded, laying his arm over the chair next to

him and splaying his long legs out in front of him. "I can't believe she was a spy for Galton. I was getting behind the idea she was Stepuli."

The stupid hope I'd harbored for that still ate at me. It's what caused the ache that wouldn't go away. It had caused so much damage to this family. Lilly, exposed. The one thing we'd been working so hard for all these years to prevent. I couldn't believe Shaw hadn't already shown up to tell us we were to report back to the community. Article IV of the treaty, any independent persons must report at the expression of latent powers due to the danger and inability to possibly control their powers. Just one more way the government had gone back on their words to us.

"Why haven't we heard anything?" I asked, voicing my concerns.

Brandon shook his head. "I was given that call to go in. I've been keeping the full strength of my abilities under wraps. I'm not expressing anything nearly strong enough for them to use on missions, but they said they wanted me to come in for mission-ready training anyway. Maybe that's the beginning of it."

I put my head in my hands. Despite being one of the strongest earth Stepuli since the ambassadors, Galton had allowed me to leave the environmental initiative, the side of the SEP that utilized our abilities. He wanted me for my DNA, and the next generation he thought he could create with me. So, he allowed me an exemption. My duties as a "father" prevented my contributions to the environmental initiative. It was just another thing the Stepuli in the community hated me for.

"Has Lilly talked to you at all?" I asked Brandon. We had raised Lilly with photos and stories of our parents, and she thought of them as mom and dad. But there was no hiding the fact I'd raised her, and sometimes she'd confide more in Brandon. My stomach sank when he shook his head.

A sound on the stairs brought both our heads around. A second later, Lilly popped into the hall, her hair tangled in a knot on one side, dark circles under her eyes. Fire Stepuli were different from the other elements. A surge of their power was met with a dump in their moods, not just their energy.

Lilly yawned wide. Even with the obvious signs of exhaustion and depression, she was adorable. She came and sat on my lap without saying a word, curling her head under my chin. She hadn't done this since she was ten. I hugged her tight, pressure building at the corner of my eyes. Brandon's lips turned up a bit at the corners and he said, "Hey Lills. How's it shaking?"

She yawned again, straightening and moving into the seat next me. "I'm fine. I'm just tired."

She knew about the risk with fire Stepuli's. It became an issue somewhere around the third generation, our parents' generation. It was the first time a Stepuli/human coupling had produced a fire elemental. When one was born, something seemed wrong with him. His moods were erratic, at times making it dangerous for people to be around him. They did studies and attributed it to a noradrenaline dump. Galton used it as a reason to keep all fire Stepuli locked away.

I stood and walked into the kitchen, grabbing some orange juice from the fridge along with Lilly's pills. I poured a bowl of cereal. Lucky Charms, her favorite. Bringing everything over to the table, I set it in front of her, and she silently set to work. Brandon and I exchanged looks over the table but waited her out. It was never good to push her in these moods.

Finally, scooping out the last charm, she sat back and looked up at me. "I think maybe we should train more. This time the dump hit me hard. It wasn't just the sparks Stasia saw. I was so mad I generated heat. I don't know how someone didn't get hurt. I'm pretty sure it was hot as an oven around me. I finally heard Stasia calling my name and it snapped me out of it."

I frowned, curling my hand in my lap into a fist. Lilly was special in another way. We had always been able to manipulate the elements, not create them. But Lilly's fire was in her. She could create fire in just the palm of her hand. Whenever she did that, the fallout was worse. Her current condition made a lot more sense now.

"We're all off today. Ian is opening, he can handle it. Why don't we play a little in that cove down on the beach? Then we can go for a run?" Brandon spoke from across the table. Lilly perked up at the mention of being able to use her fire. Even with the dangers inherent in a fire elemental with the dumps, we all felt the pull, the affinity to our element. We all longed to commune with them.

I nudged her elbow. "Take your pill and we can go."

Lilly looked down, mouth curled to the side, but took her pill without further complaint. Any time her dumps hit her this hard, which had been rare, I put her on short term antidepressants to help get her through. I also always made sure that Brandon or I were home. With how strong Lilly was, I always wondered how much worse her dumps must be for her. I swore she'd grow up to have a life. A future. Even if I had to take on the US government, the SEP, and her own mind to ensure it.

\*\*\*

Brandon, Lilly, and I stood in a loose circle under a thick outcropping of trees, mostly sheltered from any stray eyes. Brandon had felt the waves for kayakers, I had felt the earth for hikers. Stasia wasn't home. I made a tributary through the beach sand to our little cave, and Brandon brought in a pool of water, surrounding our circle in case we needed to douse Lilly. I was ready to bow the trees to give us more cover if needed. I held a lighter in front of me.

"No creating fire today, Lilly. That's what got us here. We're going to play with letting you manipulate it over the next couple days. Small doses, so your body gets used to it. A run every day after, and you have to take your pills."

I sounded like a drill sergeant, which made me cringe. Brandon's cocked head only affirmed the thought. Lilly just nodded, her face a mask of concentration. She was excited, I could tell by the sudden lift in her shoulders and the way she rocked on the balls of her feet like usual. Knowing she would soon get to touch fire, barely contained energy sparked inside her.

I took out the Zippo and said, "Okay." I struck the wheel, a small pinky-sized flame sparking over the silver box with a flag saying, "Made in The USA." A private joke.

Almost instantly, Lilly's chin came up. Her tangled hair fell behind her shoulders as the tiny flame became a ribbon of fire, circling first around my body, then hers. Brandon brought up the river of water he'd made around us but held it. Lilly was beautiful. She looked like a rhythmic gymnast, but her prop was fire.

The fire left me and went to twirl around her. It singed the parts of her hair it touched, but she managed to wrap it almost flawlessly around her arms and legs. It cut into her clothes, but any skin it touched was unmarked. It undulated with her as she twirled. Finally, she looked up at me and Brandon mischievously.

My lips quirked, and Brandon braced himself right before she hurled tiny fire bullets at us. I brought up sand from the beach to catch them and dodged. Brandon doused them with the sheet of water he circled around us and threw water bullets back at her. They just sizzled off her fire. I watched closely to make sure they didn't sizzle off her, making sure she kept her promise to only manipulate the fire.

I formed little balls of dirt, careful not to pack them too tight, and threw them back at my siblings. We played the game until all of us were out. If you were hit directly three times, you had to sit. The last one standing won the game. Brandon dove to the left, avoiding a fire bullet, only to get an earth bullet to his forehead. His third hit. He was always too reckless. Lilly's mischievous look turned to concentration. She had never beaten me.

She rapidly fired three fire bullets at me. I had gone from dodging and parrying to standing directly in front of her. I merely looked at the bullets, catching them all with earth flying in front of me. Reforming the earth that had caught the bullets, I shot them at her at three different angles. She dodged one, but two struck. She huffed and slowly let go of the fire glowing around her like a halo.

"You always win," she said, a little petulant. It lifted my spirits like nothing could. If Lilly was petulant, she was feeling more like herself. She hated losing.

I smiled cockily at her, lifting my arms wide. "I'm the best Lills."

She huffed again and started stomping off, but

Brandon's hip-height wall of water stopped her. He laughed quietly and waved his hand. The water fell, slowly leaking back through the tunneled sand back to the ocean. I smoothed the sand over with a thought.

"I'm going to get ready for my run," Lilly said in a snooty tone.

"See you up there," Brandon and I sing-songed at the same time, purposely teasing her. We looked back at each other and smiled. Brandon's eyes, a light gold compared to mine, and Lilly's darker brown, shined. It made me forget the threat of Galton hanging over us. For a moment.

After letting Lilly get a bit of a head start up the path to the house, we headed up ourselves. It was always easier to let her work herself out of a snit.

"That went well," Brandon said.

I nodded. He seemed better since he'd been spending more time at home with Lilly. Since he'd quit drinking. I regretted pushing him to manage the bar, especially at such a young age. It had seemed like a good idea to give him purpose. He'd been chafing at giving himself away and having to go in for monitoring by the SEP.

I had thought it would be an outlet for him. My mistake had been assuming I knew what was best when he'd been old enough to decide for himself. I ran my hand through my hair, hoping I didn't make as many mistakes with Lilly as I had with him.

"I'll take her for a run," Brandon said, breaking through my thoughts. His voice was quiet this time. "Why don't you garden? I thought I saw your campanula wilting."

The corners of my lips lifted. The bell flowers in my cottage garden. It was Brandon's not-so-subtle way of saying he thought I could use some time to commune on my own. I put my hand on his shoulder. "Thanks B, that sounds good." As tall as he was, I'd always been bigger. But he was growing into a strong and thoughtful man. Pride helped shove that ache from this morning a little further away. The only room in my chest now was for my swelling heart, filled with love for my family.

# CHAPTER 18
## Stasia

'd become more comfortable with the job, more assertive ever since the incident with Elle. I had tried to check on her the next day, but she'd been home sick. The fear and guilt I'd felt when I heard that almost made me quit. The trainer Sue assured me she was fine, and I'd seen her after a couple of days lined up next to Caleb. The two young kids wouldn't give me more than a cursory hello after that first day, deepening my guilt.

I had rotated to the eighteen to twenty-two air group today. I sat in front of my computer, my vital machine next to me, going over charts from previous days. I had begun annotating the level and time of strenuous activity next to the effect it had on the patients. Especially when working with the younger classes, I would highlight children at risk for overfatigue so they could be watched more closely, and their workouts could be amended to meet their needs.

The bang of the door announced the presence of the older class. They came in after lunch, and from the loud voices drifting my way and roughhousing between a few boys, they were much more keyed up than the younger patients usually were. Nerves twisted my stomach, but I forced myself to stand as three students broke off and headed my way.

Two stood at medium height. One, a girl with thick black hair framing her browned skin and eyes so dark they looked black. The boy next to her looked almost identical with long black hair pulled back in a ponytail. He had bold features and a cocky smile. Another boy walked alongside them, blond-haired and freckled, his cheeks a little red. I smiled as they approached. The boy with a ponytail contemptuously flicked his eyes over me and turned smartly toward the fans. The girl next to him gave me a slight smile. The blond boy ignored me completely. Ok–ay, I thought and took a seat.

The trainer came toward us, and I started when I recognized him. Christopher Shaw walked up, all business. "We're working with grains of sand today. Let's make sure none of them escape the wind funnel. We'll be starting on medium then high speed. The goal is to show you can stop even small objects from escaping and hurting someone in a hurricane or tornado. We're working on precision with a high volume. Let's get to work."

Ponytail boy clapped his hands together, the blond boy shifted nervously. The girl at the end just stood, looking at her nails, seeming bored. Shaw wasted no time putting the fan on. He took out several pre-made bags with varying amounts of sand in them. He noticed the girl's lack of attention and released a small bag in front of her.

She had seemed like she wasn't paying attention, but as soon as the first granules hit the wind, her eyes snapped up, laser focused. The sand granules stopped their massive spray and began collecting against the strong funnel of wind. They formed into a ball in front of her, and she used hand motions to tease each stray granule into the ball.

I didn't realize I was standing with my mouth open until I heard a familiar voice to my right. "If it isn't the snake in the grass." My mouth snapped shut with a click, and I looked over, surprised. Brandon's golden eyes stared at me intently. Various emotions hit me. Guilt. Excitement because it was the first time I'd seen one of the siblings. A little fear.

"Hey Brandon," I said, voice small.

He curled his lip at me and walked away. He was making sure I knew the measure of his disgust but also wanted me to know I wasn't even good enough to talk to. I watched his back as he walked languidly toward the pools. He needed a haircut.

All thoughts were abruptly cut off as sand smacked against my left cheek, the force of it like a slap. I gasped. Ponytail boy narrowed his eyes at me, his lips turned up in a sneer.

"Sorry, Boss," he called. "I lost control of it." The boy next to him smiled wickedly too. The girl shifted uncomfortably, shooting the ponytailed boy a look of reproach. He must be her brother.

Shaw started toward the boy with a darkness on his face.

Panic clenched in my gut, and I called out, "No problem, I saw it. That whole spread went far right."

Shaw's steps slowed at my words. I was sitting to the right of where the sand would have been thrown at the boy, and I hoped Shaw would think the miss was his fault. I didn't want to get the punk air Stepuli in trouble. I was on their territory.

I didn't really know what these kids were going through. My intuition seemed off these days. I felt nothing but animosity and fear from the proud ponytail boy, excitement from the blond, and an odd sort of sadness from the girl.

Ponytail boy had a bit of doubt on his face now, but he nodded. "I'll be more careful."

He turned back toward Shaw, who had stopped his advance but continued with a lecture. "You should have been able to catch that, Lusio."

The boy's eyebrows slashed down. "It's Lucy."

Shaw rolled his eyes. "Pay attention and do what you're supposed to." He walked back to his place behind the fans, his movements jerky and agitated. When he stood facing the group of airs, he said, "Again."

The girl turned to me. Her lips lifted in a small show of thanks. I nodded back to her and turned to my computer, my cheeks reddening. I didn't dare look over at Brandon. I had heard the trainer over there call the class to attention anyway.

The day felt long as Shaw put the class of older Stepuli through their paces. Finally, he called our class to a close. I took the blond boy's vital signs. He said nothing before trotting off toward the gym door. Ponytail boy sat arrogantly in front of me, his legs thrown wide, propping his arm up for me with a wide grin. I placed the blood pressure cuff on his arm.

"I'm Lucy. That's Lola," he said, staring at me carefully while he pointed over his shoulder to the girl I'd suspected was his sister.

"Hi," I responded. "I'm Stasia."

I finished and removed the cuff. After finishing his

other vital signs, he got up but didn't leave, hovering as I did the same for Lola.

"We heard about what happened with Elle," he said after a moment. My gut clenched, and this time the heat in my cheeks spread down my chest. Refusing to shy away, I looked up.

"I didn't have a handle on my job. I should have taken her out for the day or stopped her session."

The doubt was back, a speculative look in his eyes at my words. He nodded, smacking his lips. I finished up with Lola, who had been quiet the entire time. She stood, and Lucy wrapped his arm protectively around her, guiding her in front of him toward the door.

"See you around, Doc," he called over his shoulder.

"I'm not a doc," I shouted after him, reflexively. He didn't look back, just waved his hand in the air.

Shaw came up next to me, and I jumped a little. The interaction had been so oddly intense. He looked after the two retreating backs. "The air twins," he said. "The brother is nothing but trouble. The girl is a mouse. Their mother was from a Native American tribe. They came from the original community in Roswell when she died. Cancer."

I nodded at him, wondering how many jobs he had. Liaison at the naval hospital, orienteer, trainer to a top-secret government initiative. I had been shocked when I'd seen him come through the doors. He indicated toward the catwalk that led to the second and third story entrances from the gym above us. A silhouette stood waving at the second-story window.

"Galton wanted to speak with you before you go."

"Thanks." I cleaned up my station and walked toward the stairs.

Shaw's voice stopped me. "It's good to see you again Stasia." I turned toward him. We'd hardly spent time together, but his tone spoke of familiarity.

"You...you too," I called back, social niceties drawing the words out of me. Before climbing the steps, I couldn't help glancing over at Brandon one last time. Nerves returned to my stomach when I saw he stood facing me, eyes dark, looking between me and Shaw. I silently pleaded, willing him to understand I had no connection to this man. He turned away from me, back to the instructor at the front of his class, and I continued up the stairs to Galton's office.

Once I reached the door, I knocked. Galton hadn't waited for me. His door was closed when I arrived.

"Come in."

I walked in gingerly like I'd been called to the principal's office.

"Hi, Dr. Galton." He gestured to one of the chairs in front of him, and I took a seat. My foot tapped against the floor.

He felt excited. Dr. Galton always felt excited. At first, I had attributed it to his love of the job, but it had begun to make me uneasy.

"Hello, Stasia, how are you finding things at SEP?" Every time he spoke, he reminded me of a grandfather having lunch with his grandchildren. I wondered if that was intentional.

"They're certainly interesting. The work is rewarding," I responded. This time, I could give a more honest depiction of how I was finding a new job.

He hummed, a smile on his face, spectacles drooping down his nose. "Good, good to hear that. I hear you're wonderful with the subjects."

He used that word again, subjects. I often thought of them as patients by default, or students, since their workouts were in a building attached to the university that educated all the students in the community. I found it odd that he always referred to them as subjects. Or was I looking for things since what Jack said?

"They're smart and sweet kids."

"Right, right. Something else has come to my attention."

I stopped my eyes wandering around the room, his words catching my full attention.

"Okay?" I prompted him to continue.

"It seems there was a mistake when you first came to town. You were allowed to move into a house reserved for a different kind of family. I'm afraid I owe you an apology for that oversight."

My thumbnail pinched into my pointer finger, the pain keeping me from reacting. My breathing became shallower. I forced myself to respond, my eyebrow furrowing. "What do you mean?"

Dr. Galton searched my face as he continued. "Well. You see, certain families, with provisions in the treaty, have been allowed to live among humans on a probationary period. Most have broken the treaty in one way or another. Usually, latent or hidden elemental expression has brought them back into the main community. But we have one family in Washington that still qualifies for their probation. Jack, Brandon, and Lilly Walker."

I couldn't feign surprise. My face went still. I kept my nail dug into my finger. I swallowed, thinking fast on what to say. Brandon was here today, there was no hiding the fact that I knew he was Stepuli. Dr. Galton gave me a piercing look.

"I was wondering when I saw Brandon walk in today," I finally said. "I just assumed I misunderstood, and Stepuli also lived throughout Washington."

Dr. Galton continued his intense perusal for a moment before he responded.

"No. No." He looked down, shuffling some papers on his desk. Looking back up, he continued. "There used to be. Like I said, most have broken the treaty and were required to return to the community."

"What does that mean, broke the treaty?" I asked. He had repeated it several times.

He was pleased I'd asked. I realized he had repeated it on purpose, waiting for me to pick up on the cue.

"Well, you see. Sometime around the last group of children, Stepuli started suppressing their powers. We aren't sure why. Maybe they wanted to be more human? Either way, it leads to dangerous eruptions of power. These workouts not only help those who participate in the SEP environmental initiative, they also help young Stepuli learn to control and channel their power. Article IV of the treaty states that anyone with latent expression of elemental power must return to a community."

That's what Jack meant when he said now Lilly would end up in a lab. "I see."

"The three siblings have expressed wonderful abilities. Jack, of course, was given an exemption while he raised his younger siblings, but he has been using his earth power since he was a child. He had his abilities well in hand. I do wonder about the other two sometimes."

I thought about Jack's beautiful cottage garden surrounding the front of his house. Earth. It suited him. His solidness, how he seemed to center those around him.

Dr. Galton spoke again, dousing the warmth in my chest with ice cold. "Have you noticed them using their powers? I often worry about Lilly especially, as young as she is."

I realized what Galton was doing. The excitement was back. I adopted a confused look and said, "I hadn't realized any of them had powers until I saw Brandon today, Dr. Galton. I've certainly never seen any kind of power from Lilly."

Dr. Galton's eyes sharpened, his grandfatherly act faltering. "Are you quite certain?"

I smiled sweetly. "Of course. I would tell you." No, I wouldn't, I realized. I would never tell him. All of Dr. Galton's grandfatherly concern, excitement, and talk of subjects settled in my gut like a stone. Jack's words came back to me. I would never tell anything about his family to this man. Or anyone else involved with SEP.

Dr. Galton nodded his head slowly. I felt frustration and disappointment. "Well, thank you. There is another matter. The environmental initiative has a training mission coming up. We have a small class of older Stepuli this year, but they all qualify for integration into our hotshot program."

"What can I do to help?" I wondered where he was going with this. I had heard about the environmental initiative. I knew it was technically the part of the SEP I worked in. The students here practiced their skills until they were strong enough to participate on missions.

"We're taking the class out to assess where they are in their skills. It's a couple weeks out, but we'll need a medic with the team. How would you like to be that medic?"

I was stunned. The idea of participating in something

like that sounded exciting. Like I'd really be making a difference. "I'd be honored to go."

"Good, good. You'll be briefed in the coming days. Your job will be like here, monitoring the Stepuli for overfatigue and ensuring they work within their limits. You'll also be tending to any acute injuries. As an emergency and trauma-trained nurse you seemed the perfect choice."

A smile broke across my face. I hadn't forgotten the probing questions about Jack's family, and I wasn't fully comfortable with Galton. But I couldn't help being excited at the prospect of helping people in such a big way. "Great, I look forward to it."

We both stood, I kept the smile on my face as we said our goodbyes. As I turned to go, I realized his door had been left slightly open. I must have forgotten to close it when I came in. Light golden eyes flashed and footsteps retreated as I walked to the door. By the time I made it to the hall, nobody was there.

# CHAPTER 19

## Jack

A howl echoed from outside. I glanced at the window, then determinedly back to the book in front of me. Anytime I heard Stasia outside, I quickly came back in and drew the blinds. I didn't know why someone hadn't shown up yet, forcing us back to the community for our violation of the treaty. Either way, I wasn't going to give her anything else to report on.

The heavy steps on the stairs told me Brandon was finally up. He always slept later for several days after he worked out at the school. He walked into the kitchen, stopping at the coffee pot to start it, and looked over at me. Red lines showed on the right side of his face. He must have slept on something.

"We need to talk." His serious tone juxtaposed against his relaxed appearance. Messy hair, wrinkled shirt, and red-lined face. I tensed.

I stood and walked over to him. Propping an arm on the kitchen island, I waited.

"Galton called Stasia into his office yesterday."

My muscles locked so tight my shoulders ached. This was it. Maybe she just hadn't had a chance to report before now.

Brandon's brow furrowed, and he tapped his fingers against the counter. "She didn't tell him anything."

My face screwed up in confusion. "Explain. Everything. From the beginning."

Brandon told me how he had snarked at her when he first walked in for class. He had been irritated at seeing her standing so casually in front of an air class at one of those medical stations. I felt a prick of annoyance at him for that. We didn't need to poke at the spy. He told me how she had covered for the air elemental. My jaw tightened. Despite myself, I angered when I heard how he'd slapped Stasia in the face with sand.

Conflicting emotions continued filling me as Brandon went on, recounting the odd interaction between Stasia and Shaw. "Shaw left early, so I snuck upstairs. Nobody was paying attention. The way Galton was talking, Stasia didn't know she was living next to Stepuli. He apologized for the mistake. He talked about Lilly like she already had powers, telling Stasia some bullshit about how he worried about Lilly the most. When he tried to get Stasia to confirm, she bottled up. Said she'd never had a clue until she saw me come into class that day."

I swallowed hard. Hope formed in my chest, but I ruthlessly crushed it. "Did she see you?"

Brandon straightened as the coffee machine beeped. "Yeah. I mean, at the end. I think she caught me as she was walking out."

The small bud of hope wilted before it ever had a chance to grow. "It was probably just a trick B. Don't mention this to Lilly." I couldn't stand the thought of her getting her hopes up too. Knowing Lilly, she was ready to forgive and reform a relationship with Stasia so they could talk about boys and braid each other's hair.

Brandon shook his head at me. "She didn't see me until after Jack. And nobody has come knocking on our door."

I refused to even consider the alternative, that Stasia was an innocent party. I thought about her little breaths when I came close. About the way her lips had felt under me, her body pushed up against mine in her kitchen. My body responded, and I walked angrily back to the table, grabbing my glass of water. After a drink, I put my hand on my hip while I got myself back under control.

"Whether it was a trick or not, she isn't Stepuli. She knows who her parents were. We never should have gotten so close to a human."

"Jack, you can't live like a monk forever. We were born here. Our ancestors born on another planet didn't eschew humans as much as you do."

I turned back to him, sure none of my feelings for Stasia still showed. "Our ancestors didn't have generations of exploited Stepuli to hold against their race."

Brandon's shoulders fell, his face troubled. He was worried about me, and it chafed.

"Listen, Lilly is going to come back any second. Let's do another session with her. You stay with her tonight. I've got to close the bar. Ian was busy, so it's just me and Nadine."

Brandon's worried face lightened. Knowing what direction his thoughts had taken, I rolled my eyes. He said, "Well, you haven't always hated all humans I guess."

"No." I grinned slightly. "I guess I never would have

qualified as a monk."

He laughed. "I have other news. Galton tapped me for an environmental training mission. Wildfires in California. They're thinking about bringing along one of the older fires."

I raised my eyebrows at that, several thoughts rushing through me. The first was worry. Brandon had been underplaying his skills ever since his affinity was discovered last year. They shouldn't rate him strong enough to be useful. The second was shock. Fire Stepuli hadn't proven to have much of a practical role in any of the environmental missions, proving to be too unstable. "How do you feel about it?"

Brandon sipped his coffee, taking his time answering. Finally, he shrugged a shoulder. "I know I was messed up when I first got discovered. We live with this worry of the SEP forcing us back into the bracelets, back into the community. But it's kind of nice being able to use my powers for a purpose, to use them openly. I don't like that it's only at their discretion, and I don't like not having a choice how I use them, but at least I get to keep this part of me."

I nodded. Anger caused a dull ache at the back of my head. I was angry that we had to choose between being ourselves under the thumb of the government or hiding the most natural part of ourselves and being free. I kept the thoughts to myself. If Brandon saw a bright side to being discovered, I wasn't going to ruin it for him. His attitude was slowly changing from that surly teenager. It was improving from that reckless young adult. He was twenty-two and really seemed to be coming into himself. Maybe part of the change was being able to channel the tide inside him. I cursed myself for being so stupid and not recognizing that earlier. "I'm glad there's a silver lining. When's the mission?"

"A couple weeks, maybe less. By the way—"

The front door opening cut Brandon off. Lilly walked through, sweaty and red but with a smile on her face. Brandon and I passed a look between us and dropped the mission topic for now without verbalizing it. Lilly chattered at us, her old energy beginning to come back with her new regimen. I wouldn't allow hope to grow and feelings for Stasia to return. But I felt grateful that this time with my family, that the freedom and life we'd found, might not be over yet.

\*\*\*

Nadine walked up and down the bar jeering good-naturedly at customers here and there. The pool table was packed, the chalkboard sign up on the wall full. I walked behind the counter letting my hand slide against the live oak. The tree was long dead, but I could still feel remnants of earth in its sealed veneer.

Nadine looked over at me, bent slightly while filling a shaker with ice. Her dark hair framed her delicate Pacific Islander tan face. She was a beautiful girl, lighthearted and carefree. Her dad had brought her mom back from a deployment, and the family had settled in Washington State when Nadine was young.

"Hey Jack. Come to join the party?"

"If that's what we're calling work these days."

Someone called from the crowd, "It's always a party when Nadine is working!"

She winked at the man. His crew cut and golf shirt gave him away as military. I distantly wondered if she was seeing anyone. Girls her age on the island rarely stayed unmarried. Nadine must be around thirty now. She had spent a lot of her twenties traveling, leaving for long stints, but always ended up back where her parents were. We had a thing for a short while, but like with other relationships, I ended things before it got serious.

Someone walked up to the counter, and I held up a finger, walking behind Nadine. She brushed me as she straightened to go for the liqueurs. She sent me a saucy smile as I held up my bike helmet.

"I'm going to stash this and be back."

"We'll be waiting," she said, swinging the shaker to indicate the rest of the bar. I felt my mouth lift back. Things had been so heavy lately. A carefree night with Nadine didn't sound so bad.

The night was busy from the start, so Nadine and I didn't have much time to talk. We ran to make drinks until almost midnight. There was a local game on the TVs. The music drowned out the commentary, but people cheered for the Seahawks anyway.

Whenever they made a goal, which wasn't often, everyone would order a round of shots. A couple hours earlier, I'd made sure there were Uber drivers on tonight. As small and quiet as this town could get, they didn't run every night, and our customers were getting sloshed. We didn't cut people off often, but we had a strict no-drinking-and-driving rule. You handed in your keys to get a drink at a certain point.

As I leaned down to empty the sinks, refilling them with clean water for washing, a stream of water hit my back, soaking it. I turned around, surprised. I almost expected to see Brandon. Nadine stood there, a playful look on her face, water gun in hand. Behind her, two of the regulars high-fived, and one handed her a bill.

"I'm going to get you back for that," I said, my grin spreading.

She wiggled her eyebrows. "Bring it."

We spent the rest of the shift making a huge mess but having fun. We made a game of catching each other by surprise with the water guns. Some of the regulars had fifty bucks on if one of us could get the other in the face. Nadine and I both decided it was worth it to soak them instead, and I cleared their tab to settle the bet.

After last call, we played a game of picking keys out of the key jar and handing them directly to the Uber driver. It took a while to close. We waited while each person got off to their destination in shifts because there were only two drivers working.

Finally, after counting down the drawer, Nadine and I sat down at the bar together. We each had a shift drink in hand, our nightly ritual before cleanup. Nadine had been getting closer to me all night. Subtle brushes of skin against skin clued me in that she was hoping to rekindle something we'd left behind a long time ago. I had been having too much fun to send my normal signals that it wasn't going to happen.

As we sat, she brushed her legs against mine, twirling on the barstool as she drank her vodka Sprite. I nursed my own scotch.

"Tonight was a great night for a Friday," I said.

"Summer's shining through. Tourist season is in full swing."

I blinked. She was right. I'd been so distracted by Stasia and the things going on with Lilly I hadn't even paid attention to the change of seasons.

Her hand brushed up my thigh. It was the boldest action Nadine had tried in a long time.

"How's it going Jack?" She pulled her hand back. Just a test. Gauging the temperature of the waters.

I couldn't help the smile forming. "Same as always, Nadine. How's it going with you?"

She shrugged one delicate shoulder. She was slim like her mother, her body like a dancer.

"I've been good. Been getting a little lonely though, Jack." She blinked at me obviously. Nadine had never been subtle and had always known what she wanted.

She stood up and moved slowly toward me. I hadn't given her any indication I wanted her to stop. She moved toward me, swaying her hips. The whiskey numbed my defenses. I wasn't sure I wanted her to stop. Her hand slid up my arm to my shoulder and her playful look turned serious. Her other hand trailed up my leg to my stomach, and the one on my shoulder settled on my chest. She pressed herself between my legs. I met her mouth when she leaned up on her toes and kissed her back. As my lips moved over hers, I felt the delicate flick of her tongue and opened.

We moved against each other. At some point, I stood, turning and pressing her into the bar. A small moan escaped her, I felt more than heard it, and I brought my hands up to her side. I squeezed my fingers into her hips then moved my hands up. I heard her say my name. A softly whispered, "Jack."

It brought me out of my daze. The voice was wrong. Flashes of Stasia in her kitchen interrupted the moment. Sure, I felt arousal with Nadine. There was want. But that feeling that filled my chest, the excitement and longing I had felt with Stasia, wasn't there. I looked down at Nadine's flushed face. Her breaths came faster, and her expectant gaze stared up at me. I felt like a jerk. I knew this would never be more than a hookup. This would never be more than a quickie in a bar. It was plain to see that Nadine wanted more than that. What made it worse was, if I was being honest with myself, I had been willing to hand Stasia much more. I had wanted to hand Stasia much more. I cursed myself. Nadine deserved better.

Her expectant flush slowly turned to one of embarrassment as I took a measured step back. Nadine knew I was backpedaling. The prick of guilt only worsened.

She smiled awkwardly. "Well, that happened." She laughed, but it was off.

"Nadine—" I started. Thankfully, she cut me off. I had no clue what I was going to say.

Her smile didn't fall. She didn't seem overly upset, just a little flustered. "It's okay Jack."

Despite not knowing what to say, I knew I owed her some explanation. "Things are tense back home. Lilly's going through a lot, so is Brandon for that matter. I'm just not in a space to give you anything."

She nodded, her smile going a little crooked. "I know that. You've never led me on."

She seemed like she wanted to move toward me again. I leaned back on my heels, my arms going to my sides. "You deserve more than that Nadine."

Her arm fell from raising toward me and wrapped around her stomach. She paused for a moment, but finally said, "Thanks, Jack." She laughed a little. "On that awkward note, I'm going to take the liberty of letting you clean up the bar on your own tonight."

I smiled back. "Fair enough."

We had already counted our tips, so she took her pile of cash and saluted me on the way out. I walked to the door and watched her climb into her car. I waited until she backed out to turn back inside.

Looking at the mess around me, I laughed at myself. Beer shined on the tables. Some wrappers were crumpled on the floor. I knew when I walked around the bar, the sink would be piled high with dishes, and the floors would be soaking wet. It was going to be a long night.

# CHAPTER 20
## Stasia

My hand pressed against my belly, my toes curling under the covers. For the first time in a long time my breaths weren't coming fast from a nightmare. Flynn still lay asleep next to the bed. I closed my eyes, relishing the last moments of the dream. Of being with Jack. I knew it was stupid. He couldn't have made it clearer over the last week and a half that he wanted nothing to do with me.

The glares had lessened from Brandon over time though. He'd been coming in often for workouts at the gym. I'd found out he was going to be part of the team going to California. There had been some extra workouts and briefs, and as I interacted with him and the other Stepuli more, his animosity toward me seemed to wane.

Letting the sweet feeling from my dream fade, I swung out of bed. Flynn instantly lifted his head and stood. He leaned onto his front legs in a long stretch. His customary growls called up to me. I scratched his head in greeting.

After letting Flynn outside, I wandered into the

kitchen and pulled out the notebook I had begun putting recipes in. Still on a mission to learn to bake, I had a recipe for blueberry muffins from scratch. I was trying to graduate from baked goods in a box. I had a few hours before having to leave for work, now on the mid shift with the older kids.

I pulled my mouth to the side, consternation lowering my brow as I pulled my second batch of muffins out of the oven. They still looked like they were falling apart a little. I took a crumbly head off one, bouncing the piece between two hands until it cooled enough. Taking a bite, I figured they were edible enough that at least Pat would eat them. I left them on top of the oven to cool and ran upstairs to put on my scrubs.

After feeding Flynn, I left him in his usual spot. He pouted with his head cocked, watching while I walked out the door. I locked up and headed to my car, looking next door like I always did.

Sometimes I caught glimpses of Lilly running. She must have joined track or something recently. Sometimes she hesitated like she was going to come over. I always stood stock still, willing it to happen. But she never did. And I never called out to her.

Driving to the Stepuli community was a habit now. The scenery passed in a blur. I pulled into the parking lot and looked around, finding Pat's car with no Pat. Figuring he must have gotten here earlier—this was a decent hour, even for him—I grabbed my Tupperware of muffins and headed inside. I had rotated to water elementals. I took a seat at my new medical station and checked over the equipment.

As I tinkered with the pulse oximeter, someone sat in the chair next to me. A cute little boy in a too-big white lab coat with dark skin and a bald head. His hospital socks peeked out of his shoes. He drummed his feet against the metal legs of the plastic chair.

"Hi, I'm Dr. Milo." His voice was high, the way boys' voices were before they hit puberty.

"Hi, Dr. Milo, I'm Stasia."

Milo cocked his head. "That's a weird name."

The innocence and bluntness of children knew no bounds. I laughed. "It is. It's a nickname, but I don't like going by my full name."

Milo nodded sagely. "Well, Stasia is cool. Just weird."

I laughed again. "So, what is your job today, Dr. Milo?" I sat on my chair next to him.

"My job is frustrating my guard."

I raised my eyebrows. "Your guard?"

"MILO!" Pat's voice echoed across the open gymnasium. Other students were filling in, watching on in amusement as Pat stomped over to where Milo and I sat. I had to suppress my own laugh at Pat's red face. His long lanky arms swung agitatedly at his sides. Milo had accomplished his mission.

"Milo, what did I say?" I kept my eyebrows raised, the entire situation seeming odd. So far, as medical personnel, we'd been around to monitor the exhaustion level of the patients, but we hadn't been required to step in for behavioral reasons. That was what the trainers were for.

"What's up Pat? Me and Dr. Milo were just sitting here having a fun conversation."

Pat finally seemed to notice me, his laser focus shifting from the culprit in front of him. Milo ducked his head with a gummy grin. I pursed my lips to keep from laughing.

"Oh, hey Stasia. I've been on fires for the last few days.

This little—" He stopped as I stood, resting my arm on my computer station but flicking him a stern look.

"Angel," Pat continued. Milo looked up, unrepentant, a gummy grin still on his face. Pat frowned. "Has been playing hide and seek. Which nobody else was playing. So, it has turned into a frantic game of seek."

I smiled back at Pat. He was still red, breathing like a bull, clearly annoyed. "Might be time for you to move to the older kids, huh bud?"

"You're telling me," Pat muttered before laying a hand on Milo's shoulder. "Let's go munchkin, back to your area."

I hadn't been around the fire or earth elementals yet, and part of me was curious about them. There weren't any earth elementals in the mission-ready class, and I just hadn't been assigned to the fire section yet.

Milo continued smiling playfully. Curious, I studied him. He didn't feel distressed, just mischievous. He reminded me of Lilly, I realized, humming with energy. He stood and saluted me. "Have a good day, Stasia."

"Have a good day, Dr. Milo!" I called as Milo shot me a wink and then took off back to the door Pat had just come out of.

This time I didn't try to hold back the laugh as Pat screamed after him. "Seriously!" Pat ran to catch up, and they both disappeared behind the door.

I was still looking after them and chuckling when Brandon came up behind me. He was making an annoying habit of that, I thought as I startled.

"Have a good talk with Galton the other day?"

I frowned at him. Part of me felt guilty that I worked for this government trial and that Jack felt betrayed by me.

But I had also moved on to feeling hurt and angry. I hadn't known. How could I have known? It was so out there, an alien race. And what I was doing wasn't bad. I still hadn't seen hard evidence of anything abusive other than a few feelings of insecurity, sadness, and over exhaustion around me. Which was what I was here to prevent. I cared for these kids, and I enjoyed this work.

I sighed and said with an exasperated note in my voice, "We did. He apologized for moving me next to a Stepuli family. Something I found out about when you showed up in the gym the other day." I emphasized the timeline in case the idiot was dense. I was surprised it had taken this long for him to bring it up. I thought I had caught his golden eyes as I left.

Brandon took my cue. He gave me a speculative look. "Well, we don't go around advertising it. We aren't allowed to."

"Which is what I told Dr. Galton. Apparently, you are behaving like stand-up citizens. Now, do you mind if I prepare for the day?" It's not like I had a lot to do, but he was making me nervous. Though his overall hostility toward me had lessened this past week of working together, the continued distrust hurt after so many nights spent smack-talking over spades. I missed dinners with him and Lilly. I missed Jack.

I swallowed the lump that formed in my throat as he went to walk away. Suddenly, he stopped and turned.

"You were good with Milo. He doesn't get a lot of time to interact, but he's wily. I'm sure he appreciated you calling him Dr. Milo."

I frowned. I hadn't realized Brandon was already in the gym when I had talked to the kid. But also, what did he mean that Milo didn't get time to interact? He'd seemed like a bright, lively boy. Stepuli had families outside of the school. This entire suburban neighborhood was full of movie theaters, grocery stores, and parks. Kids might stay in their insular community, but they weren't kept in a jail.

The trainer walked out, a well-built middle-aged man with a forgettable a face. I had stopped keeping track of the trainers. I never really interacted with them unless there was a problem, which admittedly was rare.

The trainer moved through the class activities. I was fascinated with the way the older water students moved the streams. The goal of this class was to take a ribbon of water through a structure if needed, to help douse the flames, giving firefighters more time to get inside structures and rescue persons trapped inside. Today was the last class before we went for our mission to Northern California. To demonstrate, the waters made elaborate shapes with their water, running it through circled arms up to the ceiling. They used their hands and arms, directing the streams midair in a wonderful swirl of watery ribbons.

Unable to help myself, I watched Brandon the most. I had grown to recognize signs of strain in patients. Droplets of sweat, higher respirations, reddened coloring. Brandon seemed almost bored effortlessly going through the motions. Every once in a while, I would catch a constipated look on his face, as if he was trying to feign strain. I remembered Jack's voice, cold and distant that day in his kitchen. The hint of desperation in his eyes as he told me they'd been hiding Lilly's abilities. Maybe that wasn't all they were hiding?

After the class ended, I did the customary vital sign monitoring. When it came to Brandon's, I increased all his vitals a little. Not enough to be noteworthy, but enough to show an increased physical strain. He looked at my paper then at me. My cheeks warmed. I could be totally misinterpreting the situation, and he could be thinking I didn't know how to do my job. But when he left me, the only thing I felt from him was surprise. And gratefulness.

The rest of the day moved by quickly. Pat and I met up in the locker room that we kept our gear in, though the type of gear I needed for my job had been greatly reduced. I kept a stethoscope just in case there was ever a more severe problem.

"God, that kid is a pain in my ass," Pat complained. I had a feeling he didn't find Milo as adorable as I did.

"He seemed like he was putting you through your paces," I said in sympathy, closing my own locker. We were both dressed in regular clothes after changing, having made plans to grab dinner after work.

"He's such a troublemaker. He knows he isn't allowed out of his section. He pushes his limits all the time."

While I felt for Pat, part of me was also a little exasperated with him. "Pat, isn't that kind of what kids Milo's age do?"

Pat looked at me, surprise on his face. He formed a sheepish smile and said, "Yeah, yeah, I guess you're right. Honestly, Stasia, sometimes I forget. I mean. They're aliens. They have superpowers."

I realized that I had never thought of the Stepuli's abilities in terms of "superpowers." Their abilities seemed like an extension of themselves. The same as my good intuition or Pat's ability to make me feel at home.

I said as much. "Well, you are a more accepting person than me, girl. Let's go."

He guided me out of the gym with a hand on my back. We made our way to our cars and met at a cozy Italian restaurant in town. Angela was going to join us later for drinks. She had texted me earlier today, excited. Apparently, she had a plus one for tonight. Unease settled in my gut as I took a seat across from Pat and the waiter took our drink orders.

Somehow, I was just realizing how much of a date this seemed like. I didn't want Pat to get the wrong idea. I liked him a lot. But that thinking brought me to thoughts of Jack's hands. Thoughts of the way he made my stomach bottom out with one touch against my hip. The way he made it hard to breath as that hand had traced up my side to my breast. I squirmed in my chair and firmly stopped thinking of our moment in my kitchen.

I liked Pat a lot. But not like I did Jack. And even though I knew nothing was going to happen with him, it wasn't in me to start something new while these feelings still lingered. While I still dreamed of him at night.

Our drinks and food came, and I sipped my wine, wondering how to signal to Pat that I only saw him as a friend without making it awkward. Pat noticed my quietness and finally asked me about it. I hadn't thought of a way to bring it up, so I asked him about what Brandon had said instead.

Nobody was sitting close to us. I scooted my chair a little closer to the table and leaned in. An eager smile on Pat's face almost made me wince. This wasn't helping, but I didn't want to be overheard. "Someone made a comment after you left with Milo, today." I looked around again when Pat stiffened. Making sure not to say anything that would be too obvious, I said, "He mentioned that class doesn't get a lot of time to interact."

Pat leaned back. Our food was almost gone, my wine about half empty. He looked at me, searching my face. His perusal confused me. He seemed so serious. "Angela wants to meet at Walker's Place. I'll drive and tell you about it." This time I did wince. I so did not want to go to Jack's bar on a Saturday.

"Any chance we could try out a different bar?"

Pat cocked his head. "It's the best one in town. Any reason?"

"Just thought we might get some variety."

His mouth turned to the side like he thought there might be something more. Annoyance came off him, which confused me more. "Angela texted a second ago and said she's already there."

I hung my head in defeat. I didn't know what I could say to convince them to change venues. I had a hot moment with my neighbor in my kitchen, and now I'm dreaming about it? Even though now he hates me and wants nothing to do with me? Seeing him might be a bit awkward, and I'm not a hundred percent sure he won't throw me out on the spot?

Keeping those thoughts to myself, I nodded my assent, and we signaled we were ready for the check. I insisted on paying half, overruling Pat's complaints. That uneasy feeling he saw this relationship as something different seeped in even further.

Pat had been an amazing friend since coming to Washington. Him and Angela were my bedrock, especially since Jack had kicked me out of his house. I couldn't imagine not having them. But I also knew that nothing would ever happen between me and Pat. I trailed behind him, heading to the passenger side of the car.

He fired up the engine, pulling the sedan out of the parking lot. I'd Uber home later. I waited for Pat to bring up the conversation from inside the restaurant, but he stayed silent, tapping the steering wheel.

Finally, I prompted him. "So...about Milo?"

He looked over at me. His face was stoic.

"Who mentioned that anyway?"

I didn't want to bring up Brandon's name. "One of the students, can't remember. They said it in passing."

I felt disappointment from him. Before I could wonder about it, he continued. "Milo is a fire elemental."

"Yeah?"

He looked over at me, before staring at the road again. We were getting close to Walker's Place. This town wasn't big.

"Fire elementals aren't like the rest, Stasia. They're unbalanced."

It was my turn to frown. Classing an entire type of people as unbalanced seemed a bit ridiculous.

"What do you mean unbalanced?"

"They're all just off. Something about the chemicals in their bodies when they use the fire makes them super hyped, but then super low. We keep them drugged up half the time. They don't get to go home like most of the other kids. They stay at the university full time in a fire-retardant section. The government is trying to find a use for them, and a program that will let them function semi-normally. That's why they're taking a fire on that mission coming up to California. But I don't know. We have to keep them and us safe, you know?"

Horror settled in my gut. I thought of Milo's

exuberant energy, his gummy smile. I thought of Lilly. Protectiveness like I'd never felt before rushed through my middle. No wonder Jack was so scared for his sister.

"They keep them in a fire-retardant section? All the time?" The reproach was clear in my voice.

Pat looked over, his eyebrows pinched. "We have to protect them and ourselves," he repeated. "Milo is probably the most normal of them. He's hyperactive, but they also don't let him work very hard. They already started him younger than the other Stepuli. I've seen the older ones. They're intense. They stare at you like there's nothing there."

I thought of Lilly living carefree and happy with her brothers. She couldn't hurt a fly. I remembered her hand sparking that day at school. I knew how mean teenage girls could be. I could imagine what that blonde-haired girl had said to provoke her. I also remembered how confusing it could be at that age with hormones scrambling your thoughts. Still, she'd held back. But what would she be like if she'd grown up sequestered in a lab? No freedom to be a kid or room to make mistakes and learn from them?

As we pulled into the parking lot of Walker's Place, I was quiet, my back stiff. "Maybe if you grew up in a cage you wouldn't be all there either, Pat."

"It isn't a cage, Stasia. It's the only way to keep them from being terminated without risking everyone in their community."

I felt sick at his comment. He put the car in park as I asked, "Terminated?"

Pat's shoulders tightened, but he didn't respond to my question. "Listen, just be careful on this mission coming up. They have one of the older fires going with you as a training exercise. It's a bad idea. A disaster waiting to happen."

Confusion and anger overrode my thoughts. I didn't want to say something I'd regret. I jerked my head in a nod to tell him I'd heard him and stepped out of the car. Pat stayed seated and looked after me. We stared at each other through the front windshield. After a short moment, he followed me. Together, we walked into the bar toward Angela's bright face.

# CHAPTER 21

## Jack

My eyes tracked her across the room, moving over her face, down her neck, her arms. I was stuck somewhere on her fingers when I heard Nadine. "Hey, Jack!"

My head jerked to the right. "Yeah?"

"The keg, the Belgian?" she called like she'd said it a few times. I nodded my head, muttering "sorry" on my way to the cooler. As I headed to the hallway, I watched Stasia out of the corner of my eye. I made short work of hefting the kegs around, hooking up the nitro, then walked back down the hall, slowing as I entered the bar's open area.

I spotted Stasia sitting at a table where Angela had been the last hour with a guy from the base. Stasia was sitting next to the guy she had been in with the last time they'd come as a group. I felt a prick of something. Annoyance maybe? As I headed back behind the bar, Nadine caught my arm.

"Everything okay? You seem a little spaced out."

I forced a smile I hoped was reassuring. "Good, just daydreaming. Crowd's picking up."

She ran her hand down my arm. "It is Saturday."

I nodded my agreement as I moved past, my gaze unerringly pulled back to where I had last seen Stasia. I caught her looking back at me, gaze sharp. The annoyance that had tightened my shoulders eased off. She didn't like when Nadine touched me? Good.

I shook my head at myself, the mixed signals inside confusing. Brandon's updates about Stasia at the SEP environmental initiative were messing with my head. I tried to hold onto the anger and betrayal I had felt when I found out she was part of the SEP. But the more I heard, the harder it was. About how she'd lied to Galton's face. How she persisted that lie and seemed compassionate to the Stepuli in the school. The more my vehemence slipped, the more the warm feelings I'd had returned, making me think of Stasia's eyes. Her lips. Her arms. Her damn fingers.

Nadine noticed something was up about an hour after Stasia and her friends sat down. After our talk, she had continued her normal flirting. The little touches and comments didn't typically bother me. They were harmless, and Nadine was a nice woman having a bit of fun. But I noticed the way Stasia's gaze kept creeping back to the bar. I thought I saw tension in the lines of her shoulders, and I knew I'd caught a frown on her face a few times.

Stupid guilt for what had happened between Nadine and me the other night set in. I lost count of how many times I reminded myself I'd done nothing wrong. Not only did I owe nothing to Stasia, she could have actively hurt my family. I passed a beer over to the next customer and sighed. Because she could have hurt my family. But she didn't.

"Hey, want to take a break?" Nadine's hip checked

mine at the question. I gave her a smile but moved my body away from the contact.

"Nah, you go. I've got this for a while."

She smiled back, but I could see the uncertainty in it, and that made me feel bad too.

"When's Ian going to be back?" she asked. I had given him a couple weeks off. After being arrested, he had come right back to work but had quickly realized he needed some time off to decompress. Afraid of losing him altogether, I had given him a couple paid weeks off.

"Next weekend. This is the last one you'll have to put up with me." I ended it with an awkward laugh.

Her smile barely lifted on one side. "I haven't minded." With that, she tossed the bar towel she'd been winding through her fingers over her shoulder and headed to the back. I watched her go, sighing at how much I felt like I was messing things up lately. At least Lilly was doing better. Her depression was waning. She was weaning herself off the pills. I never should have let her training slip. When Stasia had moved in, I hadn't known how to continue it in secret, the risk of being discovered was so great. Then I had gotten caught up in thinking Stasia could be Stepuli. So stupid.

A commotion brought my eyes back up and almost automatically over to Stasia's table. Anger and a hint of panic ripped through my chest when I realized that was where the trouble was coming from. I moved without even realizing it, halfway to the table when I began picking out the voices.

"Get your hands off her right now."

"Yeah, sir. Uhm, this isn't cool."

"Sit down and shut up Petty Officer. I'm just being

friendly. Isn't that right, young lady? Now, can I buy you a drink?"

"Let me go. I'm not interested."

I recognized the captain from the other night. Pat stood facing off with the man. The military guy with Angela was standing too, but not moving closer. His eyes shifted back and forth, his hands fisted. Clearly uncomfortable but uncertain what to do against a superior officer. Respect for Liam's situation from a couple weekends ago ran through me as I moved faster.

The captain had his arm around Stasia's back, clasping her shoulder, leaning her body into him. She used her other hand to try to get some space, leaning as far from him as she could. A grimace pulled her lips down, and discomfort etched every line of her face.

"How do you know until you have a drink?"

Pat grabbed the man's hand, and the captain turned, belligerently swinging for Pat right through Stasia. She began tipping over, and I grounded the wood of the chair down with a thought. A second later, I reached the captain and grabbed him by the back of his shirt and swung him around.

He fell roughly against the ground. I had used every bit of my strength. Grim satisfaction ran through me when he got off the floor and came back for me. That one toss hadn't been nearly enough to satisfy the rage running through me. Remembering Stasia's past, what being harassed like that might do to her, I put everything behind the fist I slammed into the captain's stomach.

He fell against my shoulder. His friends came toward us with angry faces, and I roughly pushed him off into their arms.

"What the hell? We're calling the police!"

A grim smile crossed my face, and I stepped forward. I wasn't sure whether I'd answer them with words or with fists when I felt a hand on my arm. Stasia's concerned face looked up at me. Her calming presence rushed through me. The anger leaked out like it was water running through a sieve.

She turned to the men who were still yelling. As the captain recovered and took a step toward us, I began pulling Stasia behind me, but she stopped me.

"Let's call the police. I'd like to file a sexual harassment complaint against this man."

The captain stopped his advance, his face turning red as he sneered. "Sexual harassment for what? Offering to buy you a drink, you dumb whore?"

Anger threaded through me again. The chair behind me shook. Stasia's fingers dug into my arm, the calm rushing through me like a cold bath. I looked down at her in surprise. I hadn't imagined that.

"For touching me. They have cameras. Leave. Now. Or I call."

The captain looked like he was about to say something when one of his friends spoke in his ear, pulling him back. He looked over at his friend and back at us. Where Stasia dug her nails was beginning to hurt, but I still felt the cool serenity. Intellectually knowing she was safe, I tried sinking into that feeling. Explore where it was coming from.

"Bitch," the captain muttered. He walked straight out the door. His friends shot dark looks in our direction, but one took out a hundred-dollar bill and tossed it on the table before walking out as well.

"Jack, what is going on?" Nadine walked up, looking

pointedly at Stasia's hand on my arm but gesturing toward the slamming doors.

Stasia noticed the look and dropped her hand from my arm. She'd left half-moon impressions where she had gripped me.

Without thinking, I caught her hand in mine before she turned away. Whatever look I gave her cleared her uncertain expression. I turned to Nadine.

"I'm going to call Ian to come in to help you. I need to get Stasia back to her house."

Pat, who had been standing behind Stasia with his hand on her shoulder the entire time, said, "I can take her."

"I'm taking her." I turned to her and asked, "Are you ready?"

She looked up at me, gaze unerring. "Yes. Let me get my bag." She turned back to do that. Pat and she murmured back and forth. His voice sounded angry. It made me tense, now that Stasia was away from me, and after what just happened.

Nadine looked up at me and frowned. "Why don't you let her friends take her home?"

"She's my neighbor, and she just got assaulted in my bar. I'll take her home." It was the best reason I could think of.

"I'd hardly call that assault." Nadine swallowed and crossed her arms.

She was right. The man hadn't really assaulted Stasia. I would have never let it get that far. But even the threat of it. The discomfort on her face. I needed to take her home. I needed to know she was all right.

"I'm taking her home," I said again, leaving no room for argument.

"It's like that," she said softly, raising her eyebrows. "Whatever." She turned sharply and walked back to the bar. I ran my hand through my hair in frustration. I just seemed to keep hurting people. I felt a tug on the arm going through my hair. Stasia looked up at me expectantly.

I took her hand again, leading her first to my office to get my helmet, and then back out. I called goodbye to Nadine, but she didn't bother looking up. Pat sat sullenly at the table they had all been at. Angela talked to him quietly as we left.

As we stepped outside, I pulled Stasia, her hand still nestled in mine, alongside my bike. I hadn't thought to ask if she was comfortable riding on the back. I stood in front of her and carefully put the full-face helmet over her head, visor up, and clasped the strap.

"Are you ready?" I asked. My throat was thick. This was the first time we'd been this close since that day. The first time I'd touched her. I'd had so much preoccupying me I hadn't let the sensation of it all in.

She just nodded her head. I gently closed the visor, shielding her big green eyes from sight, and sat on the bike. I steadied it for her as she climbed on. She gripped my sides, and I reached back to bring them around me more securely. She didn't resist. Just rested her head against me, laying the front of her body fully against the back of mine, hugging me around the middle. With a deep breath in, I backed us up and took us down the road.

*\*\*\**

I pulled into Stasia's driveway and set the kickstand with my foot. Stasia sat up, putting some distance between our bodies, but neither of us moved more than that for a second. After a while, the silence stretched, and I felt the pull of the bike as Stasia lifted herself off the back. She unclipped the helmet and handed it to me. We still hadn't said anything.

I set it on the handlebars. Still sitting in my seat, I looked up to her, and with my heart in my throat, asked, "Can we talk?"

"Yeah." Her voice was scratchy.

She moved back, and I followed her to her front door. Flynn was scratching at the door. She opened it, and he greeted us both enthusiastically. He grabbed my wrist, growling, and tried to lead me out to the front yard with him. I couldn't help letting a laugh escape, loosening some of the tightness that had settled in my chest.

Stasia laughed behind me too. "Soft," she called. Flynn let me go and pranced into the front yard. He ran for a while before stopping to sniff around the grass. I turned back to Stasia. She leaned against the front door jam, staring at me. I couldn't decipher the look on her face. Open, maybe hopeful? But weary at the same time. The tightness curled back as I walked toward her.

I stopped a few feet short, leaning against the wall of the house. "Hey," I said lamely, not sure how to start.

She smiled and waited. She wasn't going to help me out here. I decided to start with the obvious. "Are you okay?"

Her smile went crooked. "Yeah. I appreciate your help, but it wasn't that big of a deal Jack. He was just being a jerk."

My hand curled into a fist as I remembered her trying to create space from the man, her face a mask of discomfort.

"Nobody should touch you, especially when you tell them no."

"Obviously, Jack, but I had it under control." A V-shape creased her forehead as her eyebrows drew in. "Are you okay? The chair…"

She let the sentence hang in the air, but I knew what she was talking about. "I was losing my temper. He almost knocked you over. You could have been hurt. And then what he said." I stopped, abandoning my relaxed pose and leaning my back against the wall, crossing my arms.

Stasia drew close. "Thank you. But they were just words, Jack, hardly the worst I've heard."

That pissed me off more, but I didn't say anything, just tried to collect my careening thoughts. It was dusk. The shadows grew longer, and the porch light over our heads snapped on.

"How have you been?" I asked. I didn't know why I was prolonging this. I just didn't want to leave her. Stasia didn't come closer, but she didn't retreat either. She stood within arm's reach. She tucked her hands into her pockets and rocked back on her heels.

"Good. I've been…" She hesitated, looking at me uncertainly. Whatever decision she came to, she forged on. "I've been getting to know the Stepuli at the school. I'm even going on one of the training missions as a medic."

My entire body tensed. I didn't know how that made me feel. On the one hand, it was surreal. Talking about my people with someone. On the other hand, I still felt betrayed. The knowledge she was an outsider was something I couldn't shake. She didn't realize she was going to be a glorified handler. I thought about that calm feeling back at the bar. How sure I had been there was something more to it than how I felt about Stasia. But standing here now in the quiet, twilight creeping in, I felt as foolish as the day I had told her I thought she was Stepuli.

I ran my hand through my hair. "I'm not sure why I came over. I just. Goodnight Stasia." I turned to go, but she called out, stopping me.

"Wait!" In her haste, she stumbled toward me. Flynn looked up at her call.

I turned back to her expectantly. "Why do you hate me, Jack? I didn't know. I swear to God I didn't know anything about it. They told me in orientation the day before, and then when I dropped Lilly off and saw her hands spark, I wasn't even sure what I was seeing. I just knew I should get her out of there. I never told anyone. I would never tell anyone about your family. I'm just trying to help. This job, it started as something different I could do, something to break up the monotony, a change. I knew nothing about it going in. But now, I care about those students."

There were tears in her voice by the end of her speech, and I couldn't help walking back to her. My hand stroked through her hair to the back of her head. So soft. Her eyes turned up to me, so big and green, water blurring their color. The tightness in my chest didn't leave, but warmth surrounded it, pulsed with it. I reached down and brushed my lips softly across hers. I tasted salt, beer, and Stasia. I had only meant it to be a bittersweet goodbye, but she stepped forward flush against me, her hands going to my back. And I couldn't help but take it there.

My hand tightened in her hair. My lips stopped their gentle perusal, the kiss turning hungry, and I dipped my tongue into her mouth. She met me stroke for stroke, and I pushed her against the wall of the house. My hands reached up her shirt, over the soft skin of her belly, both our breaths coming in short pants when I heard Lilly call my name.

"Jack?"

She must have said it a couple times because her voice was getting closer. Finally, I broke from Stasia, who slumped against the wall, her head resting against it, her eyes closed, panting. "Be there in a minute!" I called, frustration lacing my words.

Stasia opened her eyes, and when she looked at me, my resolve almost crumbled. I almost said fuck it and followed her inside. I brought my hand up, my thumb smoothing over her cheek. She leaned into the touch, and my gut clenched.

"I can't." I wasn't sure if I was talking to her or me.

"Why not?" She was breathless. The sound went straight to my groin.

"I can't get any further in with the SEP. They hunt us, find any reason they can to break the treaty. They'll take Lilly away and put her in a lab if they find out what she can do."

Stasia nodded, her face going grim. "I would never tell." Her eyes shined with sadness. She knew my next words before I said them.

"I still can't. Be careful on that mission Stasia." I dropped my hand, turning away from her. It took every bit of my strength. She didn't call out to me this time. As I rounded the corner I saw Lilly in the space between our yards, petting Flynn. I heard Stasia call him behind me. He ran straight past me. I didn't look back.

"Go inside, I'll be there in a minute," I said to Lilly as I climbed onto my bike to move it into our driveway. She nodded, looking at me with questions in her eyes. Questions I couldn't answer even for myself.

# CHAPTER 22

## Stasia

A tight band wrapped around my temples, a dull pounding at the back of my head. I hadn't slept well. I kept replaying Jack's kiss over and over in my head. Sometimes his hand would finish its slow trail up my ribcage to my breast. Sometimes he'd abandon the smooth caress, pick me up, and take me right inside. Sometimes he'd leave me even more abruptly than he had. Lilly had horrible timing.

"Stasia!" somebody called.

Rubbing my fingers into my right temple, I looked up as Dr. Kimi came toward me. She hadn't been around during my shifts since that first day. I tried to perk up and plastered a welcoming smile on my face. She looked me over. I was dressed in the Nomex pants and shirt I'd been issued, my bag over my shoulder.

She jerked her thumb over her shoulder at a wall of the hangar where other bags lined the wall. On the other side, people milled around a coffee station. "You'll drop your bag there and meet up with everyone. We're leaving in thirty. I wanted to talk to you first about your role on this training mission."

I nodded, willing my headache to recede as I focused on Dr. Kimi's words. She had always seemed so hard to reach. Austere and serious, the only times I saw humanity poking through were when she talked about her job.

"This is these kids' first training mission. They may range in age from eighteen to twenty-two, but they have no experience out in the real world. All their instruction has been in simulation or a gym. I fully expect them at times to become overfatigued and overwhelmed. It is your job to make sure when, not if, that happens they take a break."

"Of course, Dr. Kimi. I'll take good care of them."

She frowned and pressed. "The trainers may fight you on this. It's their job to push the kids to get them ready. The naval hotshot team is a point of pride for both the Navy and this program. Our team has an impeccable record for both speed and safety. Nobody knows that's because we have an upper hand. This program is one of the shining examples of the Stepuli's potential benefit to the US."

I nodded again. "If I see someone getting into trouble, I'm going to step in and make their medical care a priority. They're in good hands, Dr. Kimi," I repeated, trying to reassure her.

She didn't look impressed but nodded sharply. I turned to walk away, but her hand on my arm stopped me. "One last warning. Pete, the fire elemental coming with you. I know you haven't dealt with the fires yet. He's a nice kid, but he…can be troubled. Just look out for him. We're really hoping integrating fire Stepuli onto the teams works out. It would help mitigate a lot of danger to our hotshots." Her warning unsettled me, her words coming from a different place but echoing Pat's. I nodded again and moved to drop my bag.

\*\*\*

We landed after a short plane ride from our Washington State base to the small Northern California airstrip. It was a private airstrip placed on military land but not often used for transports. The SEP tried to keep visibility of the young recruits they used to a minimum. While the veteran Stepuli hotshot teams utilized for the last couple years were closer to the average age of a typical woodland firefighter, the younger students in training would raise eyebrows.

We unloaded and began unpacking the bags from the back of the plane. Brandon, Lola, and Lucy, I knew. The fire elemental attached to Shaw, the trainer selected to monitor this training mission, was eerily quiet but always watching. Sometimes I would look back and see his lips moving as he muttered under his breath. There was one other, an earth elemental named Greg, the incident commander for this training exercise and part of the type one hotshot crews.

You wouldn't know it from how Shaw was acting, but Greg was supposed to be the leader of this exercise. As all the bags were laid out on the flight line, Shaw came to the front and spoke to the group. Greg stood next to him, frowning but not overruling Shaw.

"We're going to be heading out. There's a brush truck waiting. Everyone carries their own pack. We're going to be making a fire line on the north side of this ridge. It's one of the safest areas. The wind is currently pushing the fire south."

Greg squared himself next to Shaw and spoke during the short pause. "Now, don't let that lull you into a false sense of security. We've been practicing the different techniques we utilize to fight these fires without the safety equipment the hotshots have used for years. Because of our abilities, we're more effective and our teams are safer overall. We've sustained only minimal injuries and have had no fatalities since integrating with the human teams."

Shaw shot Greg a dark look and said, "Right. So, work hard. With the right mindset, you'll be on the level one team within the year."

This time Greg blatantly interrupted him. "The reason we've had no fatalities is not because we're invulnerable. It is because we use our abilities to take our own precautions. Though we have power over the elements, these fires are stronger than any one or even five Stepuli. Follow your training, keep your heads up, and check in with yourselves. This is training. We are assessing what you've learned."

Shaw spoke over Greg again. It felt like a volleying match. "It is important to the SEP environmental initiative that we continue the high level of skill and service to this team. We would like to get you out of your community and into real-world environments, but you have to prove yourself here first."

His incentives left a bad taste in my mouth. As beautiful as the Stepuli community was, a small town of state-of-the-art entertainment centers and beautiful buildings, I couldn't imagine only staying within that tiny square footage my entire life. I imagined many of the younger Stepuli felt the same way. They'd probably do anything to get out. Even push themselves into dangerous jobs just to see something different.

Greg spoke again. "A more experienced team is coming in to relieve us tonight. This is a one-day training session to help you understand what real-world conditions are like, and for us to gauge where your training lacks."

We all began hefting our bags behind us when Shaw spoke over everyone one last time. "Your bracelets' GPS trackers are still on. While you won't alarm unless you try to remove them, we can still locate you anywhere." His mouth twisted into a smile, but I felt a black sort of wickedness from him. "You know…for your safety." At that, he turned around and headed to the hangar where the bush truck was waiting.

We walked in a loose group behind him. Greg and Shaw wore what looked like black smart watches. I moved closer to Brandon so I could ask without raising my voice, "What was he saying about GPS bracelets?"

Brandon looked over at me. I'd learned at the coffee station he was not a morning person. Almost worse than Pat, he'd looked like he was sleeping standing up and only marginally improved after an hour nap on the plane. "You haven't noticed all of the Stepuli at the school wear them?"

I shrugged. I guess I had, but a lot of things were standard issue in the military, and a lot of how the Stepuli were handled modeled the way the military supplied gear or housing to its servicemen.

Our conversation seemed to perk Brandon up a bit. His brow wrinkled. He looked ahead at Shaw, who was already to the doors of the hangar. We had dropped behind. "Every Stepuli has a bracelet. It's like what humans use when they're on house arrest. It's how the government contains us to the community."

"You don't have one."

Brandon gave me a droll look. We got closer to everyone, and he spoke faster, keeping his tone low. "We don't wear one since we're released to live in the real world. Instead, we have a type of probation officer who checks in on us weekly."

I hadn't noticed someone coming to their house weekly since I moved in, but then I did work a lot. "Who's your probation officer?"

Brandon looked ahead, muttering one word before he moved away from me. "Shaw."

***

The drive up to where we were supposed to hike out was bumpy. Lucy, Greg, and Brandon sat on the bench seat, and Lola and I sat in a jump seat in back. Shaw drove with the fire elemental Pete never far from his side.

I noted the bracelet on Lola's her right hand. I wondered why I had never questioned it before, having spent weeks with the Stepuli. Lola caught me looking. She gripped her wrist loosely and let it drop. "Wish we could personalize it. Purple would be much better than black."

"Purple would definitely suit you better."

Lola looked to the right, the rough terrain oddly beautiful. Since we landed, the air had been thick with smoke, like the whole world was next to a campfire. "So, is being part of this fire team exciting? Is this what you asked to do?" I said, trying to make small talk.

Lucy quirked his head slightly toward us, but he didn't turn or say anything. He seemed very protective of his sister. Lola looked back at me. "We don't get a choice. They assign us based on our skill and where they think we'll be useful." Her voice was musical with a lilting quality. I'd felt sadness from her when we'd first met in the gym.

My brow furrowed, and I felt a thread of concern and indignation for her. "What if you don't want to do anything?"

She shrugged her shoulders. "That isn't one of our options."

The vehicle skidded to a stop, cutting off any more conversation. Shaw got out, the boys in front of us exiting and pulling the seats forward so we could get out more easily. Pete walked around obediently to Shaw. His continued silence began to unnerve me. I tried to get a reading on how he was feeling, but his body language lacked any expression. He felt like a black hole.

Shaw gathered us up and opened his mouth to speak, but Greg beat him to it. I wondered at Shaw's continued attempts to take over this mission.

"Okay guys. We're going to hike out to where we'll dig the fire line. I wanted you to get a sense of the physical strain, but we're only going three miles in. Our packs are considerably lighter than a typical hotshot's. But where they're burning four to six thousand calories, we're burning the same or more. Our elements take it out of us as well as the physical strain. So, use what was on your packing list and stay hydrated and fed." He looked to Shaw, giving him the lead.

Shaw seemed agitated. "Let's go." He hefted his pack, an axe hanging off the side in easy reach, and moved out to the head of the group. Pete followed, then Greg. I fell into line with the rest of the group behind me. I asked Greg, "Why does Shaw's pack seem heavier?"

Greg looked back at me. He was tall and burly with a

thick beard covering half of his ruddy face. "He packs out like a typical hotshot would. He likes the security."

I suddenly felt self-conscious, like maybe I was underprepared. I hiked up the shoulder of my pack. Greg noticed, because he said, "You're our medic. We got you. We have you pack out like us." After that, he turned forward, and we all concentrated on our steps, one in front of the other.

As I fought the difficult terrain, rocky with thick brush on a steep incline, I wondered at the fact that Shaw felt the need to carry extra precautions with him on this exercise. That he didn't trust the Stepuli would have his back. After a short while, the sound of faster breathing made me drop to the back of the line. I wanted to keep everyone in view so I could watch for strain. Lola stumbled a couple times, and I opened my mouth to call for a break, but she looked back after she caught herself and shook her head.

I waited about ten minutes so she wouldn't think it was her fault, but then called firmly for a stop. I had learned my lesson from Elle and didn't intend to repeat past mistakes.

Shaw grumbled about it, but when he dropped his pack, the entire back of his shirt was drenched in sweat. Greg was the only one who didn't look like he was under severe strain. I walked around taking everyone's pulse and making sure they drank water.

When I passed in front of Lucy, he nodded to me, a thanks in the soft look of his eyes. Though that day Galton had called me into his office, Shaw had adopted an overly familiar attitude with me, today he made no attempts to talk. The more comfortable I became with the Stepuli, the more he seemed surly and put off. I wasn't upset by that. The oily feeling from when I first met him had only worsened as I watched him interact with the students. The way he acted friendly and personable with me, only to turn around and bark a rough command at a Stepuli student or become instantly agitated rubbed me the wrong way.

After checking on everyone, I found myself sitting next to Brandon. He didn't indicate he minded, so I dropped my own pack and started drinking water thirstily. While I liked hiking, and sometimes would take a jog, this was more physical activity than I did on any kind of regular basis.

It didn't help that the thick underbrush constantly tried to catch my ankles. My sturdy boots protected my skin, but the pull of the sticks and crags made my calves burn. I couldn't imagine what traditional hotshots felt. Even my twenty-five-pound pack caused a deep ache between my shoulder blades.

Brandon's voice surprised me. "How are you doing?"

I sat slightly below him on a hill and looked up. "Good."

He watched me doubtfully. "You're breathing like you just finished the iron man Stasia."

I laughed. "You know how to make a girl feel good about herself."

His mouth quirked, and he took another long pull of his water. When he was done, his laugh turned into a cough. Clearing his throat, he said, "My specialty. Seriously though. How have you...been?"

Though he sounded unsure, the genuine question warmed me. I glanced at Shaw. I didn't want to give away how familiar Brandon's and my relationship was, but I appreciated that he was extending an olive branch. "Good. Preparing for this has kept me busy."

He nodded, having seen the direction I looked before answering. He lowered his voice. "I think we were wrong about you. And I just wanted to say I'm sorry for giving you such a hard time when you first started with the school. You've really proven yourself over these last weeks. At least to me."

I understood his unspoken sentiment. Jack had said "I can't." He may not trust me or be willing to forgive even my accidental involvement with the SEP, but Brandon was saying he could. While my feelings for Jack went deeper, I had fallen in love with his entire family. With their dynamic, their fierce loyalty and love for one another. And knowing even one of them didn't hate me helped ease some of the ache in my heart.

"Thanks Brandon, that means a lot."

"I know what it's like having Jack's disappointment. Even when it's deserved it sits like a stone around your neck. I just want you to know it's not entirely you. There's stuff. There's…" He struggled with whatever he was trying to say. He looked toward Shaw once more, but Shaw was oblivious to our conversation as he ate his protein bar and side-eyed Pete. "Jack has a lot on his shoulders. Sometimes he makes rash judgments thinking he's got to protect everyone. It takes him a while to get out of his own way."

I could see that. While Jack's solidness made him feel like a rock to lean on, sometimes his stubbornness felt more like a boulder blocking your path. "He's lucky he has such a wise younger brother then."

Brandon snorted. Shaw looked over at us. We quieted and took bites of our protein bars. Pete got up, snagging

Shaw's attention, and Brandon continued. "Yeah, right. More like a little brother who avoids everything, making the weight on his shoulders too heavy for anyone to bear."

I frowned. "What do you mean?"

Brandon kept his eyes on the dirt. He uncapped his water bottle, letting a ribbon of water come out and trace between his fingers. "After I got disc—" Brandon stopped, coughing. When he continued, he measured his words. "After I began expressing abilities a year or so ago, I was so angry. I realized my life was going to be different from what I'd fought so hard for. I just, I wanted it to all go away. And I really made Jack's life hard."

Sympathy welled inside me. "Brandon, you were under an impossible set of circumstances. Anyone would have reacted the same way."

Brandon looked up at me. His eyes were red, but no tears fell. "I'm just trying to make up for it. He's put a lot of trust in me. I used to be angry at his rules, his constant badgering. But as Lilly gets older, I don't know. I think I understand what he was going through better."

I was beginning to understand Jack's angry words from that day. His fears of Lilly being trapped in a lab. His resentment toward the SEP. "Jack's strong, and he's amazing." Brandon hung his head again, and I felt a smile pull as I continued. "But so are you. You have had so much happen to you Brandon, and you've recognized how to handle it so much younger than many would. Give yourself some credit. Jack's trust in you isn't misplaced."

He looked back up at me and opened his mouth to say something, but Shaw's bark of command cut him off. "All right, it's time to head out. We need to make it back to the flight line by dusk. Let's go."

Everyone's color and respirations looked back to normal. We all wordlessly packed our bags back up and shouldered them. We fell back into line, continuing to where we'd make the fire line.

# CHAPTER 23

## Stasia

W hen we reached where the fire line was to be dug, Greg led everyone through their tasks. The air twins would be helping to clear the air quality around us so we didn't sustain smoke inhalation while working. They'd also be monitoring the wind's direction to ensure the fire wasn't changing directions and heading toward us. Brandon's job was mostly for safety. If the fire suddenly switched directions, and the twins didn't catch it in time, or weren't able to shift it, he'd use his powers and the store of water we'd been carrying to wet the ground around us and create a barrier.

Greg's job was the hardest. He was the one creating the fire line. Instead of using axes and chainsaws, Greg would use his powers to create a trench. Since using your element taxed a person physically, Greg was only able to do this in shifts and then would need a break. It was everyone's job to monitor conditions during those breaks.

Pete's job was, once the fire line had been finished, to create a backfire. In the past, Stepuli hotshots had done this the traditional way. But if a fire Stepuli could be included on the team, they could help control the direction and extent of the backfire, eliminating a lot of the risk involved.

\*\*\*

Shaw sat back and occasionally barked commands. Mostly, he griped at Lola and Lucy that the air still smelled too much like smoke. He had a small oxygen tank in his pack but insisted the air twins do a better job of filtering the air quality. Sweat beaded at both twin's temples, tracking down the dirt on their faces, but their vitals were still good.

The shrill sound of a phone alarm clock broke through the air, and Greg shifted. He opened his eyes slowly. At this point, I was mostly worried about him. He had two-thirds of the fire line finished and had needed an hour break after his last section. I'd hooked him up to some IV fluids before he fell asleep. He'd gone through two bags of saline, and his heart rate was better, but I still worried about rhabdomyolysis.

He grunted as he stood. "Let's get this over with."

I walked alongside him as he went to the fire line. "You sure you're okay for this?"

He looked down at me. "Yeah. I'm just used to working with multiple earths on a line. We don't have any earth Stepuli old enough to begin training in this class." He looked over at Lola and Lucy. Brandon hadn't really had anything to do yet and looked the most rested. "Few of us are able to do a fire line alone. This is really just a short test to get these kids in the right mindset for the rest of their training."

"Well, I'm here if you need anything."

I started to walk away, but his words stopped me.

"You've been great. Thanks for making us stop earlier, and the fluids. Shaw normally makes these initial training missions practically impossible for me."

I didn't need to feel his gratitude. I could see it shining plainly in his eyes. I smiled and nodded before walking the rest of the way back down to the group. I felt more unsettled than ever. Before this, I had seen small signs of strain, but nothing that was unusual for a group of people working out. Whether it was working out their elements or working out physically, for the Stepuli it was essentially the same. This was the first time I really understood Jack and his family's attitude about the restrictions and treatment they received from the SEP and the government.

As I took a pull from my water bottle, someone knocked me with their shoulder. Lucy smiled at me. For once, I didn't feel suspicion from him or see calculation in his gaze. His expression was open, and his smile playful. "How you doing, Doc?"

I rolled my eyes. "Not a doc."

He laughed. Lola stood next to him looking a little peaked. "Hey Lola, why don't you take a break?"

Not only was she sweaty, but her respirations were up a little. She was also looking a little pale. "In fact, I insist," I said, guiding her to sit and feeling her pulse.

Shaw walked up behind me. I felt his resentful energy. "No, she needs to know what it's like to run one of these missions."

I looked up at his towering, sweaty frame. A sour odor came off him. Pete stood a little back and to the left, still silent, still staring intensely. I turned my attention back to Shaw. "This is a training mission, and she's dangerously fatigued. I'm taking her out."

His mouth twisted. He crouched down next to me and Lola, getting into my face. "Listen little Stepuli lover, I'm the boss here. I say she needs to continue."

Lola had shifted, starting to stand. "It's ok, I'm fine."

I stopped her with a hand on her knee. I stood and faced off with Shaw. "You may be the boss of training, but I'm the boss of medical. She's out."

He reached out as if he was going to grab me. I tensed, waiting for it, but his hand didn't make it up from a half raise. "What the—" he started angrily. Brandon and Lucy walked up, taking up position slightly behind me on each side. Lucy held Shaw's arm down with air.

"Hey Boss, everything okay over here?" Lucy's voice was casual, but the tension thickened around all of us.

"Let me go right now you little—"

"I wasn't talking to you." At those words, I looked at Lucy to my left. He stared back at me steadily. "Watcha want to do Boss?"

I smiled at him. "Shaw was just confused. It's all good." Shaw had stopped struggling with his arm. His eyes shifted between Brandon and Lucy. Lola stood and joined us. I felt fear through his resentment.

Greg's voice broke the tension. "It's time for Pete."

He was standing at the top of the hill, hands on his hip, frowning at all of us. Shaw jerkily moved back toward the silent fire Stepuli. "Whatever," Shaw muttered as he gestured angrily for the boy to stand. Pete looked at me steadily before following behind Shaw.

I took a deep breath. The confrontation with Shaw put me on edge. I had started to feel a little afraid but determined to shield Lola from him when Lucy and Brandon had stepped up next to me. It gave me a sense of security knowing they had my back. We all walked up to get a better look at what Pete was doing. The other's, I imagined, because they were curious. Me, because I had made Dr. Kimi a promise.

Pete's blank look was replaced by one of deep happiness as Shaw flicked a lighter beside him. He used hand motions to take the little flame and toss it to the ground on the other side of the fire line. His happiness turned into giddiness, and he made larger motions with his arms. The fire spread unnaturally fast along the trench. The sound of it was like it was a live thing. Pete began giggling hysterically. He said something low. Shaw nervously inched away from him. Shaw's hand went to his belt, to what looked like a taser. I raised my eyebrows and tried to interject myself between them.

As I got closer, I made out what Pete was saying. "Burn, burn, burn, burn." The darkness that had felt like an empty hole earlier undulated with crazed energy. Pete bounced on the balls of his feet, and his wide hand motions stopped. Instead, he clapped his hands, muttering, "Burn, burn, burn."

This was not normal. I looked over at Greg, whose face was a mask of alarm. "Hey, uh, Pete. It's...this is enough. This is plenty of fire. If you could, uh, dial it back man. This is just a small backfire to get rid of the brush."

Pete's movements became angrier at the suggestion he dim the fire. He looked over at Greg. "I like to watch it burn."

At those ominous words, I realized something was very wrong. I retreated to my medical bag and pulled out a sedative. I capped the shot and put it in my back pocket where I could easily reach it. Brandon had uncapped his water bottle and had water rotating steadily around one hand. Before I headed back up the hill, I uncapped a couple of our larger water containers for him. He saw what I was doing and pulled the water to him.

Lucy inched Lola away from everyone and pushed her down the hill. I passed them going back up as they retreated. Greg was trying to reason with Pete. "I understand man. I get it. It's just, we're here for a reason, remember? If you're going to continue coming out and playing with the fire, if you're going to get to keep watching it burn, you've got to keep it under control man."

Pete turned his head to Greg. On his other side, Shaw took what was definitely a taser out of its holster. I jerked my head no at him. He looked at me incredulously, but I kept inching up the hill closer to Pete.

"They're telling me to burn it all," he whispered.

Greg blanched, but I understood what was going on. "Who's telling you? Pete, nobody is telling you to burn it all. I'm telling you, you've got to back off man."

Pete turned away from Greg toward the flames. I couldn't see his expression anymore, but Brandon had positioned himself on the other side of Pete. Greg looked back at me as I approached. I motioned a bear hug. His eyes were wide, but he nodded his understanding and got ready to help restrain Pete. As I reached for the shot in my back pocket, Pete snapped around and stared straight into my eyes. "You're going to make the fire go away."

He motioned, and fire shot over his shoulder toward me. Brandon doused it with his water as Greg grabbed Pete, trapping his arms to his sides. I uncapped the shot and stuck it in his shoulder through his shirt, pushing the plunger.

"It's going to take about ten minutes," I said.

Pete's hands were stuck to his sides. He kept trying to use his fingers to bring forth tendrils of fire, but without seeing the inferno he'd created, and without being able to make the hand motions the Stepuli were taught to guide their elements, he barely brought forth sparks.

"Crazy ass Stepuli. I told Galton these fire kids weren't right in the head!" Shaw cursed and kicked the dirt. So not helpful.

Finally, the meds kicked in. When Pete realized he wasn't going to burn everything down, he had settled into staring at me intently like he had earlier in the day. His eyes drooped. He tried to fight it. His head would fall then jerk back up. Right before his eyes closed for good, and he succumbed to the medicine, he said to me, "They're mad you stopped the fire." His head lolled to his chest.

"He's out." Brandon sounded relieved.

"Jesus," Greg said, shifting Pete's body and lifting it over his shoulder in a fireman's carry. He turned to look back at the fire Pete had started then at Brandon. "Can you douse that at all?"

"Do you need it out, or just less of it?"

"Just dump enough on it so it's smoldering. It'll pick back up and do what it was supposed to do with the wind from the embers, but right now, it's going to cause a whole other section we'll need to fight against." Brandon set to work. I sectioned off some water for the trip back, but we were all going to be exhausted by the time we made it back to the flight line.

As Brandon came back down to the bottom of the hill, I checked him out to make sure he didn't need a break before we headed down. He didn't even look winded. I didn't make a thing of it, realizing it probably meant what I had suspected back at the Stepul School, that he wasn't using even half his power in lessons. Greg organized us all, keeping Pete hefted over his shoulder, and we started back down the trail toward the bush truck.

I looked around for Shaw, not used to his silence. He'd been a bully inserting himself most of the day. When I spotted him, he wasn't falling into line. He was staring at Brandon suspiciously. Brandon wasn't paying attention. He fell into line behind the air twins. As I moved to do the same, assuming Shaw would bring up the rear, Shaw's face shifted to mine. He smiled, but nothing about it was friendly.

# CHAPTER 24

## Jack

I waited in the parking lot at the small FBO. This was Brandon's first mission, and even if it had been a training exercise, I was anxious to find out how it had gone. Especially considering they had taken a fire for the first time. Greg was a good guy. We had worked together back when I was active in the community and part of the environmental initiative. Still, I worried.

It wasn't long before I saw the plane's lights on the horizon, and the small gulf stream came in for a landing. I walked up to the locked gate as the plane taxied to the office. The plane door popped, and the ladder dropped. Shaw was the first one off the plane. I leaned against the chain link as I waited for everyone else to deplane.

I straightened, fear lacing through me as Shaw turned back to help grab the edge of a stretcher. Greg came out in an awkward crouch on the other end. Blankets covered the form. From this distance, and with Shaw blocking me, I couldn't make out who lay there. I tried the door of the fence, knowing it would be locked, but fear was making me stupid. Brandon came out next, but my anxiety only skyrocketed. Stasia was on this mission.

I shook the handle more forcefully, getting ready to break the fence with earth when Lucy noticed my struggle. With a wave of his hand, the gate opened abruptly, and I wasted no time pushing through. I jogged toward the plane. Brandon noticed me and my panic-stricken face. Before he could get the words out, Stasia's form followed Lola at the plane door, and I abruptly stopped my advance.

Leaning with my hands on my knees, I took a deep, cleansing breath. *Thank God.* I straightened, close enough now that I could hear everyone's voices. As I moved toward the plane, Stasia looked at me curiously. We had left things so abrupt yesterday. Part of me wanted to reach for her. Instead, I turned toward Greg, who stood next to the stretcher with Shaw.

On the stretcher lay a young kid I barely recognized. He had been one of the younger fires at the Stepul School when I was active there. His features had slightly changed with age, his face peaceful in sleep. His chest rose and fell steadily.

"Hey man, long time no see."

I shook Greg's hand, nodding to him. Shaw didn't bother talking to me. Aggravation stiffened the lines of his arms and hard set of his jaw. Greg noticed and put a hand on my shoulder to guide me away from him toward my brother. Stasia passed us and gave me a small smile on her way to the patient.

"Yeah, how've you been?"

"Good, good. I took over taking the new recruits out to start breaking them in. Could have used you today man. I never realized how taxing doing those fire lines alone was."

I laughed. Part of the reason I used to take the new recruits out was because I was the only one who could dig a full fire line alone without nearly passing out. During years we didn't have an earth with us to help, it was useful. "It's not so bad."

He pursed his lips at me, and I laughed. "Okay, yeah, it sucks. How'd my brother do?" I asked as we drew up next to Brandon. Greg answered me, giving Brandon praise. My eyes kept drifting back to Stasia.

"—especially when Pete went nuts."

My eyes snapped back. I had been tuning out whatever Greg was saying. "What?" I looked over at Brandon. He knew what had distracted me.

He swallowed. "Yeah, that was crazy. Might be a little premature to be bringing fires out."

Greg ran a hand over his sweaty head. "Yeah, Pete's not all there. The young one, Milo, seems to have potential, but it's going to be years before we can find out if he'll function. His moods seem more stable anyway."

The rotating blue and red lights of an ambulance pulled up to the gate. Shaw headed toward it to open it up. "Gotta go." Greg slapped me on my shoulder again. "Nice seeing you man."

"You too!" I called after him but turned back to Brandon. The air twins had already headed to the smaller gate I'd come through. An idling car waited in the parking lot for them. I stepped closer to Brandon. "What happened?"

"I'll tell you in the car. Let's go." I nodded, not wanting to leave Stasia, but as the ambulance pulled up, she helped lift the stretcher onto a gurney. After loading the fire elemental onto the ambulance, she climbed into the back behind him. Right before she shut the back door, she looked over at me. She waved, and then closed herself in.

Shaw looked over at us but didn't say anything. He walked back over to the plane to talk to the pilots. I followed Brandon's lead and headed back to the Tahoe. "So?" I prompted as we walked through the gate.

Brandon sighed. "Obviously, it didn't go so well with the fire." He paused as we got into the vehicle. I pulled out and set out for home.

"Pete was a little off his rocker from the beginning. He didn't talk to anyone, and Shaw stuck to him like glue. When it came time to set the fire, everything seemed fine at first. But then he started talking to himself. The fire got out of control, and he wouldn't rein it in. Said the voices told him to burn it all. It was creepy."

My gut clenched thinking about Lilly. Not all fires ended up like that though. She was nothing like that. She had some depression after letting out too much fire, but she'd never heard voices. I swallowed. She'd never told me she heard voices.

"How did you stop him?"

"Stasia noticed what was happening, I think. Before he got too bad, she had already drawn up some medicine. She was great. Right before he got completely out of control, she had everything ready. Greg grabbed him so he couldn't move his hands to call the fire, and she gave him a shot of sedative."

The fear I had felt earlier wormed into my chest, making it heavy. "She was okay?"

Brandon looked over at me. "Yeah, I wouldn't have let anything happen to her."

I swallowed. Though I kept saying we couldn't let

Stasia back into our lives, Brandon saw right through me. "Good. That's good." My voice was rough. I coughed to clear my throat and turned onto our street. We hadn't been too far from the military-controlled air strip. "Thanks B."

We were silent for the rest of the ride. As I pulled into the driveway and put the car in park, Brandon broke the silence. "Stasia's kind of amazing, Jack. She was good with that fire elemental. Trust me, there's no love lost between her and Shaw. He tried overworking Lola, and Stasia got right in his face." My fist tightened at that, not liking the idea of Shaw anywhere near Stasia. "She's great with the younger and older students at the Stepul School. I don't think you should be trying so hard to stay away from her. It's obvious you want her. I think she wants you too."

I swallowed again. My fingers drummed against my leg. He was right. I did want her. And the more I learned since that horrible day in my kitchen, the more I believed that Stasia hadn't been some spy. But then why did Galton let her move next to us? There was no way that happened without his knowledge. And what was the calmness I felt around her if she wasn't Stepuli?

"I don't know, B. I want you to be right, but we've got Lilly to think about. I just don't know."

"I'll be here for you, Jack, either way."

I clapped him on the shoulder. "Thanks, B." With thoughts of Stasia swirling in my head, I walked up to the house with Brandon. I knew the prospect of getting a few more hours of sleep was unlikely.

# CHAPTER 25
## Stasia

I opened the school door wondering if Pat would be on today. Things had been tense since dinner the other night. I was avoiding him, and part of me felt horrible for that. I didn't want to ruin our friendship. After the fiasco with Pete, I understood some of his misgivings about fire Stepuli. I just hated how negatively he talked about them, how okay he was with letting kids grow up in a lab.

The greeter's desk, only there for orientation days, had been cleared away. I was just about to step into the locker room when the clack of Dr. Kimi's low-heeled shoes caught my attention.

"Stasia, you're assigned to the fire Stepuli today. You were wonderful on the training mission the other day and getting Pete safely neutralized before the incident became worse. I wanted to see how you work with them in a more controlled environment. I need to get you settled there before I go back to headquarters."

Headquarters? I wondered if she meant the basement gymnasium, the place Pat and I had gone for our first day with the deprivation pods.

"Okay," I started, but she was already walking away. I hurried to catch up, figuring I could do without my stethoscope for the day.

"The fire elementals are different from the others you've encountered," Dr. Kimi said as soon as I fell into step with her. "As you saw the other day, they can be a little more volatile, especially the older kids. We're going to start you off with the youngest, Milo. He's a good ambassador for the fires. Because of his age, we haven't tested him extensively, but his powers seem mild, and his tempers are the most even."

I nodded as we walked at a clipped pace. She stopped outside a pair of locked double doors requiring key-card access. She swiped her ID, and they opened. She walked to just inside the doors. The room looked almost like an ICU with a central station setup with computers for monitoring. Across from the station in each hall was a row of rooms with glass doors. At the end of each hall was a solid concrete wall with thick concrete doors.

"Right," Dr. Kimi began, lowering her voice. I stepped closer to hear her better. "As you saw, the fire Stepuli are a little different from the others. We're not exactly sure why, though we've come up with a few theories. We think their hybridization missed an important genome when the Stepuli-human child was born. That, or the extra power required to create an inferno causes a larger noradrenaline spike than other Stepuli use when they access their elements. There's also the possibility that they don't have as much occasion to use their powers, and so possibly don't get appropriate exposure as children, which causes shock the first time they use a large amount of their power."

"What should I be looking out for with Milo?"

"Fire Stepuli, after they use their powers, are more volatile. They can become excited or violent. They can let their fire get out of control. Afterward, they can become very depressed. After each session, every child is kept on camera and put on suicide watch. The fifth generation Stepuli, or Milo, are more stable than the fourth generation. We've also adapted our techniques with Milo, and due to his age, he doesn't use as much power. It's too soon to tell if this is the reason for our success, or if he just doesn't have the flaw the fourth generation had. For now, just treat him like you have all the other students and look for overfatigue. If he does have any odd mood changes, of course report that immediately."

I nodded, though I was stuck on something. "They're on camera after they use their powers? For how long?"

Kimi gave me an assessing look. Her tone, the one she used when she was reciting science or had a question about something, had dropped. More subdued, she said, "They live their lives on camera."

I let that settle in my gut, once more thinking about Jack. Thinking about Lilly and the enormity of what he had to protect her from. It was hard to be angry anymore when I could barely fathom how scared he must be, buried under the weight of his responsibility.

I let her lead me to the central station. Various people sat around the computers. Two people were dedicated to two monitors each that watched bedrooms. I recognized Milo's bald head in one of the cameras, but the rest of the rooms were empty.

Kimi introduced me to everyone. Their names went in one ear and out the other. Two were secretaries, and the other two were sitters. Then she led me to Milo's room.

"Stasia!" he cried when I darkened his doorway. I crouched down and caught him as he ran toward me. He once again wore a too-big lab coat. This time the stitching had Dr. Alver written on it.

I stood up. "Hey, what's up Milo?"

"Are you my guard today?" He said it so innocently, but my heart squeezed.

I cocked my head. "How about I be your friend instead?"

His smile widened. "I like that!"

Dr. Kimi had that assessing look on her face again. I opened my mouth to ask her if she was okay, but she beat me to it.

"The trainer will be here to get you for your exercise soon, Milo." Turning to me, she said, "The training rooms are at each end of these corridors. Milo works in a different area than the older kids. They've already gotten started."

I nodded to her. Milo spoke up beside me. "Are you going to play with me today, Kimi?"

Dr. Kimi's entire countenance changed as she looked down at Milo. With a smile on her face, she seemed less scientist and more human. "Not today, I'm afraid. I have a full schedule, Milo, but I promise to check in on you tomorrow."

Milo pouted. "The other grown-ups are so boring."

"I know Milo. I'll bring you a treat, I promise."

He perked up, at an age where he was easily persuaded with sweets. I kept that in mind for future assignments with him. Dr. Kimi finished her goodbyes, and Milo and I were left to our own devices. He had some enrichment toys in his room, puzzles and such. I found a life-sized Connect Four in the corner and wondered distantly how often he had playmates to play it with. To his excitement, I pulled it out, and we settled in for about an hour before a trainer came and got us.

\*\*\*

I had noticed that the same trainers worked with the same kinds of elementals. So, I hadn't met the man who came in for Milo. He introduced himself as Jason. Like most of the men who led an elemental power workout, he was generically fit with close-cropped hair. I wondered if everyone here was enlisted or an officer or if any of them were independent contractors like Pat and me.

"How are you doing today, Milo?" asked Jason as we walked. I trailed behind everyone. Milo answered, his words and movements animated. Jason led us to one end of the corridor, to a concrete door in a thick concrete wall. We passed a glass room that looked like a recording studio with a room in front of it covered with a shiny flame-retardant lining.

Milo walked into the lined room, not missing a beat as he spoke to Jason. I looked around for a medical station and found a vital sign machine in the far corner. Pulling it around, I frowned. Dust covered the blood pressure cuff, and the cuff was too big for Milo. Jason spoke to Milo through a speaker. Noticing I hadn't followed him, he motioned for me to join him. I pulled the vital sign machine with me. The sound of the rolling wheels echoed off the walls. Jason said through a speaker, "Leave it."

I frowned again but did as told and walked into the booth with him. Milo's voice filled the room, talking about how he had dominated Connect Four. Jason rolled his eyes. "This kid can talk. Go ahead and take a seat. I'm going to run him through a few exercises. We don't do anything with him to get him too exerted because of his power and age. Then, we'll take him back to his room, and you can go get lunch."

I nodded and looked back at Milo. I had seen in his file he was six years old. It worried me that he seemingly wasn't being monitored as closely as the other children, especially because of the special consideration for fire Stepuli. But I didn't say anything right now. Jason wasn't the right person to bring my concerns to anyway.

As promised, Jason ran Milo through easy exercises. Bunsen burners attached to the wall lit with a flame. Milo would flare the fire for a moment or put it out. Afterward, Jason would let him talk. Jason would ask him questions about superheroes or which Disney movies he liked most this week. He explained to me he was gauging Milo's mood, seeing if he held his normal interest in things he liked. It troubled me that the only things he had to ask him about were movies.

"Does he ever go outside?" I asked Jason as he had Milo do the most complicated thing so far, detach fire from the burner and hover it over his palm.

"Sometimes, and only when under guard."

I looked over at him incredulously at the word guard, but he was talking into the speaker again, telling Milo to put the fire out. He asked him some questions, and then told him we were done. "No need to do vitals," Jason said as he saw me eyeing the rolling medical stand.

"I'll just check him over really quick." I ignored Jason's response, and he finally shrugged his shoulders as I wrapped the too-big cuff around Milo's skinny arm and took his temperature and pulse ox. Everything was normal but his temperature, which was at one hundred one.

"Feeling okay Milo?" I asked, feeling awkward crouched down as I was. There was no real medical station in the echoing concrete anteroom between the two booths.

"Yeah, how come, Doc?"

I smiled at him. "Not a doc. You have a bit of a fever."

His smile widened. "Oh, I always run hot after a session. I feel good."

"You sure? No nausea, headache, bellyache?"

He shook his head. "Can we play Connect Four one more time before you go?"

His face was so hopeful my heart hurt for him. "As long as I'm allowed to, I'd love to play another game or two."

His face lit up as I pulled the cuff off. Before I could stash the machine, he excitedly grabbed my hand and pulled me back toward the corridor. "Come on then! I'm so gonna beat you!"

I was laughing when raised voices alerted me to a commotion just outside the door. I tried to stop our momentum so I could check what was going on, but there was no way to do it without yanking Milo's arm. We ran into bright lights and Pete surrounded by Jason and three other guards. He had something in his hand and a wicked smile on his face. I looked into his eyes, transfixed. His energy still felt black, but this time, hatred pulsed deeper than anything I had ever felt before.

Milo and I caught Pete's attention. He stared at me with that vacant gaze and said in a hollow voice, "They're mad you made the fire go away."

Milo turned back to me with wide eyes. "You need to get back in the room." He pushed me toward the concrete door we'd just exited. I looked at him, confused, then back up to the scene in front of me just as a large boom and Milo's shout of "No!" rang in my ears. And then I was flying.

I smacked sideways into the concrete wall behind me and slid to the floor, coughing. My ears were ringing, and plaster fell from the ceiling. Dust-covered bodies entered up the corridor, but I ignored them and looked around frantically for Milo. He stood a little in front of me, head bowed, arms out in front of him, palms facing outward. I tried to stand, collapsed a few times, and finally just crawled toward him.

I put a hand on his shoulder and spun him to face me, shouting his name, but I couldn't hear my own words. Something wet was on my neck, and I felt heat so powerful the room was like the inside of an oven. I ignored all of it, concentrating on Milo. He opened his eyes and looked at me with such sadness and fear. I pushed as many feelings of calmness and safety toward him as I could muster and pulled him roughly into me with one arm. I checked him over for broken bones, my other arm still supporting me. The heat in the room eased off, and people swarmed us. Someone helped me to my feet, and someone else took Milo away from me.

I called for him, my arms outstretched. His mouth moved, but I couldn't hear anything. I looked forward and saw charred bodies. Four charred bodies. Pete stood naked with a wicked smile. He shielded himself, his hands folded as if they were already restrained in front of him. All I could sense around him was satisfaction and that undulating hate. Around him stood four men. Brandon was one of them. He looked at me with concern.

The people bracing me on each side walked me past

him. His eyes followed me. Each of the four people surrounding the fire elemental had water in their palms. Vaguely, I realized I was soaking wet and looked up into the source. Sprinklers spit water from the ceiling. My legs barely worked. The two strangers dragged me to the double doors. Right before we exited, I looked over my shoulder and met Brandon's eyes. His brow furrowed as water circled his palm.

*** 

I woke up in an infirmary with bandages wrapped around my head and a saline drip IV in my arm. My mouth was so dry I started to cough. I tried to sit up, but every part of me hurt. I felt like I'd been hit by a truck.

"Hey, hey. Wait." The head of the bed started to rise. Pat sat at my bedside, the bed remote in his hand.

"Hey," I croaked.

He smiled at me, but his face twisted in worry. "Hey, yourself. I'm so glad you're awake." His voice sounded like it was coming through a tunnel, but I could hear if I concentrated.

"How's Milo?" I asked. I didn't remember passing out, didn't remember anything past the look in Brandon's golden eyes. But I did remember Milo, remembered reaching for him and him for me as two people had dragged me from the corridor. "Did he make it out?"

Pat's concern morphed into frustration. "Milo's fine, Stasia. Jesus, that fire elemental almost killed you. Are you okay? They said your CT exams didn't show internal bleeding, but your ears were bleeding, and you look like one giant bruise."

I coughed again, the dryness scratching my throat. Pat reached for a white plastic cup with a straw sticking out on my bedside. Tepid water met my lips. It was the best thing I could ever remember tasting. I hadn't heard everything he'd said, but I heard CT, and he wasn't freaking out.

"I'm sure I'm fine then," I finally said when I could speak. "Milo was so scared, and he was standing in front of me. He…"

Pat sat again. His mouth twisted down. I watched his lips move and concentrated as he spoke, making sure to catch every word. "Milo is fine. They put him in a temporary holding cell while they fix the fire quarters. The other fire elemental has been relocated. Milo has more power than any of us guessed. He saved your life actually."

After he finished, I laid back with a huff, my energy spent. I remembered Milo crouched in front of me, his head bowed, his hands up in defiance. I remembered the charred bodies. God, had he held back the fire? The fire from an explosion, I guessed, based on the soreness, and the…well, the flying through the air.

I closed my eyes and took a breath. Opening them, I looked at Pat with one last question. "Can I see him? Can I see Milo?"

He shook his head, the worry seeping back in judging by the tightness around his eyes. "Milo's on suicide watch, Stasia." I turned my head away and closed my eyes tight. Tears leaked down my cheeks.

# CHAPTER 26
## Stasia

A prick stung my thigh. The sting, then a tiny bit of pressure. Then it was gone. Voices talked around me.

"I think she's the one. I think this is it." It sounded like Dr. Galton, but the voice came in and out, distorted one second, and his the next. I couldn't see anybody's faces. Everything was blurry, like I was watching an out-of-focus scene in a movie.

"Are you sure? If she's not, if she realizes what's happening, we'll need to terminate her." Another voice. This one female, but not one I could remember hearing before.

"It's worth the risk. Her father had a watered-down version of what she's been displaying."

"We won't be able to verify the clairvoyance until after the testing." The woman sounded skeptical. I tried bringing the picture into focus but struggled to sit up and look. Something weighed me down. I was frozen. Paralyzed.

"Even if all we get is the empathic qualities, she'll be valuable, Diane. It'll be worth trying." Was that Dr. Galton? The voice kept changing.

*"Then let's begin."*

I woke up to rumbling underneath me. I was still in the infirmary, an old-fashioned setup with metal beds lining both walls and an empty nursing desk at the head of the room. The other beds rattled lightly. My brow wrinkled. I had read that earthquakes happened in Washington State but that they were rarely felt. The rumbling soon stopped, and I looked around in the dark to get my bearings.

When I had woken up before, Pat was here. It had helped orient me, though I'd been on so much pain medicine, I hadn't stayed that way for long. He'd promised to pick up Flynn and look after things. I wanted to leave, but when I asked before, the doctor had refused. Some man named Shepherd. He said I still needed observation. I didn't understand why if there was no internal bleeding, but Dr. Galton had come in when I'd gotten upset and insisted I let them take care of me. I didn't have enough energy to fight.

I was still on a saline drip. I looked at the clock overhead, and luckily, the date with the time helped me realize it was still the same day. At least for the next five minutes. A noise at the doors to the right brought my head around. A nurse I had seen at orientation came through.

"Hi," I saw her mouth. My hearing was still muffled, and she'd started talking too far away. She was pretty, with dark red hair that looked dyed.

"Hey." My voice still didn't sound right. It still croaked like I was coming out of a trek in the desert.

The girl, I couldn't see a nametag, came alongside my bed. She picked up the remote Pat had used earlier and raised the head of my bed. I braced my hands against the bed to sit up, but collapsed back with a cry of pain. I brought my hands up and saw a splint on my right wrist.

"Just sprained," the nurse said as I rotated my arm. I'd only been awake in spurts, mostly complaining to leave, since the bomb.

"When can I leave?" I don't know why I bothered to ask. It was nearly midnight. If they wouldn't let me leave this afternoon, they wouldn't be letting me go now. But I felt trapped. The redhead felt oddly excited, and the disorientation and lack of Flynn was getting to me. I felt unmoored, like a ship lost at sea.

"Not for a couple days probably. Dr. Galton will be in in the morning. I think it's time for another pain shot."

She inserted a syringe of something in the needleless port.

I tried to stop her, my hurt arm even made it to her, before she pushed the plunger. My eyes rolled back. Her doll-like face framed in red hair and odd excitement were the last things I registered before sleep took me again.

*** 

The next time I woke up, it was morning. Light blasted into my eyes. I went to sit myself up with both hands, but the stiff ends of the brace poked into my right hand, and I remembered it was hurt. Leaning heavily on my left arm, I scooted back until I was in a sitting position. My eyes blurred everything around me. I rubbed at them to bring the room into focus.

I coughed, my head hanging to my chin. Whatever drugs they'd been giving me for pain left my entire body feeling weak and exhausted. I looked to my left where Pat had grabbed the plastic cup of water last time, but it was empty.

Someone called my name. It still sounded like it was coming through a tunnel. I looked around, surprised to see Brandon sitting on the right side of my bed. His eyes were tight like they'd been last time I'd seen him. His white-knuckled hand gripped the metal side rail of my bed.

He said something again, but he must have been practically whispering because all I caught were distant tones.

"You have to speak up. My eardrums are perforated. It's still hard to hear." His eyes widened. He looked back at the door. I followed his gaze, but the doors sat still, the room empty except for us.

Instead of shouting, he scooted the metal chair closer and spoke near my ear. "How are you feeling?"

He leaned back and waited for me to answer. Tears welled in my eyes. I tried to blink them back. Still, I felt wetness on my cheeks. His brow furrowed deeper in concern. "I want to go home. I'm worried about Flynn. And Milo. They won't tell me anything, and they keep giving me pain medicine."

It felt good to voice my worries. I had fallen asleep after Pat had told me Milo was on suicide watch. Grief and worry had combined with the drugs and pulled me under. I hadn't seen him since, and nobody else had been helpful in getting me what I asked for. They just gave me pain medicine and told me I needed to be here.

Brandon leaned in again. "I don't think they're going to let you go for a couple days. I had to sneak up here. We have Flynn at our house. Your friend stopped by to grab him, but we told him we'd keep him."

I stretched back and looked at him in surprise. Last time I'd spoken to Jack, I hadn't expected to see any of them again. He had seemed firm he couldn't have me in his life, and while it hurt, I'd understood. After what happened to Milo, if anything, I understood more. My wide eyes were enough for Brandon to understand my confusion. He leaned back to my ear.

"I picked him up after I left last night. After we secured Pete, they released everyone. Training is canceled for a couple days. Jack is kind of freaking out."

When he leaned back, he glanced furtively at the doors again. I needed to figure out why he was nervous, but first, "Why is Jack freaking out?" Panic welled in my chest, pushing back the exhaustion. Was Lilly okay? Had they pulled her in for some reason?

Brandon leaned in and said, "Stasia, when they pulled you from the room, you barely looked alive. Your ears were bleeding, your eyes were rolling back. Two people had to carry you out. I found out you were in the infirmary, but nobody was allowed in to see you. I didn't have a good reason to push it."

He eased back. "Is Lilly, okay?" I asked, still trying to figure out what had upset Jack.

Brandon looked at me like I was an idiot. He leaned in. "Lilly is fine, Stasia. Jack is freaking out because he can't get in to see you. He caused an earthquake. I had to slap him, literally, to get him to come to his senses."

When he leaned back out, my face was slack with shock. I cared about Jack. I was in love with him. But I didn't think for a second he returned my feelings. Not after finding out I was in the SEP. His family came first for him, and they should. He didn't have room for more. Especially not someone involved with the very entity that could threaten his and his family's freedom.

Brandon just shook his head at my open-mouthed speechlessness. "I promised him I would come check on you." He placed his hand on mine, and I looked down. I felt slow, like I was wading through Jell-O to keep up with my emotions, this conversation. The fact that Jack cared that much. "I would have anyway, but I can't stay. I shouldn't be caught in here. The only people who have been allowed in are staff. A few of the Stepuli have asked after you."

I looked up again, my mouth still hanging open. The pressure behind my eyes increased, and warmth spread through my chest. Even with Pat checking on me, this was the first time I hadn't felt alone since I'd woken up that first time. I loved Pat, but things had been strained since I let Jack drive me home instead of him that day at the bar. I suspected his feelings for me had changed, and it had made things awkward for us.

Brandon squeezed my hand and leaned in one last time. "Get better, Stasia. As soon as you get out of here, we'll be waiting for you back at home. We've got Flynn until then. Lilly is lavishing love on him and can't wait to see you. Judging by the Richter scale of the earthquake Jack's dumb ass let out, you can guess how excited he is."

Brandon went to get up, but my hand snatched out for his, stopping him. Pain flared in my wrist, but I ignored it. "Wait." I coughed. "How is Milo? Is he okay?"

Brandon's face softened, and the warmth I had felt while he was talking returned. "He's been pretty sedated on antidepressants. He probably will be for the next couple days, but they're watching him closely. He's going to be okay."

I shut my eyes and let the few tears I'd been holding

back fall. "Thank you," I whispered. He squeezed my hand one last time, and I felt his retreating footsteps through the vibrations of the metal bed. I lowered myself back down, exhausted after the longest conversation I'd had since I'd been blown into the concrete wall. The door swung after he exited. I closed my eyes, and this time when I let sleep take me, it felt peaceful.

\*\*\*

Whatever medicine they'd been giving me, they must have weaned off. When I woke up next, I didn't feel as groggy. Everything still hurt, but it was bearable. I would take my clear head and some aches and pains over the medicine. I looked around. The room came into focus more quickly than before. Dr. Galton sat at the nurse's desk to my left, and Dr. Kimi leaned on the desk talking to him. Arguing with him, from the way her arms gesticulated, but I could only hear the impressions of sound.

Dr. Galton's face brightened when he noticed me sitting up, the annoyed mask falling. Dr. Kimi looked around, concern pinching her expression. They both walked over to me, one taking up a post on each side of the bed.

"How are you feeling?" I assumed Galton had shouted because I heard each word.

"I'm feeling better." I looked up at the clock and realized I had lost the entire day yesterday after me and Brandon had spoken. Judging by the light, it was early morning. That made it…two days after the blast? God, Flynn. He was probably freaking out.

A hand on my right shoulder brought my eyes up to Dr. Kimi, the concern still on her face. Her lips moved. I could just barely make out her words. "Sure… okay…don't…"

I smiled at her crookedly and asked her to repeat herself louder. She smiled weakly back and said, "Are you sure you're, ok? We have some questions, but you don't have to do this now."

I looked between them. Dr. Galton's annoyance was back at her words. "I'm okay. Don't have to do what?"

At my reassurance, Dr. Galton reached back for one of the chairs that sat on each side of my bed. He pulled it closer to the metal side rail. The excitement coming off him made me uneasy. Or was it Dr. Kimi's unease I was feeling?

"Stasia, we wanted to talk to you about something important." He spoke loudly enough that I could hear him. I nodded for him to continue. "We have noticed something about you, something that was reinforced during the incident. How do I begin?" He looked down at his lap, and my brow pulled down. I wanted to go home.

Dr. Kimi looked over at Galton, and then back at me. She seemed to sigh, her shoulders hitching, then lowering. "Stasia, you seem to have inherited your father's empathic abilities. He was known for being able to change the moods of those around him. It was a subtle ability but helped in diplomatic situations."

I was completely lost. I barely knew who my father was. He was a man on a page a private investigator had handed me who had died young in a car crash. I said as much, but Dr. Kimi just pinched her lips. Her eyes went to Galton, and so did mine. He shook his head with a broad smile on his face.

"No, Stasia. I mean yes, he did die in a car accident. Tragic. But He was a CIA operative who helped on diplomatic missions. You see, the SEP was created to work with the Stepuli population. Over time, and through the genetic research, we began to ensure the safety of Stepuli-human children. We also discovered introns in the human side of the DNA that were replicable. Humans with this wild-type DNA all seemed to have a sensitivity. It led to breakthroughs in parapsychological research. The headquarters you went to your first day, with the deprivation pods, that is the hub of human research. We don't have complete heredity with these abilities like the Stepuli. The sensitivity seems to run in families, but it can skip generations or develop in families where it was never seen before. But these findings have allowed us to make developments in human extrasensory perception."

My mind spun. I began to wonder if I was still on drugs. I looked to Dr. Kimi, but I didn't see a gotcha face. Just stoic concern. I looked back to Dr. Galton and said, "What does this have to do with me?" My voice was still dry, and I felt Kimi get up. A moment later, she sat down and held out a bottle of water. I took it gratefully and sipped.

Dr. Galton tapped the bar, and I looked over. "We found you after your father's death. We watched you through your military service, and you displayed the possibility of his empathic abilities. We brought you here to see if they were something we could develop through our program. I was uncertain, but Milo proved it for me the other day. He said that, following the explosion, fear had taken root, and he had been unable to let go of the heat in the room. But looking into your eyes, he'd felt a calmness. It helped center him enough to let go of the fire completely."

The unease that had slithered through me at Galton's

excitement wound through every part of me now. A few things stuck out at me from his confession. *Watching you. Brought you here.* He forged on like the ground wasn't opening underneath me, making me question everything that had happened in the last year. Everything that had happened since I graduated from high school and joined the military.

"We want to take you into the deprivation pods today. You're healed enough to be able to do some initial testing."

I swallowed heavily. Dr. Kimi's face looked grim. Her worry mixed with mine, leaving me sick to my stomach.

# CHAPTER 27
## Stasia

D r. Kimi helped me into the standard-issue one-piece in a locker room that led out to the deprivation pods. I was covered in scattered bruises from the blast. After lying for two days in bed, my limbs were stiff, and it was difficult to support myself. But I was getting stronger.

The woman I had always seen as so poised seemed troubled. Thoughts had been swirling in my head since talking with her and Dr. Galton. First, there was incredulous disbelief. Then fear that these people who currently had control of my care were off their rockers. Then sheer terror that they weren't.

It's not like I didn't know what they were talking about. I'd always had good intuition and could sense what people felt. But that wasn't some magical ability. I was simply good at reading body language and nonverbal cues. I thought back to the dream I had of the pods before I was in them. Even that could be explained by me picking up hints of what I was getting into before that day. Couldn't it?

Dr. Kimi's words interrupted my thoughts. "Are you sure you want to go through with this Stasia?" She spoke close to my ear like Brandon had.

My face felt frozen, my chest a solid block. Like it was seized with all the uncertainty and trepidation thrumming through me. "Do I have a choice?" I asked finally. Because really, if I had what I wanted I'd be home right now. With Flynn, Lilly, and Brandon. And Jack.

Her sad eyes only increased my dread. "No. No, I guess not. None of us do."

She picked up some probes and placed them at my temples. My forehead furrowed, and I asked, "What do you mean none of us do?"

After pressing the adhesive onto my skin to make sure it stuck, her shoulders moved, giving away her sigh. "There's a Dakota proverb, the neighbors of my people. It talks about how the legacy we leave behind is how we will be remembered. How the things we do in this life, the actions we take, and those we don't, how they will mark us for life. I often wonder about the tracks I leave."

She reached behind me for a robe and pulled it around my shoulders. "Dr. Kimi—"

"Call me Kimi, Stasia."

The corner of my lips lifted. "Kimi. What's happening right now? Is this real?"

Kimi swallowed hard. "Stasia, something is happening that I didn't even realize I might need to protect you from. The worst thing I thought I'd have to do to you was what I did that first day in the deprivation pods. Even if you had shown your father's abilities, his were so subtle. A way to tip off someone in negotiations. Maybe slightly push someone already leaning a certain way. What you seem able to do, without even trying, without even knowing you're doing it, Galton isn't going to let that go."

I swallowed hard, thinking of Jack and his family. Of how panicked Jack was when he realized I worked with the SEP and might be spying on them. I thought I'd understood him before. But the fact he still cared, the fact he saw through that, and apparently, I still mattered to him, meant even more. Because if I were in his shoes, I'm not sure I would have been brave enough to look past it to who the person really was. Because what Kimi said, what she inferred, it was terrifying.

"What do you mean he isn't going to let that go?"

Kimi frowned. She stood and held her hands out to me, and I used them to pull myself up, steadying myself on her when I swayed. When I had my equilibrium back, she studied me intently. "I mean, he's not going to let you go." Then she led me out to the pods.

\*\*\*

We walked out to the pools. After we left the door, I had taken my hand off Kimi's arm, determined to walk on my own. Something about it made me feel less weak, even if I was a little dizzy. There was activity all around. I noticed the redheaded nurse from the middle of the night at one of the stations with the portable EEGs. She watched my approach, practically bouncing on her feet. Beside her was Dr. Galton and a woman I'd never seen before.

The woman wore a smart French twist and an expensive suit and heels. Her face was timeless, but not young. As I approached and she looked at me, I felt no excitement or anxiety or worry like I did from others around me. I imagined if imperious were a feeling, that's what she emanated. The thought caused a pang of panic in my chest. I often thought of my impressions of people as their feelings coming toward me. It has always been my way of understanding others' nonverbal communication. Could it really be something more?

"So, this is Anastasia Smith?" The woman had a sophisticated accent I couldn't place. Her tone alone made me feel at an instant disadvantage.

I wasn't sure what to say, so I just stared back at her. Dr. Galton broke the building tension. "Yes, Diane. This is Stasia. With Milo's help, she survived the attack at the school. We believe she is to thank for Milo not creating a secondary catastrophe."

The panic spread through my chest, and I stiffened. Did he say Diane? I remembered my dream from this morning. Kimi's hand on my shoulder forced me to relax. I understood it as a silent warning. Don't give them anything you don't have to.

Diane stared at me steadily, but at my continued silence, she cocked her head. "Do you speak, Stasia?" Everything she said was given in such an even, measured tone. I didn't imagine this woman was ever out of control.

"Should I call you Diane?" I wanted to make sure I had heard correctly.

She straightened her neck. "If you'd like. You'll also hear me called Dr. Cutler. Are you ready for today's exercise so soon after your ordeal?"

My forehead creased. "Since I'm not really sure what today's exercise is, I don't really know how to answer that." I was in a bathing suit, so I could guess. But fishing for information never hurt.

Diane Cutler easily realized what I was doing because one side of her mouth tilted up. "Today, we are going to give you a medication that will put you into a hallucinatory state. Then we're going to run a series of tests, sending you information we want you to identify. We'll measure your brain activity through the probes Dr. Alver placed. Afterward, we'll take an EEG to identify differences in your brainwaves."

"What will this prove to you?" I asked.

Her words were so well enunciated, even through the tunnel I heard everything through, I had no problem following the conversation. "It will prove your value to the SEP, Stasia."

At that, Diane turned away, obviously done with me. Dr. Galton stepped in, his ever-present excitement saturating my senses. He wasn't talking to me, so I heard some of what he said but missed every other word or so. Kimi gestured her head toward the pod, and I followed.

Trying to keep my voice low, though I wasn't sure if it was low or not, I asked, "Who is that nurse with the red hair?"

Kimi looked back to the EEG station. "Cora. She's Galton's niece. She worships Dr. Cutler. Even dyes her hair to look like her." I could tell from Kimi's tone she didn't like her. Judging by the fact she didn't lean close and spoke loud enough I could easily hear, she didn't care who knew it.

I looked over, and the girl, Cora, was shooting daggers at us now. I turned back toward the pods. The gears vibrated under my feet as the technician brought the pod directly in front of me toward the edge of the pool. As I had before, I followed the edge to sit in the middle of the little shallow pool.

Cora had walked up with a syringe. She followed

along the same edge to reach me. "This goes intravenously." She said it loudly, and I realized why her excitement had made me uneasy the other night. It felt a lot like Galton's.

"I don't have an IV." I said as she lowered the syringe to my elbow, pushing the needle directly into the large vein there and injecting the medication in.

I looked up in annoyance. That was not the way you injected IV meds. I opened my mouth to say something, but suddenly, the room exploded into swaths of color. The last formed thing I saw was a concerned Kimi. Then it was all swirling patterns of orange and red with intermittent splashes of black. I distantly felt myself laid back and water surrounding me. I was locked away with the colors. I didn't know when or how it happened, but there was no more sound. But at the same time, sound was everywhere.

I heard excitement and expectation. I heard fear and anger. It rushed at me, the deepest shades of magenta, followed by snaking tendrils of black intertwining with starbursts of bright orange.

Interspersed through everything was faint traces of blue.

I tried to make sense of everything, but it was overwhelming. I couldn't take the chaos. The heightened emotions pressed on me until I finally pressed back. I tried to order it, to calm it. I tried to tease the blue to touch every color, to surround it. To follow the veins of black and outline the pulsing groups of red.

Eventually, I had a strong boundary of blue, enough so that the weight I hadn't even realized made it hard to breath lifted enough for me to take a couple of deep breaths. After the cleansing exhalations, I let the relative serenity, compared to the previous chaos, suffuse me. I uncurled my tightly clenched fists, and I consciously relaxed my scrunched face. I allowed myself to float in the darkness.

Slowly, the complete black made way to fields of gray.

*From the gray came his hand. Strong, but so gentle. I felt like a piece of porcelain.*

*His fingers traced my chin, along my jaw, up to my ear. His fingers slowly threaded through my hair.*

*We were moving, swaying back and forth. My heart felt so full I was sure it would burst. My lips parted. To ask a question? Say a prayer?*

*His confession stopped me. Stilled everything. "I love you, Stasia."*

*My hands tightened on his hips. My breath hitched. I stood on a precipice. His chocolate eyes came into focus. They melted my fear. Any hesitation. I jumped.*

*"I love you too."*

I woke up gasping for air. I still sat in the shallow pool. It took me a while to get my bearings, almost like when I woke from a nightmare and needed time to reconcile the dream world with the one I was grounded in. Except that last dream hadn't been a nightmare. My heart clenched thinking about Jack's touch. About his words.

The situation before me came into focus, and as it did, the fluttering that came with the dream left me. In its place was ice cold dread. Dr. Galton stood smugly in front of my pod. Dr. Cutler stood to his right, a vaguely satisfied look on her face. She nodded her head and said to Dr. Galton, "She'll do." She turned around and walked out of the cavernous pool room. Even my muffled hearing could detect the clack of her heels as they resounded off the walls. To me, it sounded like doom.

Kimi helped me out of the pod, but Cora put me into the seat with the portable EEG. She hooked me up and ran some tests. Galton stood over me the entire time, humming his pleasure. The excitement coming from him was tempered with a deep satisfaction. It reminded me of the deep reds I had seen with splashes of orange intermixed. Realizing what that probably meant, I felt sick to my stomach.

Finally, after looking at a computer read out of my EEG findings and speaking over my head like I was an object and not a person, Galton addressed me directly.

"Stasia, did you have any visions when you were in the pod?" His face was glowing. I thought of Jack hiding Lilly's abilities. Of Milo, who must have known he had more in him than the ability to flare a Bunsen burner but had never let on until the explosion.

They already felt like they'd confirmed empathic abilities in me. "I saw colors." Galton's face didn't change at first, his excitement a maniacal mask. "They burst at me, but it was too much. I tried to temper them."

He nodded vigorously. "How did you temper them?"

I wondered if I was already saying too much. I had felt like the important thing to hold back was the vision of Jack. Having gone too far to stop, I pushed on. "I-I traced everything in blue. It felt calmer than the reds and oranges that were screaming at me."

Galton leaned back on his heels, his satisfaction so deep I imagined this was what it felt like to win the lottery. He looked up at Cora, who sat on a high-backed chair at the computer station.

"You see? That calm wash we all felt. She was tempering our excitement." He looked at me then. "Stasia, you didn't just trace colors with other colors. We all felt that calmness. Every person in this room reported feeling a coolness, a serenity sometime in the first hour after you entered the pod."

I started at that. I stared at Galton wide eyed. "Hour? How long was I there?"

I looked around for Kimi, but she wasn't anywhere to be seen. Disappointment weighed me down at her disappearance. "We leave you in for three hours. We may adjust that time in the future, but that's the baseline."

I couldn't wrap my head around it. Sure, enough late afternoon sun streamed through the windows lining the top of the wall across from me. I looked back at Dr. Galton. A deep sense of weariness invaded every part of me. "Can I go home now?"

His excitement hadn't abated. In fact, it seemed to have taken on a desperate edge. "What else did you see while you were in the pod?"

"Nothing. I didn't see anything else."

His frown gave away his disappointment before the feelings hit me. For the first time, I accepted maybe I wasn't reading the slump of his shoulders. The downturned corner of his mouth. Maybe I really was feeling his disappointment. Like a deep plum. Dark, with a hint of color.

Dr. Galton didn't hold me long after that. He'd had Cora lead me back to the locker room, much to my discontent. I'd insisted I'd get along fine on my own, but he insisted more forcibly. I wondered where Kimi had gone.

Cora watched with a smile on her face as I changed back into my loose-fitting sweats. She never said a word. It was creepy as hell.

When I finished and said I was ready, she spoke. "Henry called your friend Pat for you. He's out in the lobby to bring you home."

Surprise and suspicion suffused me. It was an oddly thoughtful gesture. "Thanks," I said and walked slowly toward the door that would lead me out to the lobby. I expected her to escort me. She just stood in the middle of the locker room and watched me go. Her eyes as I turned my back were like tiny needles against my skin.

After walking around all day, I felt stronger but still supported myself here and there with the wall. I was a little out of breath but thankful that I only had to endure that creepy woman's stare to the door of the locker room and not all the way out to the lobby. I didn't encounter anyone from the exercise on my way through the halls. They were empty all the way to the elevators.

They brought me back up to the first floor, to the lobby where Pat and I had stood when this all started. As the elevator doors opened, his lanky form stood waiting for me, hands in his pockets, head bowed. I wanted to cry when I saw him. "Hey, friend."

My joke landed flat. His head jerked up at my words. "Stasia," he said loudly, remembering my hearing difficulties.

He gave me a big bear hug, lifting me off my feet. I hugged him back weakly, relieved when he put me back down. The feelings coming off him left unease sitting heavy in my stomach. I'd always thought I was full of myself for thinking Pat was into me. But staring into his eyes, the affection coming from him was decidedly not friendly. I hadn't been fooling myself for thinking he liked me. I'd been fooling myself for thinking he didn't.

I didn't know what to say as Pat supported me out to the car. I appreciated the shoulder to lean on. A lot of my energy had been spent by now. His car was parked right out front. He insisted on buckling my seatbelt, only making that uneasy feeling deeper. As we drove toward my house, he peppered me with questions. I answered as best I could.

What had I been doing at the headquarters? Why did they release me from there and not the infirmary? I wasn't sure how much I could tell him and didn't want to talk about it anyway. I laid my head back against the headrest and pretended to fall asleep, hoping I could save the conversation, both what had happened in the last twenty-four hours and what the status of our friendship was, for later.

As I felt the car slow through the tighter turns, I knew we were close to my house. Pat pulled into my driveway, and I unbuckled my seatbelt before he could get there. He turned to me with a nervous smile on his face. He opened his mouth to say something, when suddenly his entire countenance changed. Resentment poured off him, and I realized he wasn't looking at me anymore.

I looked out the passenger window to where his gaze had gone. My breath caught in my chest. Charging across the yard with an intent look on his face was Jack's tall form. The beard he had grown looked unkept. His eyes were like lasers on my face.

"Stasia. You are breaking my heart."

My eyes swung back to Pat in surprise. My mouth an O, I wasn't sure what to say.

"Why him? Why not me?"

I opened and closed my mouth a couple times.

Finally, I said simply. Quietly. "I'm sorry." There was nothing else I could say. I turned and opened my door. I didn't have time to step out of the car before Jack was there, lifting me out and cradling me in his arms.

# CHAPTER 28

## Jack

Rain soaked into my shirt as I held Stasia, the weather in Washington as mercurial as ever. I knew I needed to lift my head up, I needed to say something. Just not yet. I breathed her in, taking in the smells of antiseptic soap, something lemony, and then something that was just her. A door slammed, and I knew my time was up. It was time to lift my head from her hair. My hand was buried in her nape, the other pressed into her back, pulling her into my chest, close to my heart, which slammed against my ribs.

"Hey Jack." I looked up, the rain a gentle trickle. Pat didn't look happy. His hand was on the hood of his car, but he looked like he wanted to come rip Stasia from my arms. They only tightened around her. Her hands fisted at my back in response, and it soothed something in my chest.

"Hey, Pat. Thanks for bringing her home." Part of me was resentful. I wish I had known she was coming home. I wish she had been home the entire time.

He looked pointedly behind him at her house. "Yeah, I was just going to take her into her house and get her settled."

I shifted Stasia to my side. Small winces told me she was in pain. Anxiety curled through every part of me, making me antsy with undirected energy. I wanted to end this conversation. Get her inside. Check her over. Make sure she took pain medicine. And if I didn't let Lilly see her soon, she might set me on fire. Literally.

"No need, we've been waiting for her to get home. She's going to stay at my house until she's recovered." Stasia looked up at me, my gaze drawn to hers. Surprise showed in her eyes, but she hadn't spoken a word yet. I wanted to hear her voice. I needed Pat to hurry up and leave.

He shifted next to the car, looking annoyed. "Is that really necessary? Me or Angela can stay with her, make sure she recovers. It was a...terrible work accident." My eyes were drawn back to him, my brows turned down. Did he not know we were Stepuli? Brandon had seen glimpses of him at the Stepul School, did he not realize the connection?

"I've got her, Pat. Thanks for bringing her home." I made my tone as final as possible. I was tired of this conversation, and my need to talk to Stasia, to look her over, was beating at me. The trees around me swayed, responding to the turmoil thrumming through me.

"Pat."

My gaze shot down. Her voice was a little creaky, but it wasn't as bad as Brandon had described it. Her hand had found its way to my chest, soothing the ache, the anxiety, the wild feeling that had been winding around me. Around us, the trees quieted.

"I'm okay. I'm going to go check on Flynn and lay down. I'm good for now. Thank you."

Pat looked at her with some kind of expectation or reproach I didn't like. I wasn't sure exactly what, but finally, he gave a sharp nod and turned around. He drummed his hand on the hood of the car as he rounded to the driver's door. Right before he folded his tall body into the small sedan, he looked over the hood at Stasia. "Bye. Feel better Stasia." She nodded at him, and then he was backing away.

I turned Stasia in my arms, so she was slightly in front of me again. I wanted to look at her fully. I opened my mouth to say something, but I closed it again. I was feeling so much. Regret for being an idiot and pushing her away when it had been clear she'd done nothing wrong. Pain when Brandon told me she was hurt. Badly. That even while blood was leaking from her ears, and she'd been too hurt to even stand, she'd fought to get to Milo.

Something deeper I couldn't quite name at the realization that it wasn't because I'd thought she was Stepuli that made me feel so connected to her. Fire at the memory of touching her.

Not able to leave it only a memory a second longer, I reached for her. She was hurt, and I didn't know where. To me, she was precious. My thumb lightly brushed her chin. She leaned into it. As gently as I could, I traced my fingers up the side of her cheek. They came to rest behind her ear. She stared up at me so intently, and I was so in tune with her, I could feel her breaths coming faster, feel the slight change in her body as she swallowed. I buried my fingers in her hair at the nape of her neck.

Slowly, I drew her toward me. Her body swayed as she

walked and came toe to toe with me. The feeling of her body so close to mine, like before in her kitchen, on her front porch, gave way to weightlessness in my chest. She parted her lips, and for a moment, I thought she was going to say something. As much as I wanted to hear her voice, I needed to tell her something first. Something I had just realized. Something I probably knew the second the earth rioted when I'd heard she'd been hurt.

"I love you, Stasia."

Her breath hitched, and her eyes filled with so much feeling. I leaned back just enough to gauge her whole expression. I could see her pulse jumping at her neck. I fell into her big green eyes, wanting to stay there. I held my breath waiting. And then her words, the certainty in them, grounded me like I once thought only the earth could.

"I love you too."

*\*\**

Brandon stood in the hall, leaning against the wall, a smile on his face. I guessed he'd figured what was up when I went charging out of the house from my seat at the kitchen table. Lilly appeared at the top of the stairs with Flynn. I thought she and the dog would break each other's necks rushing down the steps, trying to beat each other to Stasia the way they did.

Alarm gripped me. I didn't want them to slam right into her. I moved to intercept, but Flynn was completely undeterred. He wound his way around my legs, his butt wiggling back and forth as he rubbed himself against Stasia's hip. He reached for her arm. Grasping it in his mouth, a growl emanated from him as he led her down the hall. She let out a helpless laugh. I scratched my head. I wanted to stop it. I worried she was going to hurt herself.

She said, "Soft," before I could say anything. He let her go and set off to find a toy he could grasp instead. I relaxed marginally.

As I walked toward Stasia, Lilly ran around, beating me. She hugged her tightly around the middle. Seeing a wince on Stasia's face, I'd had enough. I moved quickly toward them, but before I got there, Stasia met my eyes and shook her head.

"I'm so happy Jack stopped being dumb. I've been wanting to talk to you forever. Did you know that I went back to school? Things have been *super* awkward with the girls there, and Letty doesn't talk to me anymore, but I decided I don't care. How are you feeling? Oh, gosh, am I hurting you?"

Lilly noticed Stasia's tension and jumped back.

"I'm fine, Lilly, it's good to see you." Looking up at me with a mischievous smile, she said, "I'm glad Jack stopped being stupid too." I chuckled, the warmth that had settled in my center spread at her playful words.

Brandon walked up the hall behind her and laid a hand on her shoulder, drawing the water from her hair and clothes into his palm. "Jack let you get soaking wet."

"Thanks, show off." He chuckled, leading our group into the den we hardly seemed to use. Stasia followed and sat on the couch that faced a TV. Flynn, who had finally calmed, sat at her feet. I sat in the corner of the couch and drew Stasia against me. Everyone else sat around us.

Brandon bounced the water on his palm a couple times before directing it to a plant sitting in the corner of the room. Stasia followed the action, a small smile on her relaxed face.

I looked at her questioningly, and she shrugged. "It's

so mundane. I imagine it's something you do when there are no humans around. It's nice to feel trusted."

I gently squeezed her, my own heart clenching. I did, I realized. Trust her. So did my family by the looks of duh on their faces. "How are you feeling?" Brandon asked from the other end of the couch. Lilly was on the floor, petting Flynn.

Stasia looked at Lilly uncertainly. Lilly noticed the look and rolled her eyes. "I'm sixteen," she said in such a young voice. We all let out a laugh.

Lilly's face soured, but I spoke up, unruffling her feathers. "It's okay. You can talk about what happened, she already knows most of it."

Stasia swallowed. "I'm not so sure that's true." My brow furrowed, and across from me Brandon tensed. Lilly looked up, rapt but barely moving. She didn't want someone to send her from the room.

"What do you mean?" Brandon had clued us in to the details of the attack, and what he knew happened after. He had seen Stasia yesterday in the infirmary.

"Jack...guys." Stasia swallowed. She picked at her sweats, and my hands fisted and unfisted, scared at what she could be struggling to tell us. She took a deep breath and started. "It turns out, the government hasn't only been testing on Stepuli. And I didn't know exactly who my dad was."

Brandon and I exchanged a look over Stasia's head. "Explain," we said at the same time.

Stasia told us about Galton ambushing her this morning in the infirmary, and how he'd insisted because of a familial connection she participate in deprivation testing a little less than two days after she was in an explosion.

Anger thrummed through me. The plant in the corner started rustling, and Stasia's hand settled on my arm. The cooling feeling from the bar when the captain had grabbed her slowly traced up my arm. As I listened to Stasia's words, and that cooling balm spread up my arm through the rest of my body, what she was saying sunk in.

Lilly was open-mouthed; Brandon's face was grim. Stasia moved her hand off my arm, settling back into me. With the absence of her touch, panic ripped through me. Because while the abilities she was describing—abilities I had already picked up on, just attributed to the wrong thing—were amazing. They were just one more way Galton could take her away from me.

"Are you feeling okay after the testing?" Brandon asked. I looked down, waiting for her answer.

"Yeah. I was a little disoriented afterward, like when I come out of a nightmare, but I'm fine now. It just feels like what I always thought it was. Being good at reading people."

I swallowed. Stasia had also mentioned Galton fished for something more to her abilities. How she had heard the word clairvoyance thrown around. That the night she got drunk, the first time they'd put her in a pod, she'd told me she'd dreamed about it the night before. How she'd always had dreams but had figured her mind was just working out what was happening around her while she slept. Thank God she hadn't told Galton about that.

"Don't give him anything else. It was good to give him a piece of what you can do. He would have known you were outright lying otherwise. But don't give him anything else."

Stasia looked up at me, her head against my chest.

Love and fear warred as I looked down at her. Lilly did what she did best and broke the tension thickening the room.

"I'm hungry." Flynn flipped up from his upside down, cockeyed position at her words, making us all laugh. "What's for dinner?"

Stasia smiled up at me. "Yeah, what is for dinner Jack?"

Despite everything we had just talked about. The revelation that Stasia was more than just a nurse in the SEP project. The revelation that I was in love with her, and she had somehow, in the months since she'd moved here, wormed her way into my heart as securely as the rest of my family. Into all our hearts, really. I set it all aside.

I smiled back slyly. "I don't know Stasia, what are you cooking?" Her lips pursed back at me, and we all laughed as we got up and made our way to the kitchen.

# CHAPTER 29

## Stasia

Strong arms and Jack's earthy scent surrounded me. His arms tightened around me from behind and pulled me gently into the curve of his body. Despite my best efforts, I hadn't been able to get him to go further than third base. He had been gentle, insisting on waiting until I'd healed more. My toes curled, thinking about what would happen then.

As if reading my thoughts, I felt his lips on my neck, tracing up my jaw until they met my own. This was surreal. Just a couple days ago, I didn't think Jack would ever forgive me. It was weird. I had grown up with no one, and Jack and I had never made each other any promises. But even losing the possibility of him, of what was building between us, had felt devastating. I wasn't sure what changed his mind, but feeling his arms around me, waking up in his bed with his smell cocooning me, it just felt right.

"Good morning." Jack's voice was a little gruff. Flynn sat up at the sound, his growl letting loose to say good morning. He came to my side of the bed for a quick pet. I thought he had abandoned me for Lilly last night. He must have wandered in sometime while we were sleeping.

"Morning," I answered, rolling over to look at him. My ears felt a little better this morning. Sound was still slightly muffled, like I had cotton stuffed in them, but I heard his gentle rumble.

"How are you feeling? Any pain?" Jack's face was pinched with worry, and I moved my hand up his side to his back, drawing myself closer to him.

"I'm ok. I'll take some Tylenol in a bit. I already feel a lot better than that first day. My hearing is a little better too."

Jack leaned away from me. I instantly missed his warmth. Before I could object, he was back with a bottle of water and some pills. "I put them on the bedside. I figured you might need them when you woke up."

I smiled at his thoughtfulness and swallowed the Tylenol. Capping the water bottle, he took it from me and set it back on the bed stand.

"You're a very good nurse," I teased.

He smiled sinfully down at me. "You're a motivating patient."

Our legs twined together under the covers. Right as Jack lowered his head to mine, the bed dipped, and Flynn jumped on. Apparently annoyed at being ignored, he sniffed our faces with his wet nose, making me laugh and Jack groan. Satisfied, Flynn walked to the end of the bed. He shook the whole thing as he settled and rested his head on his front legs.

"On a more serious note," Jack brought my attention back to him, "how are you feeling about everything else? About finding out more about your dad, and Galton putting you in this program."

Cradling my right arm against me, I struggled to sit up. Jack was instantly there, helping me. "To be honest, I don't know yet. Everything happened so fast after Milo. They had me pretty drugged up in the infirmary. I guess I don't plan on participating in this parapsychic program he has going on."

Jack looked so worried. I wanted to lift my hand and smooth the wrinkles in his forehead. But this conversation was important, so I kept my hands to myself and waited. "Stasia." He hesitated to continue, his mouth open, but his words stalled.

"Go ahead," I encouraged, wondering what he was so scared to say.

Jack looked away from me for a moment, his jaw tight. "Are you sure you're going to have a choice? Don't get me wrong. I wish more than anything I could protect you from this. I wish you weren't involved in the SEP at all. But from my experience, if you have something they want, they don't let you go. And a few people with powers isn't enough to stop the might of the US government."

My forehead furrowed at that. "What do you mean a few people with powers isn't enough to stop the government?"

Jack stalled, playing with my fingers and smoothing his hand over my splint. I gave him time to collect his thoughts. I could feel his fear and anxiety. Now that I knew I wasn't just wishing for calm for the person I was near, but giving it to them, I tried to force some his way. He seemed to understand, or maybe even feel my efforts. The corners of his lips lifted, and he laced our fingers together.

"It was the Stepuli environmental initiative that started first. The Stepuli elders were okay with it. Our people apparently traveled the galaxies trying to help developing worlds. Our version of the Peace Corps. My grandparents, the first children born of Stepuli and humans, they were directionless. The communities were nice, but small. There was no room to grow. Not as a people, and not as an individual. The elders saw the initiative as a way to fix that."

"It does sound like it."

"Right. So, our people were okay with the environmental initiative. It was a voluntary program at first to help with natural disasters. We do the kind of stuff you saw with the hotshots. We also have teams that help in Antarctica, and there are some emergency response teams for things like typhoons. The children of the Stepuli who had been stranded settled down, and things seemed to get better. Right around then, my parents' generation started being born."

I nodded, encouraging him to go on. Jack shifted to get comfortable. He took his hand from mine and sat looking at his hands in his lap. "The humans started encouraging us to have our children in hospitals."

Jack got quiet for a while after that. Finally, I asked, "Why is that bad?"

He heaved a deep breath. "The Stepuli weren't young when they landed. They tried to impart their ways to their children. But when faced with the environmental initiative and relative freedom, it wasn't much of a competition. The government had a lot of influence over my grandparents' generation, and the original Stepuli were beginning to get too old to put up much of a fight. We were told a few of the first women who gave birth in their hospitals died."

I covered my mouth with my hand. "Oh, my God."

Jack shook his head and met my eyes. "That's not the horrible part. The horrible part is they didn't really die. Galton used them in his eugenics program. He wanted to create a fire. The only fire Stepuli who came with the original ambassadors never took a wife, and he had died. Scientists who studied us told us our elemental abilities were like eye color or blood type. We have dominant and recessive genes. Galton thought, with the right couplings, he could bring back fire Stepuli on Earth."

My eyes widened. "What happened when your people found out? Oh, my God, Jack, that's insane."

Jack's face was grim. "Galton succeeded, and when he did, it all came out. He claimed that the women had volunteered but asked that their participation be kept secret. The women had all conveniently died in childbirth, so the Stepuli couldn't ask them."

"So, what happened?" I prompted him

"When Galton revealed the fire, people were angry. Pressure started building then. I was young, but I remember as I grew up that the fire was off. He would get into strange moods. Things seemed to get better when he took a wife, but then they had a child. Shortly after, he killed himself. At that point, my dad and the other rebels who had been organizing had enough, and they fought back."

"Fought back how?"

"They tried to force their way out of the community. They were determined to tell the rest of the world about the Stepuli. As you can guess, they never made it. There was a showdown a little way outside the community. The government said it was a militant extremist group the local police had a shootout with. I was so mad. I was eighteen at the time, Brandon five. I obviously knew why my father kept him out of it, but I didn't know why he didn't ask me to help."

Horror filled me as I understood Jack's words from before. I echoed them. "Because a few people with powers weren't enough to stop the might of the government. Your dad wanted to keep you safe."

Jack hung his head. "After that, after everything died down, Galton started offering freedoms for people who participated in the eugenics program voluntarily. An addendum to the treaty was made. Mom was determined to get us the freedom dad died wanting us to have. She participated."

I stayed silent, scared of what was coming but also needing to know. He searched my eyes before saying his next words.

"Nine months later, Lilly was born. It turns out children born from the inseminations are harder on the mother. Mom didn't make it out of childbirth."

Deep sadness for Jack filled me. Horror at the audacity of the government spread through me. I wanted to say this wasn't possible. That things like this couldn't happen. But a quick reflection of history made me realize how naïve that was. If the government could force people indigenous to this land onto reservations, indoctrinate their children, and forcefully sterilize their women. If they could use minorities for syphilis studies, letting them endure painful symptoms and death in the interest of curiosity. Then was it really a far stretch to believe the government could commit these same kinds of atrocities against an alien people they had kept secret from the world?

"Jack. I don't even know what to say. I'm sorry isn't enough. Does Lilly know?"

Jack laid his head against the headboard and closed his eyes. "No. I don't know if I'll ever tell her. Right now, she's so young. She's already so confused about who she is. I keep her away from the Stepuli events, so she doesn't accidentally give herself away. And she has so much trouble at school making friends. I don't want another thing to make her feel like she doesn't know who she is."

The love I had already acknowledged for this thoughtful, selfless man bloomed. I thought about his original question. "You don't think Galton will give me a choice with whether or not to participate?"

Jack got out of bed and stretched. I followed his lead, moving a little more stiffly. He moved to my side of the bed to help me up. Flynn perked up at our motions. "If you have some kind of ability Galton has been trying to develop, no. I don't think he'll let you go."

We took turns using the restroom. When I came back out, Jack looked ready to go downstairs. Flynn was up, accepting some scratches from him. Jack's emotions were flat. He felt sad and hopeless after our conversation. I wanted to fix it for him, but I didn't know how.

Something struck me. I thought about the fact that Jack and his family had been able to stay out of the community when everyone else was called back. And that Jack was given an exemption from participating in missions despite Greg saying he had been one of the strongest earth elementals.

"Jack. Why don't you have to participate in the environmental initiative? How did you stay independent when all the other families had their freedom revoked?"

He straightened at my question, and the hopelessness in him yawned. I felt like I was in a freefall when I heard his next words. "Fire elementals aren't the only ones they're trying to create from the Stepuli left on earth. There's a type of elemental that were our leaders back on our planet. The government wants to unlock their abilities here, and I have a recessive gene for them."

I swallowed. "A recessive gene? What type of elemental? Are you saying…?"

Jack put his hand on my back, leading me toward the bedroom door. "The only way I could keep us free. Keep Lilly out of a lab. Was to agree to do what my mom did. Galton plans to use me to create a spirit elemental."

His words fell like an avalanche. He opened the door, and we walked down the stairs to the kitchen. Jack started coffee and breakfast. He set a steaming mug in front of me. As I sipped the caffeine, Lilly and Brandon wandered down, and I stared at the family around me. I wondered how they had grown up under this oppression. Wondered how they had grown into these people considering what they faced. Lilly's bright optimism. Brandon's sarcastic wit. Jack's bottomless nurturing. And inwardly, I swore, this wouldn't be their lives forever. I'd find a way to get them out.

# CHAPTER 30
## Stasia

I put my Jeep in park and stared up at the Stepul School. It was my first day back. Galton had called me yesterday asking me to come into work. It had been about a week since the accident. I had fallen into a surprisingly easy rhythm with Jack's family. It hadn't felt right to stay at his house, so I'd gone home after that first night with him.

I found myself back at his house every night for dinner. We'd spent a lot of time walking on the beach with Flynn, playing cards after dinner, and learning how to be in each other's space. It felt surreal how quickly our lives clicked together.

A rapping on my window made me jump. Pat stood near the window, shoulders slumped, but with a hopeful smile on his face. I waved, grabbed my coffee, and opened the door. I tentatively tried to reach out to see what he was feeling.

I normally didn't actively try to get a read on people, it was just something that happened for me. Ever since the deprivation exercise though, I'd been experimenting.

"Hey, Stasia." His voice was unsure, and while I felt the contriteness, I also felt an underlying resentment from him. Nervousness fluttered in my belly.

"Hey, Pat. Have enough coffee this morning?"

He laughed. "Never."

Some of the tension leaked from his shoulders, and we headed toward the front of the building. Part of me wanted to broach the topic of what had happened with the explosion and being in the infirmary. With Jack after. A larger part of me was happy to hide from it.

"So, are you excited for your first day back?" I knew he was trying to open with something easy, but the small talk felt painful. I had texted Pat to let him know I was coming in today. It seemed odd not to. Since I had moved to Washington and we'd become friends, we talked most days, even if it was about something mundane. I had handled his budding feelings for me badly, and I didn't want to lose our friendship completely.

"I am. I'm hoping to see Milo, and it's nice to get back into a routine. I'm not used to being infirm."

"I bet Jack was enjoying convalescing you," he said bitterly.

I winced. I guess this was it. "Pat..." I wasn't sure how to even broach this topic, but I knew I should say something. Luckily, Pat saved me.

"No. It's okay." He jerked the door open and hung his head, motioning for me to go ahead of him. As we walked through the main lobby, he said, "You don't owe me anything. And I was a jerk. I just, I don't know. I don't even know what I thought. But what are you thinking, Stasia? Getting involved with one of them."

I felt his revulsion, and something dark slid through

me. Anger. Disappointment. I turned to him, stopping our advance toward the main gym. "What do you mean by one of them? And I wondered if you even knew. You acted like he couldn't know what had really happened here."

Pat threw his hands up. "He's an independent Stepuli! He shouldn't know what happened here, it's none of his business. It's top secret! He's not even human, Stasia. Look at what that little fire kid did to you. You're going to get hurt!"

Pat's voice grew more intense as he went on. He wasn't louder exactly, but the amount of anger and conviction in it told me how much he meant every word. So did the emotions rolling off him. Pat had been my cornerstone. Him and Angela. It had been the first time I felt like I had a support network. But I couldn't differentiate his bigotry against Jack and the Stepuli any differently than I could if he was showing this kind of prejudice against anyone else.

I clenched my jaw, breathing through the anger. I concentrated on the gym door, unable to look at him. Exhaustion hit me hard as I came to a decision. "Pat, that's not how I feel. I don't think that's how anyone should feel. They're people just like—"

"That's just the thing Stasia." He stepped closer to me, his voice taking on an aggressive edge. I wasn't scared, but I was beginning to be done with this conversation. "They aren't people, are they? They're from another planet."

"Stasia? You, okay?" Brandon stood at the gym doors looking between me and Pat, his brow drawn down. Warmth helped crack the hard shell forming around me. I walked toward Brandon without bothering to look back at Pat.

"I'm great."

Brandon stood with the door open, waiting for me to go through. His eyes were hard over my shoulder. Pat's resentment grew at my back, but I ignored it. I accepted I probably just lost my best friend.

Pat had made me feel welcome when I first came to Washington, made this feel like home. But I knew even if I wasn't involved with Jack and his family, I wouldn't accept this level of hatred for someone just because they were different. Just because they didn't fit the mold Pat expected them to. And realizing how he found Stepuli, inferior, somehow. It helped put into perspective how easy it had become for the government to exploit the Stepuli people in the first place. They didn't see them as people.

Brandon and I walked toward the water side of the gym. The older class was already setting up for their exercises. A nurse sat at the medical station there. The medical station at the air class was filled as well.

"Everything okay with Pat?"

I looked over at Brandon. He was watching me with concern. I shrugged. "It'll be fine. I'm not sure where I'm reporting to. Galton told me to come into the gym, I assumed I'd be at one of these stations."

Right as he was about to say something, we heard my name called. Galton stood on the catwalk, his grandfatherly smile that made my skin crawl was in place.

"See you later," I muttered, not wanting to bring too much attention to Brandon. I headed to the stairs, trying to walk confidently, but feeling nervous as I thought over my conversation with Jack. Galton wouldn't give me a choice. He wouldn't let me go.

I swallowed as I neared Galton. He felt determined. I clenched my fist discreetly, sure that couldn't be a good sign. When I reached him, he brought his arm behind my back, making me tense. Galton ignored it and guided me into his office.

"Stasia, how are you feeling? You look much better." My bruises were healing, and the stiffness was all but gone. Even my ears felt much better, my hearing almost normal.

"I feel much better, thank you Dr. Galton. You asked me to report to the gym today?" I wasn't interested in having a long-winded conversation. I wanted him to get to the point.

He got the hint because his smile took on an annoyed edge, and he walked around his desk to his chair. I took one of the seats in front of him.

"That's good news. Yes, I wanted you to come in today so we could talk about steps forward with you in the human ESP program."

My gut clenched. This was it. Jack and I had a lot of long conversations while I was recovering after that first morning about the governments compulsory testing. Both in relation to him and his family and the possibility of what Galton would ask of me. We hadn't really come to any conclusions. Jack's solution was to commit more of himself, if he had to, to the SEP to give me as many freedoms as he could. I wasn't going to let that happen.

I tried to play dumb at first. "Oh, I see! I thought you needed me to return to work. I appreciate your offer, Dr. Galton, but I'm not interested in participating in the ESP program."

He smiled like I'd said something funny. "Your parapsychic skills are extraordinary. I suspect you can do even more than we realized in your last session. We can't let that go to waste." The knots in my stomach tightened.

*He doesn't know,* I told myself. He couldn't know.

"I appreciate that vote of confidence. But it isn't an area I'm interested in exploring. The deprivation testing after the accident was upsetting, and I don't see how being intuitive to those around me could make a difference in more of a way than they already do, as a nurse."

I tried to go with firm. I was a United States citizen. I wasn't a hidden Stepuli that the American public didn't know about. He couldn't force me into this. I pinched my thumbnail into my first finger and waited.

Galton stood and walked around the space behind his desk. He looked at the pictures on the wall behind his chair, moving one arm to his hip. I followed his gaze. There was his PhD in biochemistry hanging proudly. And a photo I had never noticed before with him and Dr. Kimi. There were a couple other people in the picture, looking years younger. I swallowed when I recognized one of the faces as Diane Cutler, the imperious woman from the deprivation testing. Galton's words broke me out of my study of the picture.

"Stasia. You see, you have a skill that not only not many have, but that is uniquely useful to both your country and the SEP. As more than a nurse. I think it is in your best interest, and the interest of your country, to develop it, don't you?"

The determination I felt from him was laced with annoyance. *He can't force you,* I reminded myself.

"I appreciate your faith in me, Dr. Galton. I'm simply not comfortable doing the medical testing. Between the hallucinogenic drugs, and the hours of deprivation testing, I'm not comfortable with it. I'd like to continue as a nurse. As I have been."

Galton sighed. He dropped his arm from his hip and shook his head as he sat again. Meeting my eyes, he said, "You know, I got into eugenics inspired by my grandfather. He believed in bringing out the best in the human race. Our leaders agreed with him then. It was a long time before we could convince modern administrations of the merit. I hoped you would see the potential in these studies. I'm sorry to hear you don't."

For a moment, the knots eased. I took my first deep breath. I knew it. I knew he couldn't force me. As I opened my mouth to apologize, thank him, and ask what the next steps were, Galton went on. There was something in his eyes, a calculation.

"You've grown close to the Walker family, haven't you?"

His words knocked the wind out of me. Knowing Jack's story, I could already guess where he was going with this.

"Yes. They're my neighbors."

"I think we both know they're more than that."

"We're friends." I swallowed. My heartbeat picked up.

"I once asked you about Lilly's abilities, but you said she didn't have any."

"That's right."

Satisfaction came from Galton before he said his next words. And already, I knew Jack had been right that morning.

"Footage at Lilly's school shows her exhibiting elemental powers. A very rare and dangerous elemental power. Right before you stepped in and rushed her out."

Any pretense I had any rights here was gone. I was strung so tight my muscles began to ache. "What do you want?"

For the first time, I think I saw one of Dr. Galton's genuine smiles. "Your full participation in the parapsychic testing. Whatever is required of you. And an accurate portrayal of your experiences."

"What do I get in exchange?" I needed to tell Jack that Galton knew about Lilly. I had wanted to find a way to expose this government corruption, the horrible things they were doing to his people. I wanted not just freedom for his family, but for all the Stepuli. But now all I cared about was making sure Lilly was somewhere safe and out of the reach of this grandfatherly-looking sociopath's grimy hands.

"You get Lilly. Kept at home. For now."

"For good."

Galton stood. "You don't have any cards to play, Stasia. I'll expect you to report to headquarters in the next couple hours. Cora is there waiting with Dr. Kimi to begin your training." Part of me felt a spark of hope at Kimi's name. She had shown the most humanity toward Stepuli. There was no hiding she cared about the kids she interacted with.

"I have rights. I'm a US citizen. You can't force me to participate in medical testing if I don't want to."

Galton's expression didn't change. Neither did the satisfaction and victory, I realized, that I felt coming from him.

"You have rights." He looked toward his door. Toward the gym. "But they don't. I have agents at Lilly's school right now. They'll take her if you don't agree."

Pressure built at the back of my eyes. A weight like an elephant sat on my chest. This was how Jack must feel all the time, I realized. I stared at Galton with more hate than

I'd directed at someone ever before. It only seemed to make his smile wider. "I'll go. I'll go report to headquarters."

He nodded, like he'd always expected that to be the answer. "Good."

I turned for the door, but as my hand reached for the handle, he said, "Oh, and Stasia?"

I stopped, not wanting to turn around. "Don't forget, a full accounting of what happens in the pod. You see, it seems you held something back last time." My shoulders tensed. How could he know that? "We've found, over time, certain abilities create certain patterns on your EEG. Even through the less sensitive temporal probes that you wear in the pod, yours were off the charts. Something we never could have expected, and something you express more powerfully than any before you."

I turned back to him. I wondered if he was fishing. I stayed silent, waiting. "Even better than what we hoped for. You expressed precognition. You're exactly what we've been looking for. See you at headquarters, Anastasia."

I didn't bother to answer. I walked out. Jack had been right. A few people with powers weren't enough to stop the might of the US government.

# CHAPTER 31
## Stasia

I tried calling Jack before leaving for headquarters, but he wasn't picking up. Since all pretenses were gone, I stopped and told Brandon he needed to go pick up Lilly and take her home. Realizing something was wrong, Brandon hadn't wanted to let me leave, but I believed Galton when he said if I didn't go to headquarters, he'd have Lilly taken right then and there. I told Brandon I'd explain later.

I walked into the dimly lit building, the windowless inside like a cave. The security guard at the desk to the right looked up as my steps echoed through the hall. I didn't recognize him. He wasn't the guard who'd checked me in last time I was here. Before I reached his desk to check in, someone called my name.

"Stasia." Dr. Kimi was waiting for me, her hands tucked in the pockets of her lab coat. Her shoulders were stiff. She seemed as poised and distant as the first day I'd met her. Anger mixed with nervousness when I remembered her leaving me with Galton and Cora. At Dr. Kimi's entrance, the guard turned away from me, dismissing me. I turned direction and went to meet her.

Dr. Kimi had always seemed so earnest about the Stepuli. She was amazing with the children and militant about their care. At times she'd been disappointed or angry if she didn't think someone was taking their job seriously enough. I thought of Galton's picture behind his desk. He had fooled me at first too.

As I neared Dr. Kimi, I reached out and tried to get a sense of her feelings. Searching for people's emotions instead of just letting them come to me was becoming second nature. Shock ran through me when I realized terror was rolling off Dr. Kimi. Her face was a mask of bored professionalism.

She gestured to me sharply and walked toward the elevators. She continued past them to a corner door I hadn't noticed before and took me down the stairs to the basement level. When we were about halfway down the stairwell, she stopped. Dr. Kimi looked up and down furtively, her mask falling to reveal the tension I felt pouring off her.

"We only have a few seconds before this gets suspicious. I need you to listen." Confusion warred with the nervousness I had already been feeling, but I just nodded. "I've been working with Galton for a long time. We were PhD candidates together. We were tapped at the same time by Dr. Cutler to join the SEP."

Suspicion threaded with my other emotions, which combined with hers and began to overwhelm me, making me irritable. "Yeah. I saw your picture on his wall."

Dr. Kimi's eyes tightened. "It was an amazing program, Stasia. We were helping an alien people find their place on Earth and making so many strides in human technology and medical testing. It was exciting and so rewarding. At first."

"They're your prisoners. You keep children in labs and force people to let you run tests on their bodies against their wills. You force them to have children. Pregnancies that kill them."

Tears tracked down Kimi's cheeks. She wiped them away like an afterthought. "I know, but that's not how it always was. When I began to see what the SEP was turning into, I knew I had to do something. I've been working to get people out when I can."

"Why are you telling me this?"

Kimi looked up and down the stairwell again. Her voice took on a sense of urgency. "Galton plans to use you to create a spirit Stepuli. He's been trying for decades. Since his initial success with the fire Stepuli. You have certain DNA factors. It has to do with your ESP abilities."

Fear laced through me. I needed to get to Jack. "What do you mean you get people out when you can?"

"I have a network through some of the reservations. But we need to do this soon. Tonight."

"I need to talk to Jack. Explain what's happening—"

She shook her head. "The Walker family is safe for now. This isn't easy, Stasia, Galton watches everything. I can only get you out."

Horror spread through me. A couple things clicked. One was that Galton planned to put me in a breeding program with Jack. The second was while Kimi was offering to get me out, she was going to leave Jack and his family to keep being used. Probably in even worse ways if I suddenly disappeared.

Kimi started walking down the stairs, continuing toward the basement level. I hadn't moved. "I'm not leaving without Jack and his family."

Kimi stopped, frowned up at me. "Stasia, that isn't possible. It isn't possible to get that many people out at once."

I realized something then. No matter what I would face if I had to stay, I wouldn't leave without Jack and the others.

"I'm not leaving without them," I repeated firmly, walking down so I was on the same level as the doctor.

We stared at each other for a minute. "If I make arrangements to get you all out, I can't promise you'll make it. This many people have never left at once."

"I understand."

She gave me a searching look. "Okay."

Kimi walked the rest of the way to the door leading to the waiting deprivation pods. I readied myself to walk behind her, into testing I didn't want to do, because I and those I loved were being threatened if I didn't cooperate. I needed to find a way to tell people about this. I needed to find a way to tell the world what the SEP was hiding. Who they were hiding.

\*\*\*

I stepped into the gym ready to submit to whatever testing Galton asked of me. Whether it was embarrassing or taxing. Even if it hurt, I wouldn't complain. I'd get through this day, and I'd get back to Jack. I'd tell him all that had happened with Galton and Kimi, and we would escape. Together.

That resolve crumbled as we walked into a door-lined hallway with gray carpet. Pat stood next to one of them up ahead.

"What are you doing here?" I asked as we drew closer. I looked to Kimi when I felt her discomfort.

"I'm going to be the sender in today's experiment."

My brow wrinkled. "You know what's happening here?"

Kimi cleared her throat. "Pat is one of our handlers. He's in a division of the CIA that works with the SEP. He helps find subjects who may be valuable to the human ESP side of the project and brings them in."

The ground opened underneath me. My mouth hung open in disbelief as I looked at Pat. He was shooting daggers at Kimi. She just stood, her aloof mask back in place.

Taking in my expression, his annoyed look turned to a pensive one. "Stasia, listen. I was assigned but—"

I held a hand up, cutting off his words. What a cliché. "Don't say anything. I don't even care."

Pat's brow drew down. "That's not true. Stasia, I care about you."

I felt exhausted. I had already started emotionally distancing myself from Pat after our confrontation earlier today when he'd said those things about Jack and his family. About the Stepuli. Suddenly, his beliefs made more sense.

I looked back at him. "Is Angela a part of this?"

He swallowed. "Don't make me lie to you."

I nodded. My last attachment to this place, or at least to the humans in this place, leaked out of me. "Got it."

"Stasia."

I held my hand up again. I turned to Dr. Kimi, who watched me curiously. "How about we go over what my job is today, Kimi."

She smiled. "You got it."

We went through several exercises where I would sit in a room by myself, Pat in an adjacent room. They wanted to use someone I was familiar with for a baseline. He would send me emotions someone in the room with him would help elicit. I was supposed to identify those emotions within a set time.

We went through that for hours. I had a seventy-five percent success rate, which was unheard of. My apparent success made me sick.

Next was more pod testing. I changed into my suit and met everyone at the pool. The pod I was to use already sat at the pool edge, top open, waiting. I sat in the shallow pool, nervousness turning in my gut. I didn't want the hallucinogenic drugs again. I didn't even really know what they consisted of, and I didn't trust Cora, who jammed the needle in my arm like this was a bad sci-fi movie.

I laid back in the pool, letting the water buoy me. Cora moved toward me with that sick excitement she shared with Galton floating around her. Sure enough, a prick in my arm told me she was injecting the drugs. As the colors from last time began to swirl, I closed my eyes. Before the darkness closed in, and I felt truly suspended and alone, I felt another prick in my thigh. Before I could question it, the colors enveloped me, blackness pressing around my periphery, and I was lost.

*** 

Much to my relief, and everyone else's disappointment, I hadn't had any precognitive visions this time, only colors swirling around me. Like last time, I had lined everything in blue, the calmness and order helping me float in the turmoil of so many chaotic shades.

I threw my car in park after pulling into my driveway

and looked between Jack's yard and mine. Flynn ran toward me, and the sight helped the tight ball of worry in my middle loosen, just a little. Lilly's red hair came flying after him. They tumbled to the grass, Flynn's back end sliding out from under him as he tried to pivot. He was five years old and still didn't know how to handle his large size. The mundane thought teased out a smile.

I stepped out of the car just as Jack's front door opened. He came toward me, his face grim. I looked past him to his cottage garden, one of the most beautiful I'd ever seen. Against a backdrop of lady's mantle were golden hops, interspersed with bell flowers and winter hazel. He had worked in the yard a couple times while I recovered from the explosion. It had been soothing to see him on his knees, his hands in the dirt, serenity on his face.

I hated that I was about to ruin all of that. I hated that what I was about to tell him would probably take him from this garden forever.

He stepped to me, his hand going up to the nape of my neck. Brandon would have gotten a hold of him as soon as I left the Stepul School. My phone had several missed calls and texts when I left headquarters, but I had waited to talk to him in person. I started to say something when he dipped his head, kissing me soundly.

Instead of stopping him, my hands went to his shoulders, and I lifted up on my toes, kissing him back. His other hand tightened on my hip before he pulled back. I felt his regret as he looked between the yards toward where Lilly ran off.

"She's going to shoot us with embers if we keep letting her catch us making out."

I smiled at his attempt at levity. "We need to talk."

"I know."

"Let's go to my house?"

He nodded and followed me when I started toward my house. To tell him about Galton's ultimatum. About Kimi's warning. And about the fact that we needed to get out. With her help or without it, we needed to run.

# CHAPTER 32

## Jack

A low simmer of worry wormed through me. The first day Stasia had gotten back from the Stepul School and the deprivation testing, things had been heavy. They only got more intense that next morning when everything had come out of me. About my dad, about what I had agreed to do for Lilly to be free. But since that day, we'd fallen into a steady rhythm. Things had begun to feel normal.

We walked into the kitchen and sat down at her kitchen island. "Brandon told me Galton brought you into his office and said something. That you said he should get Lilly home right away. What happened?"

She took a deep breath. "Jack. Have you ever thought about just leaving?"

The question surprised me. We had talked about the looming threat of Galton and the government a couple times over the last week. Stasia had been sure she'd be able to refuse being a part of the parapsychic program. I hadn't been so sure, but I didn't want to scare her. Galton must have said something to her today in his office. Brandon had said she'd looked spooked but wouldn't tell him more. Worry went through me. I wondered if the reality of being a subject of the SEP instead of a nurse was finally hitting her.

"The last time a group of Stepuli tried, they were killed." I tried to keep anger out of my tone as I thought of my dad. It was mostly for him, not her. I was still mad that he hadn't come to me, hadn't asked me to help. Still mad he was gone.

Stasia nodded and looked away from me for a minute. I shifted in my seat, waiting. "It might be time to risk it."

My shoulders stiffened. "Stasia, listen. I know you mean well, but—"

"Galton threatened me today." That shut me up. I closed my mouth, waiting to hear the rest. "He knows about Lilly. I don't know how, but he knows she's a fire. He said there's footage of us that day at her school. He said if I didn't participate in parapsychic testing, he would take her. He had agents outside of her school today."

Fear punched through me. I stood, the sound of the chair against the tile jarring. I paced, the emotions running through me compelling me to move, to do something. Stasia continued.

"That's not the worst of it, Jack."

I took a deep breath and studied her face. It was set in grim lines. She watched me but gave me space. I let out a long breath and sat back down next to her.

"What do you mean that's not the worst of it?"

"Kimi Alver took me aside in a stairwell today. Galton threatened Lilly to get me to report to what he calls headquarters, where they conduct the human ESP testing.

When I got there, she stopped me where we wouldn't be overheard and told me Galton plans to use me in a eugenics program. To create a spirit Stepuli."

All the anger and fear punched out of me, leaving only shock. I didn't know how much time passed, but eventually I realized Stasia was staring at me, waiting for me to process her words. As I did, fear like I'd never known swept through me. Stasia was the faceless woman Galton planned to inseminate, whose life he planned to risk trying to create a spirit Stepuli.

"You said it was time to risk it?" Maybe she was right.

She nodded. "Kimi…I don't know how much we can trust her. But she said that the SEP used to be something she believed in. That it had changed over the years, and she's been trying to get those in the most danger out. She offered to get us out."

"Just like that?" Suspicion blossomed. Nobody was that selfless, not when faced with what Galton would do to you if caught.

Stasia swallowed. "Not at first. At first, she said she could only get me out. I refused to go without you, Brandon, and Lilly too."

"And she just agreed?" Stasia wasn't telling me something. I waited as she shifted her eyes, not meeting mine now.

She heaved a sigh before admitting, "She said that this many people have never left at once before. That she couldn't guarantee it would work."

I sat back. Fear and worry ran through me. I tried to work through everything. Stasia was right, it was time to risk it. I thought of what had happened to my dad. But he had been trying to make a point. He had been loud about his intentions, and they hadn't been to go quietly in the night. No matter what, I couldn't let Galton do what he wanted to Stasia. Most pregnancies of inseminated females resulted in the mother's death. And that was Stepuli females. I had no idea what a pregnancy would be like for a human, or even why he thought Stasia was a match.

"What if we listened to her? If you went first?" I had to at least get Stasia out. I wouldn't watch her die because of me. I wouldn't watch a child that we didn't even get to create together be ripped from us.

Stasia shook her head, her jaw set in stubborn lines. "No. I'm not leaving without all of you. If I left, and even one of you were left behind, Galton would take you instantly to get me to come back."

Stasia laid a hand on my arm, and I felt calm quiet the turbulent emotions warring in me. "It would work. I'd just come right back. I'm not leaving without you guys."

I looked down at her. The calm set aside my emotions enough for me to feel the love, the affection. Stasia was a nurturer. I had never felt like I could have a relationship with a human because they could never know me, and I had never met a Stepuli woman I felt could be my equal.

But Stasia did know me. And she was more than my equal. She was stronger than any person or Stepuli I'd ever met. After years of feeling like I had to be the bedrock of my family, having nobody to lean on, I had become exhausted. I felt like a tree that bowed to the wind, the constant pressure bending me to its will. I protected those under me, but I had felt like I could never stand straight again. Until she came along.

"So, Alver said she'd try to get us all out?"

"She said that it was riskier than sending one person, but that she'd set it up."

"So, we risk it," I said.

She nodded back to me.

"We risk it."

\*\*\*

Ian stood across from me, looking up at my bulletin board of pictures. "This seems a bit drastic Jack."

I looked down at the papers. I had printed a durable power of attorney form off a website. I had no idea if it would hold up in court, but I didn't know how much time we had.

"Listen, I'm planning on taking an extended vacation, and you're the only one I trust with this. You'll have full management of the bar, and you can have fifty percent of the profits while I'm gone. When I get back, we can talk about making you a full partner."

I had built this bar from the ground up. I didn't have time to dissolve everything and get the money before we left. I wouldn't be able to anyway since that would tip off Galton. But I couldn't just leave it to crumble.

Ian leaned against the desk next to me, his mouth turned down, his sardonic wit absent. "Are you in trouble Jack?"

I trusted Ian more than I trusted most people. Before Stasia, he was the only human I would have trusted with anything even remotely personal. But this wasn't something I could talk to him about. "Do you want it or not?"

He stared at me a moment longer. "Let's head to the bank. This needs a notary."

Relief filled me. I looked down at the paperwork. Damn, he was right. "Okay. Thanks Ian."

His face was suspicious, his jaw hard, but he jerked his

head in a nod. We headed out of the office. It was Wednesday, and the bar was busy. Nadine stood behind the live oak. She hadn't really been talking to me since the incident with Stasia. We'd both been avoiding the other. As Ian and I headed toward the front door, she surprised me by calling out my name.

"Jack!"

I looked back. Nadine patted her hands on her pants and looked around. Nobody was at the bar asking for a drink. She hooked her thumb to the hallway. I looked back at Ian. He shrugged.

"I'll meet you at the bank."

"Okay, see you in a minute."

I turned back. Nadine walked ahead of me to the hallway.

"What's up?" I tried to keep impatience out of my voice. I hadn't been fair to Nadine.

"So, I guess you ended up having space to give someone something?"

I grimaced. She got right into it, calling out my lame excuse when I had backpedaled after our kiss. "Nadine."

She shook her head, waving her hand at me. "Were you seeing her when we…when that happened in the bar?" There was a tenseness to her voice. An anger. I felt guilty, but I hadn't made any promises to Nadine. She had been the one coming on to me that night.

"No," I said, unable to completely keep the impatience out of my voice now.

She pursed her lips at me. "Is it serious?"

I took in her face. We'd had a fling a couple times over the years when she stopped in from her travels. She often came back to work at the bar, but I figured she just liked the flexibility that being a bartender offered, able to take off on her next overseas adventure whenever she wanted. I thought about her question.

Fleeing for our lives and clandestine government conspiracies aside, I stopped and really thought about her question. About my feelings for Stasia. I wondered what it would be like if we didn't have this insane situation hanging over our heads, if she would be as drawn to me, or if the danger, the excitement, was part of it.

I remembered our nights when everything first started. Flirting with each other over spades. Her warm smile when she offered to pick up Lilly. If there wasn't the threat of a eugenics program over our heads, if I hadn't thought Stasia was someone undercover trying to hurt my family, we'd probably be even closer by now. I'd have wanted her at my house every night. In my bed.

"Yes, Nadine. It's serious."

Instead of the reproach I'd expected, there was sadness. She coughed, looked away for a minute. "I think I should give you my two weeks, Jack." She stared at the floor, the wall, anywhere but into my eyes.

"I understand. But I'm going away for a while. Ian is taking over the bar. Think about it, and if you want to leave, you can do it whenever you feel you need to. Tomorrow or a month from now. But if you want to stay, I won't be around."

She looked at me then, the shimmer of unshed tears in her eyes. Nadine straightened her shoulders and gave me a tight smile. "Thanks. Better get back to work." With that, she walked past me.

I took a deep breath and turned. I said goodbye to a few people who called out to me as I worked my way to the door of Walker's Place. I looked over my shoulder one last time before I walked through the front door.

Nadine was back behind the bar already shaking up some cocktail. Her smile might not have been the wide playful one, but it was still there. She spoke to a customer who eyed her appreciatively. A few of the regulars laughed at one end of the bar.

I swallowed, realizing I was saying goodbye to this forever. I gave it a moment to appreciate it, and then pushed through the door. Into my future.

# CHAPTER 33
## Stasia

Jack walked in just as the sun was fully setting. I was in the kitchen packing up some nonperishables for the road. We were going to take both vehicles for now. If we needed, we could always sell one on the fly for extra cash. I had contacted Kimi and was waiting for her to call me back. She had given me a name and the reservation where a person would be waiting for us.

Lilly and Brandon were upstairs packing their clothes. Used to having to pack out quickly from my days in foster care, and then later in the military, my go bag already sat by the front door. As Jack walked toward me, the familiar worry coursed through me.

His emotions had been all over the place earlier. I had felt anger toward me, but then worry and guilt. Part of me wondered what was going on inside his head. I wanted to fix it for him, but I didn't understand the kaleidoscope of feelings he was turning through. As he reached me, sureness suffused him, and his confident arms wound around my back. His hand found the nape of my neck, under my hair the way I loved.

"Hey."

"Hey," I answered, stepping back so I could get a look at him.

He looked down at me, his face serious. "How are you doing?"

I looked around the kitchen trying to see what I could be forgetting. "I'm okay, I think I have things mostly packed. I—"

"Stasia. How are you doing?"

I looked up at him and swallowed. "I feel horrible. I feel horrible I'm putting your family in danger. You're in danger if I stay, or if we go."

Jack smiled a little crookedly. "You're putting us in danger?"

I wrinkled my brow at him making light of my words. "Yes. Galton wants me for this eugenics thing, and he'll take Lilly if I don't cooperate. If I leave on my own, he'll take her. I just…"

Jack laughed. All I could feel from him was this odd sort of glowing, but his laughter hurt. "What?" I felt myself getting defensive.

His face softened. "Stasia, all of this is because of the government. Of their depravity and corruption. And because an alien species landed on your planet and went along with their plan thinking they'd live out their lives in peace. None of this is your fault."

I relaxed at his words. "Your family was doing fine before I came along."

His amusement cleared. "We were existing before you came along. I love you, Stasia. None of this is your fault, and you've brought nothing but happiness into our lives." Jack's mouth quirked. "When I wasn't being an idiot, of course."

I smiled up at him as I realized what that glowing was. It was his love for me. "I love you too, Jack."

Warmth spread through me, and I stepped closer. Jack's back hit up against the counter, and our legs tangled together. My body fit flush to his, and I felt his need. I felt it just as strong. I ran my hand up his chest to his neck, ready to reach up and kiss him. My phone interrupted us.

Centimeters from his mouth, I whispered, "Dammit."

He huffed a laugh, but I felt his aggravation. We were always being interrupted. I grabbed the phone, expecting to see Kimi's name. Instead, Galton's flashed across the screen. Alarm shot through me. Looking at Jack, I hit the button to pick up the call.

"Stasia speaking."

"Stasia, this is Dr. Galton."

"Yes?"

"There were some problems with your testing earlier today. I need you to come back in so we can sort them out."

My eyebrows lowered. This was my first real day of parapsychic testing, so I didn't know how regular this was.

"Can't this wait until the morning, Dr. Galton? I'm very tired."

His disappointed sigh grated against my nerves. "Stasia. I thought I made it clear in my office today. Your full cooperation with this program is what guarantees Lilly Walker's freedom. Any deviation will result in her immediate detainment."

Anger burned in my gut, but it was one night. A handful of hours. No matter what he wanted from me, I could keep him happy tonight, and we would be gone by morning. I couldn't risk him making good on his threat, trying to take Lilly, removing any kind of head start we would have. Jack shook his head, worry pinching his expression. I held up my hand. "I'm on my way."

I heard the satisfaction in Galton's voice. "Good. I'll see you soon."

We hung up the phone. Jack placed his hand on the kitchen island, leaning on it heavily. "What was that about?"

"Some problem with the testing earlier today. He needs me to go by headquarters for a couple of hours."

Jack shook his head again. "No, Stasia, this doesn't sound right. Let's just go."

My mouth twisted. "Jack, we need a bit of a head start. If we just leave suddenly like this, they could put out a BOLO instantly. We won't make it across state lines."

Jack reached his hand out and cradled my face. I leaned into it, a smile pulling at my lips. I kissed his palm and looked up at him. "I'll be back soon, and we'll go. Go ahead and get everything ready. All of Flynn's and my stuff is at the door."

He nodded, his jaw hard. His worry was so strong it was like a live thing between us. He walked with me to the door, pulling me around right before I stepped over the threshold. Cradling the back of my head, he kissed me deeply. "I'll see you soon. I love you, Stasia."

I smiled into his beautiful warm brown eyes. "I love you too, Jack."

*** 

I pulled into the parking lot. A light had been left on outside the steel door leading into the headquarters lobby. An odd sort of trepidation sat in my gut. I chalked it up to the fact that I was ready to be on the road, putting distance between me and this place. I was ready to get Jack's family and myself away from the SEP. I walked quickly across the parking lot. The chill seeped through my sweater.

Stepping inside the door, I looked up. Surprise and terror froze me. My eyes widened. Christopher Shaw stood in front of me with a wicked smile. In front of him stood a grim Kimi Alver. Shaw had a gun to her head.

My eyes caught on the scene, but steps coming from the elevator bank pulled my attention. Cora and Galton walked from that direction.

"Ahh, Stasia, glad you could join us."

"What's going on here?"

"Well. It would seem that our dear friend Kimi, one of the founding members of the SEP environmental initiative, is shockingly betraying us." He twisted the word shockingly in a mocking tone.

Kimi didn't react, she just looked at me steadfastly. Fear turned in me. I went over our interactions at headquarters earlier, but I couldn't pinpoint a time when we had given ourselves away.

"What are you talking about?" I decided to play dumb until I knew what Galton thought he knew.

Galton's mouth twisted, and he looked at me condescendingly as he drew closer. Cora stood beside him, her badly-dyed hair shining under the fluorescent lights. That odd excitement coming off her churned my stomach.

"You didn't think we didn't have eyes on you, did you?"

I swung around at that. Eyes on us?

"You represent billions of dollars. The opportunity to indefinitely ensure national security. An edge on other nations that they could never have access to. You don't think we'd just leave all that to chance, do you?"

Galton's condescending tone grated on my nerves. "You tap our phones?" *Please, God, let that be it.* His smile curled evilly. That wasn't it.

"We've been listening and watching everything since you stepped foot in Washington, Anastasia. There are agents converging on Jack's house as we speak to take them into custody. Your little plan to escape. The fact that all those missing Stepuli over the years were a product of Dr. Kimi Alver's deception. We heard it all."

I looked at Kimi, regret in my eyes. She gave me a small smile. "You couldn't have known. I didn't even know." It was the last thing she ever said. I wasn't close enough to feel the spray, but the sound of the gunshot in close quarters pounded against my still-healing ears.

I looked at her prone form on the ground, a deep pool of red seeping out around her, brain matter on the floor in front of her. Everything moved in slow motion. I looked up at Shaw's gleeful expression, the sidearm hanging at his side.

My breath came quicker. I had no idea what to do. I prayed Jack got his family out at least. Shaw walked around Kimi's form toward me. Roughly, he grabbed my arm and pushed me forward, toward Galton and Cora. We all headed to the elevator bank.

Galton spoke as he pushed the button to take us down. "This time, it's going to work. We are going to create something special." I recognized the words from the dream I'd had when I first came to Washington. Bile rose in my throat.

# CHAPTER 34

## Jack

The trees thrashed all night due to my turbulent emotions. But a sudden increase in the violence felt out of place to me. I stopped packing the last few things in my bag and felt the earth around my house.

It was how I felt Stasia coming home that day after the explosion. It was how I felt secure letting Lilly wander around the property. And it was how I realized a large group of people were moving toward our house that shouldn't be.

"Brandon, Lilly!" I called sharply. A crescendo of feet crashed down the stairs at my alarmed tone. My brother and sister and Flynn skidded around the steps, and I met them coming down the hall from the kitchen.

"What?" Brandon barked, panic on his face. Both had been on edge since I'd caught them up with what was going on with Stasia and the SEP. I put a finger to my lips.

Flynn howled next to us, and three voices shushed him. He grumbled and sat, confused by the tenseness. "People are surrounding the house."

Lilly looked fearfully toward the front door. She sank her hand into Flynn's mane then grabbed his halter near the front door and quickly put it on. I knew Brandon well enough to detect fear in the tenseness of his eyes, but his voice was even when he asked, "What do we do?"

I didn't know. Goddamn it I didn't know. Fear beat at me. If the house was surrounded, that meant Stasia was probably walking into a trap. Knowing what Galton's ultimate plan for her was, fear thrummed through me. What if he had somehow found out what we'd planned?

I felt the bodies converging up the street and at the tree line from the water. "Get as many of our packed things as you can carry in one go. We're going to make a break for the Tahoe." I looked down at Lilly. "You stay in front of us. Do you understand me? You dive in that car as fast as you can. If one of us gets left behind, or if both of us get taken, then you throw fire and start running. Keep running."

Lilly's lips trembled, but she nodded. We had always lived under a cloud of uncertainty, but it had always been distant. The normality of the day to day had lulled us into a false sense of security. Brandon and Lilly did as I said, and in less than a minute, we were all poised at the door.

Flynn's nose pointed toward the door, the hair on the back of his neck and back stood up. He might not understand what was happening, but he knew something was wrong.

Lilly had the car keys in her hand along with some bags. Brandon had two circles of water rotating around his hands. He had turned all the faucets in the house on while I had been talking to Lilly. My mind sank into the soil under the men nearing the back door. I started turning the earth under their feet.

At the cry of alarm at the back door, we readied

ourselves to run. The steps of those at the front picked up, and with one push that made me feel like I had taken a quick sprint, I opened the ground beneath them. Brandon, Lilly, and I rushed out the door. Flynn lurched forward to run with us.

Outside, the world around us exploded into shouts of alarm and anger. "Stop!" they yelled. Men in black clothing rounded the house and ran toward us. Lilly was almost to the truck when someone roughly grabbed her arm. I shouted in alarm.

Brandon had been focused on the men still mobile in the front yard. He looked around at my shout, ready to redirect the spigot of water he was knocking people off their feet with. Flynn gave a rare bark and jumped on the man grabbing Lilly. The hundred-and-fifty-pound wolf dog slammed into the man, launching him off his feet and away from Lilly.

The man yelled and tried to roll Flynn off him. He grabbed a gun from his side and pointed it at Flynn. Before he could pull the trigger, Lilly, face streaked in tears, screamed, "No!"

She threw her hands out. Fire streamed from them, catching on the man's pant leg. The fire spread faster than was natural up the man's body, intensifying his screams. Flynn jumped off him, circling back around to stand by Lilly. The man continued screaming, rolling, trying to put out the flames.

I made the ground quake outside the circle that Brandon and Lilly and I stood in, dropping those running toward us for a minute. "Get in the truck!" I screamed, running again. Lilly was already there. She dove into the back seat, Flynn jumped in right behind her. Brandon slammed the door shut on them, and then folded himself into the passenger seat. I threw the keys in the ignition and hit the gas. The smell of burning rubber filled the inside of the truck as we sped away. Shouts of pain and anger followed us down the road.

***

"Damn it!" I screamed for a second time, slapping the dashboard. Lilly sat behind me, silent and still. It was unnerving, so different from her natural state. I checked on her in the rearview mirror. She sat looking forward, Flynn's head on her lap. I didn't have time to dwell on my worry. Brandon's words broke into my thoughts.

"Do you know where the headquarters are?"

"Yeah, Stasia told me."

"We need to go get her."

I chewed on my lip. I agreed that I needed to go get her. But it was probably another trap. "You drop me off at the edge of the parking lot and keep driving toward the reservation I told you about. Use the name Stasia gave you. We'll hopefully be right behind. At most, a day."

I eased off the accelerator. All I needed right now was to get pulled over for speeding.

Brandon shook his head. He opened his mouth to say something, but it was Lilly who spoke. "We all go together, Jack. If we all go together, we have a better chance of making it out."

Brandon looked back, worry pinching his brow, but when he looked back at me, he said, "She's right."

"This is too dangerous. You can both make it out—"

Lilly cut me off. "I'd be growing up in some lab somewhere, not allowed to see or speak to anyone if it weren't for you and Stasia."

I looked back at her in the rearview mirror. Lilly knew I had a deal with Galton that kept her from being tested too closely, but she didn't know the details. Neither Stasia nor I had told her about his recent threats.

She rolled her eyes at me, and the move was such a typical surly teenage move, it soothed some of the anxiety curling through my chest. "I'm sixteen, Jack. Do you really think I'm not always listening around the corner?"

I swallowed, and Brandon smiled. I'd swear he was proud of her eavesdropping.

"I don't know what to do," I admitted, looking back to the road and hanging a right. We were getting close to headquarters. There were still no lights in our rearview mirror. If anyone back at the house was in a condition to chase us, they weren't anywhere close.

"We go get Stasia as a family. She's part of our family now, isn't she?" The question from Lilly, her innocent perspective so simple, was what decided it for us.

"Yeah," Brandon said quietly in agreement.

I swallowed. "Yeah."

***

I pulled into the parking lot of the windowless concrete building Stasia had told me about. It looked like a reinforced warehouse. Two people stood in front of a steel door. One was a blond-haired boy about medium height. The other was Lucy. They advanced toward us as I put the Tahoe in park.

"Here we go. Leave Flynn in the truck, Lilly. Come with us but stay close. And stay behind us." I didn't want to leave her in the car for anyone to grab if they pulled in while we were inside.

"Duh."

God, teenagers could be sarcastic in any situation. We got out of the truck and walked toward the two men. I began collecting little rocks, the scrape of them audible as they skidded across the asphalt. Breaking the blacktop was harder than soft earth. I had plenty of energy and could do it if I needed to, but we didn't know what we were walking into after this. Brandon had no source of water, and I didn't want Lilly using any of her powers if I could help it.

"What's up Jack? Brandon?" Lucy nodded at us as he and the blond stopped a short distance away. The wind picked up in my hair, and I tensed.

"What's up Lucy?" Brandon kept his voice casual.

"Out for a stroll?" Lucy sounded amused. It put my teeth on edge.

"Quit playing with them Luce, let's put them down." The blond brought his hands up. The air picked up enough my feet were pushed back.

I brought the pebbles up around us, ready to hurtle them at the men's faces. Hopefully it would be enough of a distraction for Brandon and Lilly to get by them. With them clear, I could try burying them in the ground or incapacitating them some other way. Before I had time to try, Lucy brought the Maglite in his hand up. I tensed as he smashed it against the back of the blond's head.

Blondie looked at Lucy in surprise, his arm going up to the back of his head.

"Oh, for fuck's sake," Lucy said, exasperation clear in his voice, before he swung again at the blond's temple. The guy dropped in a boneless heap.

I stood shocked. Lilly fisted her hand in the shirt at my back. Beside me, Brandon didn't seem surprised at all.

Lucy shrugged. "Doc Kimi said you might need some

help. Said this was such a risky escape anyway, me and Lola could join in if we wanted."

Brandon walked forward, jolting me out of my haze. Brandon walked up to Lucy and with one hand yanked him close, kissing him. Lucy returned the embrace, drawing Brandon closer.

"Thank God. If you were with them, I think I would have lost my mind."

Lucy smiled up at Brandon. "Thought you knew me better than that."

"It's been a long night." Brandon looked over at me. "We need to hurry."

"What were you two doing here?" I pointed at the crumpled boy at Lucy's feet.

Lucy looked down. "Galton assembled an elemental task force years ago. Muscle for him, for the community, whenever anyone got out of hand. Better we fight each other than bringing in more independent contractors that know his dirty secret. He called us tonight and said he needed someone to guard the door. I volunteered, guessing why."

"You're on this task force?" Brandon shot me an angry look at my question, but I wasn't willing to risk anything because he had a crush.

"What better way to be in a position to stop them?"

"We don't have time for this." It was Lilly who spoke, surprising us all. "We need to get Stasia and get on the road."

"Little tyke is right." Lucy started walking toward the steel doors. "Galton was doing something with Stasia tonight that I don't think boded well for her. Kimi was going in to try to stall it for us. Me and Scott got here not too long ago, our instructions were to post up at the door and stop anyone trying to come in and disturb them."

We moved quickly across the parking lot. Flynn barked, and inwardly, I begged him to stop and be quiet. Lucy went through the door first, discreetly motioning behind him to stay back a moment. After he stepped through the entrance, his hand dropped, and the door slammed closed. Brandon, Lilly, and I rushed it, running into Lucy's back as we stepped across the threshold.

I grabbed Lilly, my hand covering her face as I turned us away from the gory scene. A dark-haired woman lay face down in a pool of blood. The thick smell of copper permeated the air around us. "No…"

"Lucy." Brandon spoke sharply, getting his attention. Lucy swung around, and tears shined in his eyes. Sympathy moved through me, but Brandon's next words kept us on track. "We need to get Stasia and get out."

Lucy swallowed, his voice thick when he spoke next. "Let's go."

He led us to a bank of elevators. The idea of being trapped in an elevator car pressed on me, but I didn't say anything as he hit the button for the basement. The doors opened onto an empty pool area. It looked like an Olympic-sized pool with multiple pods, similar to what they put us in at the Stepul School. There was a section of numerous medical stations I remembered from my time at the environmental initiative. They had those helmets with wires attached all over. We moved past everything to a door on the other end.

"Do you know what they're doing to her?" I whispered, as we neared the doors.

Lucy looked over at me, taking a deep breath. His eyes

were red, but he kept it together. "I know what they planned on doing to her. I'm hoping they haven't succeeded."

A sick feeling turned my gut. Kimi had told Stasia she was the subject Galton had picked for the breeding program. Fear suffused me as we stepped through the door and walked down the hall past empty exam rooms. We neared voices toward the end of the hall, the darkness giving way to a pool of light pouring from a room up ahead.

As we stepped into the light, the sick feeling became a heavy weight in my stomach. Stasia was strapped to a bed. Her hands and legs were tied down, her knees bent into stirrups. A red-haired girl stood over her. Dr. Galton stood up and brought a sheet down around her legs.

"It wasn't always this painless a procedure. When we first started, we tried to make embryos in a lab then implanted them in the mothers. We thought it was a better control for the outcome of offspring. We didn't have the budget for anesthesiologists during follicle extraction. But with Cora's help, and healthy, fertile subjects, we can implant much easier now."

A rush of air pushed the red-haired woman against the wall. Her eyes opened in surprise. Lucy went to do the same to Galton when someone stepped out from behind the door and smacked him over the head. Lucy collapsed, and the girl fell from the position she'd been pinned in, sliding down the wall and landing in a heap. She slowly sat herself up, huffing. Brandon stooped to check on Lucy. Lilly stood behind me, her fingers digging into my back.

Christopher Shaw stepped from somewhere in the room, the gun in his hand pointed at me. I swallowed.

Stasia was awake, tracks of tears on the sides of her face, duct tape over her mouth. She struggled against her restraints. Rage ran through me. My jaw clenched so tight I thought my teeth would crack. The room began to shake.

Galton spoke in a calm voice. "Ah, ah, ah, Jack. You'll bring the building down on all of us."

He was right. I swallowed, trying to control the anger thrumming through me. Stasia closed her eyes, but when she opened them, determination shined through. Cora got to her feet and walked up beside Stasia. Seeing where my eyes had gone, she stroked Stasia's face.

"Her screams were getting annoying." A trickle of blood at Cora's temple mixed oddly with the shade of red she had dyed her hair. She walked around the medical table toward Galton. Shaw kept the gun trained on me as Galton spoke.

"Here's what's going to happen, Jack. We are all going to go back to the Stepuli compound. You're going to behave. We've been injecting Stasia with hormones during her deprivation training. It's highly unlikely the insemination tonight wasn't successful. That means she's carrying your child. A child that I will take if you don't cooperate."

The ground beneath us rumbled again. I couldn't contain my anger enough to stop the tremors. Galton didn't seem disturbed. He even smiled. "We'll talk about everything that happened in the morning. At your attempts to leave. I thought you would have learned from your father, Jack."

The ceiling cracked at his words. Plaster rained down, some of it hitting Stasia in the face. She shut her eyes and turned her head, blinking the dust out of her eyes. Panic cut through me, and the tremors finally stopped.

"Enough of this. Turn around, hands behind your backs." Shaw thought we needed our hands to use our powers, even with the quakes I'd let out, I realized. That's how they taught them in the environmental initiative. It was a crutch that handicapped elementals.

Brandon looked at me, anger warring with helplessness in his eyes. I imagined mine looked much the same. I swallowed, looking back at Stasia. She lay defenseless, tied down to the table. I nodded at Brandon, not seeing any other choice. We started turning around when Lilly spoke, her voice laced with steel.

"No."

Galton looked at her, amusement in his expression. "My dear. I look forward to seeing what you can do. I've been so anxious to get you in a lab. I'm afraid this room, however, is completely flame retardant. There is no fire for you to work with here."

She shouldered her way to stand side by side with me and Brandon. The heat coming off her had us looking at each other in alarm. There was a sink in the corner of the room. I brought the ground up until a pipe burst. We rushed forward. Brandon grabbed Lucy by the back of the shirt and dragged him with us as we ran. From the corner of my eye, I saw Shaw lift his gun. Before he could discharge it, it exploded in his hand. He cried out, clutching his forearm, the end a bloody stump.

Brandon and I draped ourselves over Stasia, and Brandon brought a curtain of water over us.

Through the water's distortion, I watched Lilly face Galton. I could just make out flames in her eyes. Fire traced from her hands up her arms. Galton backed into

Cora, retreating against the wall, surprise and fear evident on their faces. Lilly's voice was toneless when she spoke.

"I *am* the fire."

# CHAPTER 35

## Epilogue

I stared at the white lines of the road and listened to the low hum of everyone talking. I sat in the back seat with Flynn's head in my lap. Lucy hadn't quit complaining that the dog got a bench seat while he was in the hatchback. Lola sat on the other side of Flynn, Lilly in the front passenger seat, Brandon in the back with Lucy.

When Jack had untied me from the bed, I hadn't been able to stop the explosion of tears. Tears of fear, of anger, of relief. The hours I'd spent with Galton and Cora. The way they'd forced me to… I swallowed and closed my eyes against the tears that continued dripping. I felt Jack's worry in front of me, but I closed myself off from it, from everyone in the car.

A hand touched my arm, and I looked over at Lola. I managed a tremulous smile at her attempt at comfort. She had been waiting for us outside, hidden in the tree line around the headquarters building. Lucy had managed to get her listed as one of the task force members so her bracelet wouldn't alarm. Before we'd left the parking lot, we broke the bracelets off the air twins' wrists for good.

We'd left everyone behind in that room, too injured to chase after us. Galton and Cora were both badly burned, the stump of Shaw's arm bled around him as he cried pitifully on the ground. Lucy had come around as we'd carried him through the gymnasium, thank God. Or we wouldn't have known to collect Lola.

Kimi Alver was apparently Lola and Lucy's aunt. She had been working with them on the underground network they had set up for Stepuli who needed to escape the government. We were headed toward a different safe house than Kimi had originally set up. After realizing how deep the government surveillance went, we figured that place was burned.

"Jack, can we stop for food?" Lilly asked from the front. Fear went through me at the idea of stopping. We were about two hundred miles from Whidbey. It still felt too close.

"Not yet, Lills. We'll get something when we stop for gas."

"Okay." Her voice was unnaturally subdued. Hesitantly, I opened myself up, trying to feel her emotions. She felt...empty. A hand dropped on my shoulder, and I looked around. It was Brandon.

"She'll be okay." He kept his voice low. "It's normal after how much power she let off. We'll keep a close eye on her and get her turned around."

I looked forward again. Lilly's red hair framed her face. I nodded and settled back against the window. I looked back out toward the road and traced the white lines leading us to freedom. The uneasy feeling in my gut mocked my optimism.

## FIND OUT MORE ABOUT MAGGIE AND HER BOOKS HERE:

Website: Maggiemaxfield.com

Facebook: https://www.facebook.com/Maxfield.Maggie

Goodreads:
https://www.goodreads.com/user/show/154136083-maggie-maxfield

Instagram: https://www.instagram.com/maggie_maxfield/

Thank you for reading The Tracks We Leave and joining Stasia and Jack on their journey for independence. The story continues in The Steps We Take coming soon. In the meantime, please support indie authors and leave a review! Your words help others find our work.

Thank you so much!

Maggie Maxfield